NO ESCAPE FROM DEATH

ALLAN KEVORKIAN

First Stillwater River Publications Edition.

ISBN: 978-1-963296-84-6

Library of Congress Control Number: 2024919348

1 2 3 4 5 6 7 8 9 10

Written by Allan Kevorkian.
Cover & interior book design by Matthew St. Jean.
Cover assets by fran_kie / Adobe Stock.
Published by Stillwater River Publications, West Warwick, RI, USA.

Publisher's Cataloging-in-Publication
(Provided by Cassidy Cataloguing Services, Inc.)
Names: Kevorkian, Allan, author.
Title: No escape from death / Allan Kevorkian.
Description: First Stillwater River Publications edition. | West
Warwick, RI, USA : Stillwater River Publications, [2025]
Identifiers: ISBN: 978-1-963296-84-6 | LCCN: 2024919348
Subjects: LCSH: Witnesses—United States—Fiction. | Private investi-
gators—United States—Fiction. | Murder—United States—Fiction. |
LCGFT: Detective and mystery fiction. | Thrillers (Fiction)
Classification: LCC: PS3611.E955 N6 2025 |
DDC: 813/.6—dc23

*The views and opinions expressed in this book are solely
those of the author and do not necessarily reflect the views
and opinions of the publisher.*

To my Italian mother, Paula Ann Vescera,
who raised me in the ways of the Roman
Catholic Church—a blueprint that remains
deeply ingrained in me today.

To my Armenian grandmother, Rose Kevorkian,
who never gave up on me, especially during
the challenging days of my young adulthood,
when my life lacked a sense of direction.

PART 1

1

ENTER THE GORILLA

THE STREETS OF THE UPPER WESTSIDE, NEW PARIS neighborhood called Roosevelt Heights, were dark as death on one cold November 1947 Saturday evening. A crescent moon hovered over the chilly, murky, Eastern USA, Mid-Atlantic metropolis as time edged closer to the witching hour. Wayne Palmer, enjoying the new Packard's smooth ride, nodded a narrow jaw up and down in tune with a Benny Goodman standard playing rhythmically from the car's speaker. The engine purred like a kitten as the vehicle cruised through a series of green lights amid a sleeping Empire Avenue. A tad over six feet tall, Mr. Palmer's head nearly grazed the inside roof of the magnificently clean, jet-black machine.

Mr. Palmer's perfectly horizontal green eyes shifted off the road and gazed into the rearview mirror bearing confidence—admiring an unaged full crown of blonde hair combed neatly to the side, starting at a flat temple. Upon a subsequent look, glistening white teeth brought more self-praising as arrogant smirking lips whispered inaudibly, "*You lucky son of a bitch.*" A black fedora rested on the bench seat next to his hip, alongside a dozen snug, long-stem roses. The roses were where he was heading. Striking his olfactory nerve, the residual feminine perfume odor that radiated from his black suit, blue tie, and white dress shirt reminded him where he had been.

The gold watch displaying eleven forty-seven in between Roman numerals made his left wrist sparkle. Using manicured fingers, Mr. Palmer, a man who existed for avarice, grasped the upper steering wheel and directed it left, turning on 18th Street. The suave insurance salesman, a scion of New Paris old money, kept the automobile to the left side of this one-way street, his street. Ten seconds later, the Packard's whitewall tires slowed beside a row of five connected brick luxury houses featuring matching grandiose stairsteps and railings. Pulling up on the driver's side, the front left side tire stopped two inches from the curb at the four-hundred block.

All in sync, the physically fit, fair-skinned, angular-faced Mr. Palmer silenced the radio, killed the ignition, and shut off the headlights. He reached inside the glove box, took out a bottle of cologne, and then sprayed his body, attempting to conceal where he had been. Mr. Palmer's whistling replaced the jazz band. The thirty-nine-year-old opened the driver's door, stretched across the passenger's seat for the bouquet, and advanced leisurely upward out of the vehicle.

The busy Saturday was coming to an end; however, it never crossed the priviledged individual's mind that November 15th would be his last day on Earth. For some, death comes as a relief, mollifying the agony of life, but friends could argue strongly this successful sybarite certainly relished his short life to its fullest. Mr. Palmer did not sense doom but satisfaction.

If there happened to be a witness on such a desolate, noiseless block, one would have seen a gorilla of a man possessing a bushel of black hair take a robust swing of a thirty-four-inch brown Hillerich & Bradsby baseball bat against Wayne Palmer's head as he stepped atop the curb. The first strike hit the temporal region 'thud.' The second crushing blow was occipital, another 'thud.' The third landed on the upper cervical, making more of a 'squish' sound. Following the cervical region clout, Mr. Palmer's body encountered the pavement, seizing, while his right hand loosened its grip on the roses, which settled on his thorax. The socialite's final breaths of life were agonal.

The three hundred-plus pound man stood over his bloody, distorted victim, giving additional blows with the baseball bat, guided by oven mitt hands until the seizing stopped. Compound fractures of the cranium were present, and a puddle of blood now covered the square sidewalk section. Next, a folded newsboy cap was taken out of the killer's huge gray trench coat's right front pocket and perched on his jumbo head. As sort of a trade for the cap, the warclub was placed inside the trench coat deliberately. An instant later, the beast ambled away, heading west nonchalantly—comfortable with his environs, like an old man strolling through a city park on a spring day.

But there was a witness...

2

THE WITNESS

THREE MINUTES AFTER THE MURDER, ACROSS A deserted street, out of forsaken shadows, stepped a thin, smaller-than-average-height, oval-headed man. His dull-complected face appeared several days unshaven. He was garbed in a rumpled tan raincoat and light gray fedora hat. Amidst a bristly mug, the man originating beyond the shadows carried a shaggy brown mustache.

Thirty-seven-year-old Bruce Ellory's hands trembled uncontrollably—gin not yet swallowed swished in his mouth like an electric washing machine. He spit out his lit cigarette violently. Alongside a closed sausage shop, the thin man hesitantly edged out of the gloomy alley, overcome by panic after being the sole audience member for an off-screen horror show. Besides a racing heart, his palms were drenched with sweat as he advanced to the curb adjacent to 18th Street, which separated him from the fresh crime scene.

Mr. Ellory entered the alley just thirty minutes before, then crouched in the darkness, contemplating ways to take his own life. Before he exited this world, the broken man wanted just one more look at the perfect man—Wayne Palmer—who had destroyed his will to live just two short days ago.

The perplexed murder witness stooped and put a small paper bag in his right hand down to the ground at his feet. Going unnoticed, the bottle inside caused the bag to fall on its side; a pencil-thick stream of gin trickled into the gutter. Taking dubious steps, like a ten-year-old boy being sent to the principal's office, Mr. Ellory crossed the temporary quiet street approaching the corpse. The driver's door of Wayne Palmer's Packard remained swung wide open—one dead man's body lay beneath.

Mr. Ellory's aghast brown eyes became fastened to the cement as he stood motionless in a cursory, catatonic state above Wayne Palmer's lifeless body. *"Mona's going to think I did this,"* he thought queasily, as trepidation set in.

After a few seconds of viewing the squashed skull, Bruce Ellory's nausea intensified. He jerkily twisted his torso right, laterally from the corpse, expelling a vigorous blast of spew via his oral cavity. Avoiding hopping over the human remains, the witness awkwardly stepped through his own pink secretions, walking towards the automobile's rear. Calling for help was of no use, so instead, Mr. Ellory forlornly wandered west, facing Empire Avenue in the direction of the Gorilla's path.

Tailing the trail of the colossus, Mr. Ellory attempted to cautiously turn left at a neon sign that read *Cocktail Lounge* at the corner of 18th and Empire Avenue, but immediately collided against a traversing mass of bodily tissue, knocking him to his buttocks.

3

MAX WEATHERBEE

AT THE SAME TIME OF WAYNE PALMER'S MURDER in lower downtown, known by locals as 'Old Downtown,' a black metal elongated sign hung atop a ninth-floor office door. This modest sign in the architecturally outdated, eleven-story, cement Keiser Building advertised: *Max Weatherbee Private Detective for Hire.*

Having nowhere to go on a Saturday night, thirty-five-year-old Max Weatherbee sat stroking his square masculine jawbone, using two wide fingers. Amid the doldrums he sensed, inside his rear office, the PI leaned backward in a red oak bendable chair. A slight mirthless smile betrayed his boredom to an audience of none. Size twelve Roblee brown dress shoes lazily rested on an enormous gray steel desk. Max had become immune to the constant humming of the two-bulb overhead fluorescent light fixture high above his head.

The half belly-up Keiser Insurance company occupied the first seven floors. Small office tenants rented the remainder at bargain rates. Many of these upper-floor businesses were managed by insomniacs who already had day jobs elsewhere. Still, the hallways were lonely at this time of night. Disrupting tranquility was the sporadic roller coaster sound of an ascending/descending elevator across the hall. With its occasional dinging, plus swooshing, the elevator seemed about the only noise that could be heard between here and Shanghai.

On a good day, Max Weatherbee stood 6'1", 190 pounds. His forehead appeared license plate rectangular, and anatomically superior existed a full head of burnished, dark hair parted all the way to the scalp by a right-side sweep. Gray strands had imperceptibly invaded this coiffure, and faint wrinkles were prematurely present on Max Weatherbee's craggy rock face. His rough face was cleanly shaven, and it made him look Hollywood tough guy handsome without the mustache. Any average-sized man who has ever engaged in a few brawls would know that this man could take your best punch. He kept his tie on, but the jacket of his blue suit dangled nearby, below a wooden six-foot coat hanger.

Max had not secured a case in over a week. Thoughts wandered in several directions—paying December's rent, war memories, scotch, and 'dames,' as he liked to call them. In betwixt contemplations, the private detective's chestnut brown eyes cooly absorbed the dozen or so framed photos of his life hanging on the painted green walls. Favorites included a picture of himself in the service, one next to his mother, the 1929 high school football team, and two photos of him with Uncle Harry. Besides providing complacency, Max felt pictures were valuable conversation pieces for him and new clients to break the Ice.

No pictures of a wife, girlfriend, or child could be found anywhere in the impeccable work space. Behind him stood two high metal filing cabinets, one six-paned window, a wooden table consisting of all sorts of cameras, and a closed white metal door featuring a black sign that read Photography Dark Room.

Max dated women, but fared unsuccessfully with steady relationships. Now reaching his mid-thirties, he considered himself a loner. He still reclined, but now with an illuminated Lucky Strike dangling from symmetrical lips, reading a men's magazine. Under a cloud of smoke, the sleuth waited desperately for the black desk phone to spark merriment. "*Hopefully, a dame in distress,*" he mused. His gut intuition told him that this was "*The calm before the storm.*"

4

THE MEETING

EXITING THE CORNER LOUNGE WAS A MID-TWEN-
ties, meticulously groomed, hatless male patron who
appeared to be fraternizing with a similar age, pretty,
auburn-haired female. Both were still on their feet. On
the pavement, Mr. Ellory looked up from his sitting
position. The bodily mass that struck him was not the
gorilla of a man who committed butchery.

Indicating the collision was purely accidental, the
boyish-faced man peered downwards at Mr. Ellory,
offering his hand for assistance. Mr. Ellory noticed that
not a hair stood out of place in this budding gentleman's pompous hairdo.

The young fellow spoke clearly, but alcohol sharply
reeked out of his breath. "Sorry sir," he apologized,
"you okay?" His helping hand remained stationary.
"Didn't see you coming around… you were moving so
fast." The voice was youthful.

Bruce Ellory grabbed his fallen hat, then hopped

up on his own and replied, "Yes, I'm fine," although his coccyx stung like a heinie whipping. The murder witness, Mr. Ellory, rebuffed additional engagement and delicately trotted south down Empire Avenue. The young couple headed north on the aforesaid thoroughfare, shaking their heads, giggling.

"*I was seen on the same street of Wayne Palmer's destruction,*" Mr. Ellory tensely thought to himself. "*I'll be the primary suspect... walk, walk.*"

The rumbling of a few automobile engines could be heard in the distance. Facing darkened storefronts, Bruce Ellory kept his head twisted left, away from the street. Cool wind billowed into his right ear's orifice. Only two blocks from the corner of the cocktail lounge encounter, Mr. Ellory's trot slowed to a dawdle. No person was seen on the street, but a burnt wood smell pervaded the air. He followed his nose, glancing past Empire Avenue at a city park, and saw flames.

With his heart racing, Bruce Ellory gingerly crossed the avenue, treading toward those flames. As he entered the park, Mr. Ellory furtively crept behind a trimmed, globe-shaped bush. He was now close enough to smell kerosene and see a metal trash barrel with a torrid fire brewing inside of it. Precisely beyond the barrel's bright flicker, an oversized, grotesque Caucasian man who just enacted murder lurked.

Through Mr. Ellory's eyes, the assassin's two-toned evil face seemed distorted in the reflection of the flames. The slayer's upper face brandished a deep red hue, but his lower face's five o'clock shadow made it appear super dirty, resembling a drunken sailor. Crouched in hiding, a fear consumed Mr. Ellory, tripped on his own foot, creating sufficient noise for the gorilla of a man to turn his bulky neck in that direction.

No longer in refuge, Mr. Ellory was now out in the open. Utilizing the best diversion coming to mind, he rose to his feet, walked up to the roasting barrel, and asked solemnly, "Excuse me, mister, do you have a light?"

The Gorilla's cold eyes looked at Mr. Ellory's scrawny body and then into the fire. His hot-dog-bun-like lips grinned while he directed with sarcasm, "Sure, there's ya light, see?" The mammoth man's eyebrows were immense in the middle of the redness as he stared inside the smoldering drum. Bruce Ellory's astonished eyes followed the stranger's own and saw the now charred baseball bat handle burning profusely in the garbage barrel amidst some two-by-four planks.

"*Burning your fingerprints*," Mr. Ellory thought as he felt the heat against his cheek like a toasted marshmallow.

The Gorilla pivoted to Mr. Ellory, employing a piercing stare down, and said gruffly, "Now beat it if you know what's good for ya." The murderer knew he could crush Mr. Ellory in a matter of seconds and wanted the puny man to comprehend such intentions. The massive fellow burst out a laugh, which began jolly but transformed sinister.

A terrified Bruce Ellory figured he had never seen such an enormous mouth and set of teeth, although numerous were missing. The killer's super-sized jaw was uneven, showcasing plenty of prior trauma. Mr. Ellory conceded, responding, "Gotcha." He egressed the scene but soon found another hiding spot amid the abundance of park shrubbery.

Distantly, Bruce Ellory lagged as the Gorilla departed the simmering blaze, and his size thirteen blockish shoes sauntered two hundred yards to the opposite side of the park en route to a tiny white brick bus station. Police sirens suddenly wailed afar. Internally, Mr. Ellory nervously reflected, "*Someone discovered Wayne Palmer's body. That street will be crawling with cops.*"

The big man presented adequately dressed—accompanied by a trench coat, dress shirt, newsboy cap, gray tie, and matching dress pants. If not for extreme torso wideness, he would have been inconspicuous among the scattered small crowd standing under an arched roof veranda in front of the well-lit station.

The Gorilla loomed statue-like, staring into outer space beside a pole with a porcelain sign attached that read: BUS #19. An attractive brunette searching for something unimportant in her purse stood eight feet away but received no attention from the beast.

Bus number 19 was unfamiliar to Bruce Ellory, who lingered frozen amongst the darkness, fifty feet behind the veranda. "*Have to clear my name, maybe a new start, a second chance to get Mona back without Palmer in the picture.*" The suicide plan stayed on hold as Mr. Ellory's diverse thoughts continued, *"This big guy did me a favor, but he's going to fry in the chair, not me. Must see where he's heading, then get out of here."*

A bus advertising Adamsville, followed by a 19 above its windshield, drove up when the clock tower displayed 12:45 a.m. Seven passengers boarded the bus, one being a vicious executioner who selected a window seat near the right rear tire.

Bruce Ellory plodded toward the bus timorously as it edged off the curb, still having its interior lights illuminated. As Bruce Ellory attempted to get a better look at the killer, the killer got another look at him. The Gorilla glacially peered out the vehicle's window, flaring two nostrils which were as wide as Washington quarters, making eye contact with Mr. Ellory, who by now had advanced to the sidewalk. The Gorilla and his black, lifeless golf ball size eyes arose to a half-standing position, utterly understanding this second meeting was not a coincidence. Mr. Ellory's countenance turned eggshell white, and his heart pulsated even faster than at any time since witnessing the murder. Bus number 19 pulled away, engulfing itself in the pitch-black night. Mr. Ellory was safe for now.

5

TWO DAYS BEFORE THE PALMER MURDER

THURSDAY, NOVEMBER 13TH, TWO DAYS BEFORE Wayne Palmer's atrocious murder, Bruce Ellory left Baxter's Department Store sulking, carrying a pink slip in his wallet. It was the price you pay when the boss warned you three months earlier that your floor sales happened to be "an embarrassment to the company."

The three months following the August poor sales warning were internally consumed with severe anxiety, including panic attacks. Congruously, his nights consisted of hitting a gin bottle and chain-smoking Chesterfields. Bruce Ellory's sales failed to improve.

While the department store salesman's mind lingered in such a pathetic state, his thirty-one-year-old, still slim, attractive wife Mona would leave the three-room, inner-city, third-floor apartment, gallivanting after supper. Bruce refrained from questioning her but instead drank until he passed out on the couch in solitude.

On the November evening, when Mr. Ellory came home sulking with the pink slip in his wallet, Mona did not venture out. To Bruce's surprise, the apartment seemed unusually cluttered; his wife had not tidied up. A strong, unventilated cigarette smell was foul, and the two small windows offered a lack of outside lighting as the rain pelted against them. The table lamps in the house stood insufficient, and the house appeared dark just as Bruce favored it.

"They canned me at Baxter's," Bruce gravely announced in a tone softer than a snake's hiss.

Five-foot-four, one-hundred-ten-pound, matchstick-legged Mona sat on the edge of an aged cloth Duncan Phyfe couch with her flat-heeled shoes grounded on the rug. The comely, pink-skinned woman shook her head in utter disgust upon hearing the news. As she did, her shoulder-length sandy brown hair floated in the air around a heart-shaped face, as diamond-shaped ears peeped out of her bouncy waves. He could not see it coming, but she had bigger news for him.

Mona Ellory lifted a meatless arm, instructing her pitiful husband to sit down in the flowered side chair, and said, "Bruce, we need to talk."

Mr. Ellory placed his fedora on the nearby blonde dining table warily, and obeyed. Once seated, he ran his fingers through his light brown, partially balding, straggled hair. Initially, silence filled the air. The woman's face featured a petite nose, umber-colored eyes, sculpted cheekbones, and a slightly pronounced mandible. Bruce's recessed eyes were oblivious to her beauty.

Mona Ellory boldly took the floor, knowing her husband's world was about to go from cracked to shattered. "Bruce, when we met, you were a highly regarded engineer. Your designs…. breathtaking." Her voice aired perfect articulation, every syllable equally balanced, passed by her long teeth as she chided, "Now you can't even hold a job at a department store."

He offered little, demonstrating a sullen tone, "I'm sorry… I failed you."

"Bruce, I never should have married you."

A speechless Bruce Ellory's brown eyes turned watery.

"I wanted children, a house, money to fix myself up and go shopping like other women." She paused, digging her long, coral-lacquered fingernail into her upper sternum, attempting to find more words—terminating words. "You see, Bruce, I've been an unfaithful wife."

Bruce Ellory tried to speak behind tan cigarette-stained teeth, but nothing came out. He sat with his hands in his face, making his U-shaped jaw jut.

A subway car thundered by, shaking the apartment briefly, then Mona continued, "I've met somebody else, and been seeing a lot of him."

"Who?" Bruce's face bitterly reddened—the spider

veins on his nose became exaggerated. He asked, "Do I know him?"

"You remember the insurance salesman who tried to sell us life insurance, obviously we couldn't afford?"

"Palmer? Wayne Palmer, that guy?"

"Yes, that guy," she replied flatly.

"I thought he was married?" Bruce Ellory rebuked feebly.

"Wayne is married but has no love for his wife, and I must confess to you, Bruce; I am no longer in love with you." She puckered her fuchsia-polished lips for an instant, then further explained. "You are not the man I remember, possessing hopes and dreams. You have regressed to a sunken human being." Mona briskly hesitated, allowing her face to exhibit contempt. "And unlike you, I still enjoy dreams," she divulged, "dreams starting with getting out of this deplorable apartment."

The conversation ceased, devoid of pother. Minutes later, in a dingy room consisting of two separate twin beds, empty-hearted Bruce Ellory began packing whatever he could inside one large red, rectangular suitcase. He paused and looked at her lone bed. It came to him. His mind reflected back to years ago when they were first married, recalling how he used to climb into her bed late at night to make love.

The fractured man returned to working unhurriedly as if hoping she would halt him, but Mona never entered the bedroom. Bruce, carrying the suitcase, moved at a snail's pace into the living room. Expressionless, Mona seemed all neck and little chin as she stood smoking a cigarette with her hair propped in a bun. She whisked the apartment door ajar. Mr. Ellory, lugging his suitcase, crept by her. Eye contact was declined by both husband and wife as the suitcase crossed the threshold.

In the hallway, leaving the apartment for the last time, Bruce glanced back, only seeing half of Mona's painted lips and purple peplum dress as the door shut swiftly. Bruce frantically bellowed at the closing door, using a high-pitched voice, "I'll make Wayne Palmer pay dearly for what he has done to me! I swear on it!"

While Bruce Ellory shouted, in the adjacent apartment, Mrs. Kerns, their elderly, petite, gray-haired neighbor, was peeping one lens of her black cat-eye glasses through the open chain-link door crack. Her mouth fell agape.

Afterward that evening, Mr. Ellory somberly sat at the Dexter's Pharmacy food counter. Following a swig from his coffee cup, he reached into his right pants pocket, took out a battered brown leather wallet, removed a folded business card, and dropped it on the tray.

Wayne Palmer
Codac Insurance Agent
Residence: 475 18th St.
Roosevelt Heights, New Paris
Phone: ST1-9054

6

POINT OF NO RETURN

PRESENT TIME. LONG GONE WAS THE BUS STATION. Under a soot-colored sky, five-foot-eight, one hundred forty-five-pound Bruce Ellory trotted south out of the park, keeping his distance from the murder scene. When he got to a dark, deserted commercial street, racing thoughts reoccupied his head. *"I can't go back to my sister's house; the police will be looking for me."* Feeling defeated, he slowed his pace and skittishly glanced up for prowl cars. Once none were seen, he resumed thinking, *"They'll pin this on me, I know what the city cops do."*

Since leaving his apartment, the last two nights had been spent crashing at his sister Susan's home on the lower west side of New Paris, but presently, he continued east. His sister's husband, Walter, did not appreciate such an encroachment anyway. Heading in this direction was not impromptu. His past work as a taxi driver while attending engineering college made Mr.

Ellory very familiar with this heavily populated city in the United States.

Fluttering thoughts lingered, *"I'll be convicted of a murder I didn't commit...The gas chamber will be my destiny... I'll take myself out before that happens."*

He walked and compulsively smoked Chesterfields throughout his excursion to the dreary lower east side of New Paris. *"Mona will never believe I wasn't involved in Palmer's demise."*

As Bruce Ellory's ambulation progressed, the streets grew even darker. Large neon merchant signs became smaller amid the fog behind him, and a lack of street lights was evident in this part of the city. The heavy smoker's hollow cheeks sucked in the air, fighting to maintain his breath. Bruce's coccyx still hurt, and now his feet and knees joined the pain club. Several times, he stopped to pull up his trousers and then tucked in his dress shirt over a soft, fried clam-shaped belly that protruded under his puny chest. He paused at a corner, removed his fedora, and ran a narrow, dirty finger around its brim, extracting a plethora of sweat beads.

Shortly after 2 a.m., an exhausted, out-of-smokes Bruce Ellory arrived wearily in one of the seedier sections of New Paris known as Webster Hills. Narcotics and prostitution were well known here. City lowlifes often joked, *"If you want the pills, go to the hills."* The sidewalks he journeyed over became loaded with litter and fragmented glass. Taxicabs searching for fares seemed bygone. Dingy bar rooms and pool halls were now prevalent—eloquent storefronts were not. Young men derived from mixed ethnic races sporadically stood on stoops, some ignoring November by displaying sleeves rolled up. Besides putrid garbage, he could also smell the East Side River—it did not smell good.

The witness snubbed the various catcalls young, night owl hoodlums sitting on stoops broadcasted, "Hey little man... What ya looking at pussy? Got a problem pal?" He recognized this environment as the dregs of New Paris; he just no longer feared death.

A gilded border, half-lit sign hanging alongside an old, rust-colored, five-story brick building about twenty feet above the pavement advertised this broken man's destination. Dispersed unlit, busted bulbs projected distortion at a distance, but as Mr. Ellory grew nearer, he read Hotel Duncan Rooms for Rent. The pouchy skin below his eyes needed rest.

7

THE HOTEL DUNCAN

SUNDAY, 2:15 A.M., PASSING THROUGH TWO SETS of glass double doors surrounded by dinged, black metal frames that might have looked dandy twenty years ago, Mr. Ellory languidly entered the lobby of the five-story Hotel Duncan. Big band music played staticky on a tabletop radio. The forty-by-thirty-foot lobby, enclosed by a ten-foot-high checker board ceiling, smelled of heavy cigar residue. It consisted of two well-used red leather couches, three matching chairs, two stand-up cigar ashtrays, and no occupants.

Mr. Ellory paused to process the environment. Surrounding the lobby were four pale Roman columns, each one featuring a plastered gargoyle sitting atop. In the rear lobby, there was a sit-down phone booth with a glass door. A set of narrow stairs covered in red carpet sat to the right. The molding on the lower wall, leading up these stairs presented as discolored white.

To the left of the lobby existed an office surrounded

by a wood frame below and a metal cage above. It reminded Bruce Ellory of a prison cell. The night manager on duty sat curled like a feline in a chair to the rear of this cage. When he jumped up, sliding his tiny shoes on, he appeared to Ellory to be about fifty years old, maybe five-foot-six inches tall, and hardly one hundred thirty pounds soaking wet. The top of his head was completely bald. Clumpy hair on both sides of his skull protruded laterally like a garden hedge needing a good trim. The hair color seemed dyed an eerie black. He had ghost-white skin, blotches of facial eczema, long piano key teeth, plus bags under his eyes. The ghoulish employee stood dressed in a wrinkled white dress shirt—no tie.

"*Zombie,*" Mr. Ellory thought as he circumspectly approached the cage. He cleared his throat. "Do you have a room?" he asked the creep in an extremely, non-threatening tone.

Large, bloodshot, distended eyes stared at Bruce Ellory, causing him to break visual contact. The night owl clerk spoke slowly, airing a flat affect. "I wouldn't… still be up… if I did not." The bat-eared manager leaned his ashen lips proximal to the closed caged door. He drawled again, "I'm Mr. Gray… at your serv…ice." Gray's corned beef breath was foul to Bruce, triggering him to retreat a few feet away from the cage.

Stiff postured, Mr. Gray dug his mushroom-shaped thumbs into the wood sill below, giving a morbid tight lip smile, then resumed, "Do you… want hourly… or nightly? He talked so slowly that one could finish any sentence for him. "And is there... a woman... you are courting?" Mr. Gray's caterpillar eyebrows elevated with every syllable.

"Nightly... I'll be here a few nights. I'm here alone," Mr. Ellory reassured.

"Pur...fect," uttered Mr. Gray, still smiling but bizarrely.

Tomorrow's fugitive stepped forward toward the caged office door and requested softly, "Can I have a room on the fifth floor?" Mr. Ellory, a man devoid of fortitude, stroked his uneven mustache in one motion while ominously reflecting internally, "*Just in case... five floors should be enough to end it.*"

"Sorry... we rent... one floor... at a time," Mr. Gray informed, "Currently... we are up to floor... number two." He further added, "The bathroom and shower... are shared ... one per floor. I must ... collect... a ten-dollar deposit." He raised his chin skywards, pointing a crooked jaw at his uneasy lodger.

"Of course," Mr. Ellory said politely, trying to terminate the undesired conversation. Compulsive thoughts assured him, "*I can always find the roof.*" Next, he removed trembling hands out of his pants pockets, dropped a sawbuck on the sill, and signed Mr. Gray's guest register as Mr. Cecil Wallace, an alias he instantly invented.

Fiendish Mr. Gray reached his hand through an Easter basket-size opening of the upper caged door. One room key dangled from fingers, which were arthritically bent at the knuckles. Bruce Ellory took the key—Gray took the ten.

Mr. Ellory looked beyond Mr. Gray's bony left shoulder and noticed a small vending area offering tobacco products, candy, simple medicines, newspapers, and soda pop on ice. Ellory bought three packs of cigarettes and four Hershey bars. He then requested, "Two packs of matches, please." Cash for merchandise was exchanged, and Mr. Ellory's items were slipped via the cage's opening in a paper bag. Following the transaction, Bruce Ellory was nonverbally directed by Mr. Gray's pointy chin to the stairs.

Mr. Ellory found that room twenty-five contained a paltry single brass bed, dresser, mirror, Winsor-backed chair, desk with a spiral-shaped lamp, three inexpensive, theater prop-type art pieces on the wall, and one green plush chair suffering from several cigarette butt holes. Two worn-out braided rugs covered half of the wooden floor.

For the moment, Bruce remained content to be off the streets, so much so that he hopped in bed and slept almost the entire day away. If he happened to go down to the lobby for a newspaper later Sunday morning, he would have seen a concerning headline:

> *Gruesome Murder Shocks Roosevelt Heights Neighborhood. Victim Bludgeoned. No suspects. Yet.*

PART 2

8

MONDAY MORNING

8 A.M. MONDAY, TWO DAYS FOLLOWING WAYNE
Palmer's murder, a freshly showered, shirtless Bruce
Ellory stood in front of the peeled, veneer-coated mirror in room twenty-five. Sunday, the day before, which
he slept mostly all away, was uneventful. Last evening,
Mr. Ellory only left the shabby Hotel Duncan once at
9 p.m. to pick up a bottle of gin and two hamburgers
to go.

This morning, like every other morning, he saw in
the mirror a skinny, upper-bodied man who carried
an incongruous potbelly, looking much older than
thirty-seven. *"What have I become?"* he internally
reflected. After combing his wet, thinning hair towards
the right side, the broken man walked into the hallway
bathroom and shaved his stubble. Strong strokes were
applied above his lip to completely remove a shaggy
mustache. Bruce was inwardly petrified as his mind
whispered, *"I can't be recognized."*

Once fully dressed in his same brown suit, tan tie, and fedora hat, Mr. Ellory covertly crept downstairs to the hotel lobby. When he reached the bottom, he counted and then recounted the modicum of his life savings, equaling one hundred fifty-seven dollars that remained in his battered wallet. *"Gotta do something here. Need a plan,"* he pondered desperately. The murder witness proceeded to the caged office's door and found its upper portion wide open. Bruce asked, "Can I purchase one New Paris Times, please?"

An aged, short, and stout gray-haired female clerk who was new to him replied, "Five cents, sir."

Mr. Ellory placed a nickel atop the lower office door's sill.

An irksome melody existed in her high-pitched voice, magnified further by a foreign accent. "What is your room number, sir?" she asked, setting today's newspaper in front of him.

"Twenty-five."

"Will you be leaving us today, sir?" Her pitch could cut glass.

"No." Annoyance coated his curt tone.

"Will there be anything else, sir?"

"Enough with the sirs," he mused internally, then shook his clean-shaven, pale face and briskly pivoted away.

At the end of the couch sat an elderly man sporting round spectacles and a plump mustache who touched the brim of his derby to say hello nonverbally. Ellory paid him no mind and flumped on one of the lobby's tattered red leather chairs. Bruce's period of relaxation was short-lived—a headline on page three grimly sent a chill down his spine.

> *City Detectives wish to speak with a person of interest in the Wayne Palmer killing. Police have yet to release a name.*

"They're not going to lock me up," Mr. Ellory rambled inaudibly, under his breath. *The real killer took a bus to Adamsville. I'm going up there today to find this gorilla, then I'll notify the cops."*

9

MAX'S CURRENT SITUATION

AT THE TINY DETECTIVE AGENCY LOCATED WITHIN the Keiser Building, the main door leading to the marble floor of the public hallway was propped open by a rubber stopper. The second door to Max Weatherbee's rear office was also gaped in the same manner. A smaller waiting room with an unoccupied desk satisfied the space in between the propped oak doors.

Wearing a white dress shirt and red tie, Mr. Weatherbee sat hunched forward at his expansive steel desk, sorting through bills, keeping his left hand nestled in his temple. He wondered if he'd get a case any time soon, which translates to income.

The hallway elevator made a swish sound. Soon, he heard the crisp clicking of high heels—getting louder. The private detective attentively looked straight ahead into the hallway, beyond the waiting room, and saw nothing. His face grew disappointed, like a kid heading to a baseball game when it starts to rain.

She then appeared. Max gazed up, observing a young, lanky, shoulder-length brunette standing in the doorway to the hall carrying her coat. *"What a dame,"* he thought. He knew his day was about to get better.

10

ADAMSVILLE

10 A.M., MONDAY MORNING, DONNED IN A BROWN suit, Bruce Ellory bent down the rim of his fedora and swiftly vamoosed the Hotel Duncan. Today's November weather aired warm for Eastern Atlantic America. In the sky, the few scattered clouds appeared sparse like holes in Swiss cheese. After traveling eight city blocks west, he located a cab stand. One hour later, Mr. Ellory rode on a blue transit bus that read *Adamsville* above its windshield.

Bus number nineteen was half full. Mr. Ellory selected a seat in the far back. Looking like a penguin, the police person of interest sat tucking his head against his breastbone. Avoiding eye contact with fellow riders, Bruce pretended to be reading the newspaper, a newspaper he already read twice. The thirty-five-minute ride proceeded ordinary. Keeping his head buried in the newspaper, the man on a mission internally reflected, *"Just got to find this gorilla and let the cops do the rest."*

The public bus ultimately arrived near the nucleus of Adamsville. A chrome overhead speaker informed riders, "This is the end of the trip… Welcome to Adamsville!" Bruce Ellory felt his skin crawling as he, the final rider in line, walked from the bus's rear to the front. He found himself making eye contact with the cap-wearing, flat-faced male driver's dark eyes in the visor mirror. Experiencing palpitations, Bruce's head quickly turned away and descended the few stairs. Any stimulation of his senses triggered anxiety.

Primarily a garment factory town, Mr. Ellory knew Adamsville to be a lower, middle-class suburb, twenty miles north of New Paris's upper eastern border, boasting a population of seventy thousand citizens. The center district, where he exited the bus, was a sizable circle full of retail shops and small food establishments constructed under a few dozen three to five-story office buildings. A burly traffic cop blaring a whistle directed traffic as buzzing automobiles orbited the circle. The weather remained spectacular.

Standing on the lawn in the heart of it all, Bruce Ellory's mind spoke, *"It's gotta be as easy as finding an elephant in a haystack. Need to find out his name… A name to put alongside that gruesome face."*

A large sign advertising *Free Coffee with Breakfast Specials* grabbed his attention. Mr. Ellory crossed the street and entered the narrow storefront, a place called Ruthie's Kitchen. He sat at a curved S-shaped counter on a round red stool, the kind that a seven-year-old boy would love to spin around vigorously. Just like on the bus, he kept his vision low, pretending to be absorbed in the newspaper. The fedora's bent brim covered his troubled eyes. Three nervous fingers of his left hand tapped, lacking rhythm on the white countertop. A visibly starved Bruce ate two prodigious orders of the establishment's breakfast special, which sparked dialogue by the two-hundred-plus-pound, black-haired waitress, who may have been Ruthie herself.

"You're eating well, my dear!" she exclaimed, displaying boisterous resonance beyond the other side of the counter, extending her large arms as she said it.

Mr. Ellory offered a pointless smile, bearing pencil-thin lips, showing reluctance to engage in conversation. His mind was a million miles away.

Soon, she ripped Mr. Ellory's receipt off the order pad using excessive arm fat and dropped it close to his dirty plate. "See you again, sunshine," she said, giving Bruce a wink from a heavily mascaraed eye. When that was done, the big woman did an about-face in the next counter customer's direction.

Mr. Ellory departed Ruthie's Kitchen and then headed south on foot. Four blocks into his travel, he approached a pair of down-and-outers, garbed in hobo fashion, leaning against one another with too much time on their hands. Articulating in an innocuous tone, Bruce asked, "Hi... where is the pool hall district?"

While waiting for any reply, Mr. Ellory disdainfully

thought, "*These two fellers could pass for a couple of carnival creeps.*"

The taller of the down and outers stood about six foot two, possessing a jug face and a Homburg hat crushed on top, featuring its brim pulled up skywards. He smelled like a dirty laundry basket. The shorter, rotund man's white tie looked so wide that you could have pinned advertising on it. They both appeared to be a little older than Bruce.

The tall, jug-faced man conversed first. "You shoot stick?"

"Not really... just need to ask some people a few questions."

The taller hobo rotated a gangly palm supine and enjoined, "A quarter for my navigational expertise."

Bruce Ellory raised his brown eyebrows, then dabbled into his left pocket, located a quarter, and paid the fee grudgingly.

Both men's facial expressions denied any knowledge of the gigantic killer's existence, which Mr. Ellory thoroughly described. The tall man answered, "We don't have anyone round here like that, pal." His lips quickly made a frown.

The stubbier, plump-faced vagrant uttered, "This ain't New Paris; we gots nice people up in Adamsville, ya know." There was a lack of education to his drawl. His filthy oval hat seemed to move in step with his cantaloupe-shaped mandible.

"Okay, how do I get to the seedier part of town?" Bruce inquired.

"Huh?" Plump Face replied blankly.

"You know where there are pool halls."

"You'll find them joints by the river," the more articulate, taller hobo disclosed.

A crude map was drawn by the shorter round man on a paper placemat that Mr. Ellory had saved in his pocket from Ruthie's Kitchen. The conversation soon grew fugacious. The tall down and outer walked away initially, trailed by the shrimpier man.

"Thank you," Mr. Ellory muttered while jitterily finger-pointing to their backsides. He followed the local's handmade map eastward.

Four hours into visiting establishments 'by the river,' Bruce Ellory became tired of playing detective, realizing all his worn shoe leather had failed to yield any search results for the three-hundred-pound bruiser. *"I wasn't cut out for this,"* he ruminated.

Nobody claimed to know Mr. Ellory's colossus. Several drunkards, gamblers, hustlers, and bartenders shaking their heads, 'No... never seen him,' replayed in Bruce's mind. Eventually, he perceived any new responses as transparent, concluding, *"This guy can't live up here."*

Exhausted, Bruce entered a spacious, nearly deserted pool hall named Sam's Pool and Drink that he had called upon previously in the day. The joint was poorly lit, but a cozy corner looked appealing. He ordered a gin and tonic through a stocky, red-faced, possibly Irish bartender who, by his gray hair, presented to be in his mid-fifties. He wore a red checkered shirt, too tight for an older body. This cagey bartender had shaken his head three hours earlier, after Bruce Ellory depicted the gorilla, then growled, "Don't know any such mugs, Mack."

Sitting backward on a round armless bar stool in a quiet corner to the right, Mr. Ellory placed his sweaty fedora atop the bar behind him. The broken man began to focus on a beer poster of a handsome man unwinding in a lounge chair. He absently pondered, *"Why can't I ever be so relaxed?"*

Bruce Ellory spun around, facing the bar, absorbing his momentary oasis in the form of a cocktail. As he did, a slender shadow projected on the wall next to him.

Originating at an altitudinous height, the oak bar stool came crashing downwards on Ellory's skull. If he had eyes on the posterior side of his head before he plummeted to the floor, Mr. Ellory would have caught a glimpse of the very tall, skinny man releasing it. As Bruce's face sniffed the floorboards, losing consciousness, a pair of immaculate, white wingtip shoes skulked away.

11

DASHING DARLENE

SHE STOOD IN THE OUTER DOORWAY. "I'M DAR-
lene," she proclaimed effervescently, "the criminal
justice college intern student. Professor Whitley sent
me." The dialogue flowed loud enough to reach Max
Weatherbee's moderately lobed ears. To a full-grown
man like Max, her voice aired cute and innocent.

Her eyebrows were thin and accompanied by elongated, lovely brown eyes. She wore a baby blue, ruffled blouse with a compact gray knee-length skirt, dark
nylons, and black patent leather pumps. Her back was
pressed against the opened door. She craved attention.

Max sharply proceeded to a standing position,
with his left palm wedded to his desk, then charmingly
replied, "Oh, I... actually forgot, but now I can't think
of a reason why I did." He added, "You present more
mature than college age."

Darlene's red lips smirked; her perfect face grew
more perfect. "Hey, I'm supposed to take your calls

from ten till five for the next six weeks, and you're supposed to show me cases you are working on. I'm a quick learner." Her tone progressed in boldness as she finished the narrative.

Appreciating the young woman's fervency, Max detached himself from his desk and advanced to the threshold. "Sure," he chuckled. "That's if I get a case. But having you here will free up some time if I do." His hands moved as he talked. "How old are you, Darlene?"

"Twenty-one. I'm a big girl who can handle herself," she disclosed, bobbing her head. Darlene advanced briskly to meet Max halfway into the empty waiting room, handing him her coat.

"I see." Max semi-smiled and continued, "Starting now, your new name is Dashing Darlene!"

Her pinkness turned to redness. The intern retreated until she felt her backside pressed firmly against the hallway door again. During this second occurrence, she flexed a knee, digging the sole of her shoe into the oak door, which made a thumping sound on impact. "How so?" Darlene quipped.

Only a few feet away, Max pointed his left middle finger at her and complimented, "You're full of adventure and confidence!"

Dashing Darlene winked a long eye, unstuck herself off the door, and brushed by his left shoulder. She settled her belongings on the small, bare, brown oak desk in the rear of the waiting room. "I guess this is where I sit," she declared, using an enthusiastic tone.

The comment went unanswered. Besides her newly

placed makeup bag, pocketbook, and notebook, only a black Western Electric telephone and white intercom speaker featuring a red buzzer button sat on the desk. Across from her in the agency's barren waiting room were three armless, padded-seat, cafeteria-style chairs—none matched another.

Max hung up her coat and returned to the desk in his office, resuming sorting the mail, but soon became startled. She loomed over him, peering downward like a vulture on a perch. "So, where did you grow up?" Darlene encroached. Her posture was erect; with elbows bent, she placed both hands on her hips, waiting for a response.

After a five-second pause, Max locked his solid fingers together, then imparted flatly, "I was born and raised here in New Paris."

She pivoted on two black high heels and took three steps toward the wall to the right. "You have nice pictures… but the green paint on these walls is so gloomy."

"Kind of like my current situation," he snickered.

She had her rear to him, facing one wall and examining the photos. Max stared at the black seams of her nylons dividing each calf's center. He gasped. His eyes then led him to a less exciting place.

Darlene, showing a lack of shyness, slid left. "Who is this man in the picture next to you?" she queried, pointing at a photograph looking over her right shoulder at Max.

"Why, that's my Uncle Harry Weatherbee," the

investigator disclosed, "an old friend of your Professor Whitley. I guess Harry is the reason you are here."

She spun her spindly body around to face him, captivated.

He orated, "Uncle Harry taught me everything I know about detective work... used to take me to work with him at the police station when I was young. By the time I graduated college, he had retired from the force, and I went to work for him at his private detective agency. That lasted a few years until I joined the Army. When I returned home after the war, I opened this place by myself, and it has been sort of sluggish."

"Where is your uncle now?" she asked, moving towards him. Her visage broadcasted curiosity.

"He had a stroke while I was overseas... he's no longer among us," Max said solemnly.

"I'm sorry to hear of his passing." Her tone possessed sympathy.

"Thank you. He had a good life, accomplished more than most," he affirmed, staying seated.

"What about your dad?" she further questioned, edging closer and glancing down into his serious eyes.

"My dad died during the influenza pandemic in 1918, so I don't remember him much." Max leaned back in his chair and reached into a desk drawer, taking out a pack of Lucky Strike cigarettes.

Her thighs now touched the side of his desk. Darlene's nails were pristine. She sported no rings. Placing four stringy fingers on the desk's border, she continued her cordial interrogation, "Your mom?"

"You are going to be good at this," he remarked, looking toward the unlit cigarette in his right hand. Darlene stood to his left, listening. Max recommenced, "My mom lives in town; she never remarried. She didn't want me to follow in my uncle's footsteps as a policeman. 'That's too dangerous,' she kept reminding me." He lit the cigarette. "So here I am, a private dick carrying no job security, and mom's okay with it." Max grinned as he completed the sentence and enjoyed his first puff.

She oddly focused on the smoke he blew.

He asked, "You want a light?"

Dashing Darlene backed up her five-foot-seven-inch slender frame halfway toward the pictures on the wall, contemptuous of the cigarette smoke. "No... I hate those things," she answered. "My dad said they are bad for you."

He exhibited a stone face. Cutely she changed the subject. "I see you played football."

"Sure, high school and one year on the city college freshman team," Max replied. "Sophomore year, I was cut."

Darlene nodded and then got out one unrecognizable syllable. Max interjected and took control of the conversation. "Now we're going to talk about you, Miss Dashing Darlene!"

12

ADAMSVILLE
PART 2

THE ROOM WAS SPINNING AS HE GROGGILY CAME to, not having an idea of how long he had been unconscious. Before changing from all fours to pulling himself up, Mr. Ellory perceived a sharp pinch in his left hand. "Ow!" he cried.

Broken glass pierced his skin, a vestige of the gin and tonic drink that crashed down alongside him. Bruce fixed one bar stool erect, then examined the other lying on the floor and mused, *"What the hell just happened?"*

None of the dozen or so pool hall patrons seemed to notice Bruce's ascent to the standing position. The atmosphere at Sam's Pool and Drink buzzed louder now. Four fishermen, who were not there earlier, played pool fifteen feet from him. They presented as inordinately loud and were engaged in unpolished, senseless conversation around a nearby green felt table. *"Nobody cares that I was on the floor,"* said the inner self of the violence victim.

Mr. Ellory sat humbly on a bar stool, palpated his pants pocket for a bulge, and grew surprised. His wallet remained. Rubbing his sore forehead, he looked about the wood-paneled bar room, studying faces. His gut intuition told him that whoever attacked him was no longer present among the remaining denizens.

Still dizzy, he wobbled to the left and, using a half wave, summoned the red-faced bartender, who was not so attentive this time. The dour, red-faced man glared at Mr. Ellory through icy eyes and continued wiping a glass with a towel at a most unproductive pace.

"I've been hit over the head," Bruce meekly confided. Next, he attempted to ascertain, "Didn't anybody see anything?"

The thickset-bodied man in the snug shirt inched toward Ellory, displaying a kisser devoid of pity. "No, mister, all we saw was you passed out drunk.... almost called an ambulance." His tone blared asperity. "You shouldn't drink so much," he jeered.

The jarring brevity caused Mr. Ellory's face to appear frozen. His frail frame did a one-hundred-eighty-degree turn, making his way to the front door, and almost got to it. A red-headed young man sitting solo at a small round table deliberately stuck out a blue-jeaned leg; Mr. Ellory bumped into it. It seemed intentional—the young man offered no apology. The kid reeked like fish and wore a green bucket hat with locks of fuzzy red hair outlined on the bottom of it. He chomped his crooked teeth once, then he uttered, "Hey, mister, I have something for you."

Mr. Ellory peered down, and the laddish man reached for something white on the round table beside him. The stranger gave a cocky grin under freckled cheeks and notified, "A friend of yours stopped by."

Bruce's eyes became alarmed.

The young fisherman sneered and resumed, "He asked me to give it to you when you woke up from your nap."

It was a letter-size envelope, blank on the outside. Mr. Ellory hesitantly took it. The post-adolescent removed his leg, which had obstructed The out-of-towner's path to the gray wooden door, and in five seconds, Bruce Ellory saw twilight. The evening temperature now aired considerably colder. Mr. Ellory moped onto the sidewalk, internally consumed with fear. *"I can't do this alone."*

He smoked and walked, returning to the vibrant center of town. Once there, he examined his wallet's contents, finding his personal papers and identification cards folded, but all the cash remained untouched. *"Why didn't they take my cash?"* He momentarily concluded, *"This wasn't a robbery."*

Thirty minutes later, Mr. Ellory found a rear seat on an inbound bus back to New Paris. Experiencing an uncanny feeling, he opened the fisherman's envelope.

On plain white stationary in remarkably neat hand-writing, it read:

> *Mr. Ellory, Be fortunate there were spec-tators around. I don't care for witnesses. You understand that, don't you? Not sure what you're looking for, but my best advice is to get out of the state before your luck runs sour. You'll need money to do so, and it's the only reason why I didn't take your petty cash.*

The letter was unsigned. *"This writing is too orderly to be written by the gorilla of a man who killed Wayne Palmer,"* his mind reasoned. *"I'm in way over my head."* Bruce's awareness of the thumping tachycardia through his chest wall made him reach for his sternum.

13

THE HOUSE WITH THE VINES

THE NEXT MORNING, FOLLOWING HIS BOTCHED trip to Adamsville, at the Hotel Duncan, a perturbed Mr. Ellory sat erect in room twenty-five's lopsided green chair. He iced the top of his swollen head using a makeshift icepack. After the ice melted, he scanned the New Paris Times from cover to cover. When he got to the classified section, his sunken brown eyes widened. In slightly enlarged print on the second to last page, a small ad read: *$500 Reward for information leading to the capture of Mr. Wayne Palmer's killer. Call HP7-1303.*

Ten minutes later, Mr. Ellory—donned in his same brown suit and gray fedora as yesterday—sat in the Hotel Duncan's rear lobby phone booth. Tomorrow's fugitive held the now torn-out classified ad up against the booth's wall with his fingers spread apart. He felt his body sweating profusely as he dialed the digits on the paper.

"Allard Chemists," a male voice announced uninterestedly on the other end of the line.

Mr. Ellory shut the glass door and then stammered, "Ugh... ugh... I think I have the wrong number." Bruce did not speak the truth. "I was calling regarding reward money." He put two fingers of his left hand on his temple, pushing the fedora up a smidge.

"You dialed the correct number," the unknown man responded apathetically.

"I... I possess valuable information for you on the murder."

"Hold on," said the voice. The tone remained unimpassioned.

A woman's voice soon came on the line. "Hello!" It blared like a prison yard speaker.

Not wanting to use Mr. Wallace, his hotel alias, Mr. Ellory thought quickly and used another. "My name is Mr. Wells. I know things about the murder. Can we meet today?" He spoke hurriedly.

The booming female voice returned truculently, "Here are your instructions --------------."

He pulled the handset an inch away from his ear. Trying to keep up, Mr. Ellory ripped a bite-sized yellow piece of paper off the pad on the wooden ledge, yanked a pencil out of his shirt pocket, and jotted down an address. Remembering his taxi driver days, he was familiar with the affluent Wickford section in the upper east side of New Paris. "Orms Street, I know where it is," he responded.

"See you soon, Mr. Wells," she said tersely. The receiver clicked.

Mr. Ellory gripped the silent handset for five seconds and hung it up. His heart started beating fast again. *"Am I really doing this?"*

An additional phone call was made. *"Mona... Mona, pick up."* His wife did not answer; the phone rang and rang. *"She's probably on to her next man... Bitch!"*

Bruce exited the phone booth, backtracked upstairs to room twenty-five, poured himself a glass of gin from one of the bottles on the dresser top, and buried it. Successively, he buried another. His hands stopped shuddering.

The cobblestone, city bus-length walkway of the burgundy house was set back on a hillock beyond Orms Street. The modular brick walls of this majestic dwelling were crawling with ivy, resembling a monster's grasp.

Due to irresoluteness, Bruce advanced, taking tentative steps on the slippery wet cobblestone. The morning rain had halted, but the noon sky lingered gray. Halfway through his ascent, a thick wooden front door opened. One portly man stepped outside of the house wearing oval spectacles and a light gray suit that looked as though it needed dry cleaning. The two men met three-quarters of the way up the path. Mr. Ellory paused, thinking the man had been coming to converse. Instead, he cut around him, bellowing, "Pardon me!"

Bruce questioned, "Mister, do you live here?"

The rotund man stopped in his tracks, puckered his forehead, and grumbled, "I, sir, do not, and may I inquire you to kindly explain your business today?"

Bruce lied, "I have an appointment to see the chemist."

Both men stood on the cobblestone and faced one another. They were about the same height, but the bigger man had a good ten years on Mr. Ellory. The big man wore a big hat. More words flared out over his double chin. "Do you know anything regarding the murder?" His breath was hot. He went on, "Are you here for the reward?"

"Not sure what you are talking about," Bruce quibbled. "As I said, I have an appointment with the chemist."

Keeping his hands in his pockets, rocking on his heels, the fat man introduced himself, "My name is Howard Stanford." His tone aired demeaning. "Well, when you decide to be truthful and don't secure all the pieces to the puzzle, call me at my hotel. I'm sure missing a few myself." Mr. Stanford squinted through his spectacles. "Again, it's Mr. Howard Stanford," he imparted, "I'm staying at the Chadwick Hotel in Queens Row."

Mr. Ellory nodded interestedly, replying, "Okay, thanks." But thought, "*Sure, buddy.*"

Howard Stanford pinched one of the rolls of fat

behind his neck using a chubby index finger and thumb. Eyeballing the house with the vines, Stanford's inflection became animated. "I've seen many a foxy dame in my lifetime," he divulged, "but never one married to a toad like that." The obese man departed toward Orms Street.

Bruce shrugged his puny shoulders, not really understanding what Mr. Stanford meant. He then proceeded up the rest of the walkway.

As he grew close to the house with the vines, out of the corner of his eye, he saw a shadow of a human figure behind the horizontal blinds of a first-floor window on his left. The blinds were open enough for an eye to peer out, but someone could not peer in. The eerie presence of the watching shadow made Bruce extremely uneasy.

The bulky, oak, windowless dungeon-type door would hurt your knuckles if you had to knock. He pressed the buzzer—the doorbell chimed with sanctity like church bells. Mr. Ellory waited. On the right of him, pinned to the house, existed a weather-peeled, white, wooden sign that simply read Allard Chemists. "*So much for advertising,*" Bruce thought.

A slim man around forty, dressed in a white lab coat with jet-black hair, combed forward answered the door. "How can I help you?" he offered in an annoying tone, as if he did not really mean to be helpful. The man held onto the archaic door by his left hand, blocking the entrance as best as his thin frame could. He possessed dark bunny eyes that leered and stood approximately two inches above Ellory's own recessed eyes.

"Hi, I'm inquiring about the reward," Bruce announced courteously.

"Do you have an appointment?"

"Yes. I phoned... I'm Mr. Wells," Bruce pitched today's alias.

The stranger identified himself, curtly informing, "Professor Allard." He took a breath via his narrow, jalapeno pepper-shaped nose, then resumed, "Come in." The man had a stoic disposition and condescending affect to his voice even though he spoke little. Obviously, he was the chemist, and Mr. Ellory was not.

Professor Allard led the visitor into an elegant foyer that appeared redolent of the roaring twenties, which briefly gave Bruce an evocative memory of his aunt's house years ago. The professor pointed by directing a supinated palm at a gold settee on the right, featuring a flowered brocade backrest. "Wait here," he instructed, "My wife Vivian will speak to you."

Bruce Ellory sat gently on the settee. Several yesteryear art deco pieces surrounded him on the walls, but none of them were interesting. He coughed a smoker's cough, removed his hat, bent his head forward, and hand-combed his tousled, thinning hair over the egg-shaped bruise acquired the prior day at Sam's Pool and Drink.

Professor Allard articulated no more. He shut the front door, locked it, ambulated to the left side of the foyer, and slid open a door that recessed into a wall.

Mr. Ellory caught a glimpse of counters full of chemistry trinkets. Shortly, the door slid closed. Bruce raised his head, noticing a red porcelain sign reading: NO ADMITTANCE. "*The same room where somebody was staring at me through those blinds. That somebody had to be Professor Allard,*" he reflected. Being alone in the foyer of the house with the vines made Bruce's nerves brittle.

14

VIVIAN ALLARD

WITHIN FIVE MINUTES OF THE CHEMIST'S DEPAR-
ture, a fit blonde-haired woman in her early thirties
fleetly entered the opulent foyer from a rear door
beyond the spiral staircase. To Mr. Ellory, the lady
presented tough-looking but attractive, if one could
handle that sort of thing. Bruce knew he could not.

She wore excessive rouge on her high cheekbones
and carried a peek-a-boo hairstyle slightly past her
shoulders. Thin brown streaks originating at the coiffure's zenith made each side of her neck look like riv-
ulets flowing down a waterfall. The woman exhibited
immoderate arm swaying when she walked towards
the decorative settee that currently housed Bruce's
buttocks. She sported a black dress featuring netted
sleeves resembling a gossamer. The dress was magnificent, emphasizing a long V-designed front terminating
well into her sternum. Her huffy facial expression and

exaggerated body language nonverbally told Mr. Ellory this dame loved confrontation.

Feeling inferior to her ostentation, Mr. Ellory rose attentively from the settee as if she were an Army colonel. She appeared even to his five-foot-eight height in her spiked heels.

Vivian Allard arched her rainbow-shaped eyebrows, making them pointy, and initiated the conversation by chiding Bruce, "You're not with that fat stooge who just left here, are you? The one who wasted fifteen minutes of my time!" This was undoubtedly the boisterous, deep female voice from this morning's telephone call.

A normal man would have chuckled, but Bruce Ellory could not foster a clue how to. Almost hypnotized, gazing at the mammoth gold swirl emblem on her necklace sitting over her cleavage, he humbly said, "No, ma'am."

She announced, "My name is Mrs. Allard." Her resonance did not change. "I presume you are Mr. Wells, who called me a few hours ago." She stood close and confident.

"That is correct, Mrs. Allard," Bruce Ellory replied diffidently.

She gave a sardonic grin using extra dark red lips, then brusquely questioned, "And exactly what information do you possess regarding my brother Wayne Palmer's murder?

"I saw the killing," he disclosed solemnly.

It struck a nerve; she seemed temporarily silenced.

Her wine glass-shaped face above a long neck turned white in the rouge-free areas. Mr. Ellory did not know what to do next. He reached out for her hand to comfort her. She pulled it away. Her nails were sharp, piercing his thumb.

"Go on, Mr. Wells. Have you notified the police?"

"I didn't want to get too involved," he lied.

He fastidiously told Vivian Allard his recollection, starting with the macabre night witnessing the murder, the gorilla boarding a bus to Adamsville, and his own trip to Adamsville. It contained facts only police would know, like the position of the dead body and exactly how Mr. Palmer was dressed. To protect his identity, he cautiously left out the part about his wife Mona having an affair with Vivian's brother, Mr. Wayne Palmer. By the time his story finished, the smaller-than-average man was back sitting on the gold settee, leaning forward, holding his fedora. Sweat poured downward on his pale visage.

She sat to his right on the bottom of the staircase, smoking a cigarette through a long black Bakelite holder. "Well, it's a good thing you didn't go to the police." She leisurely puffed and exhaled. "My brother Wayne became affiliated with some gangsters," she divulged, "bad ones."

Bruce's face became deadpan.

"Your story is vague, Mr. Wells, certainly not enough information to receive any money."

"I am not interested in reward money. Only wish to see the killer brought to justice." He spoke meekly, finishing the sentence in his mind. *"So, I can get off the hook."*

"How do I know this big ape tale isn't hogwash?" she snapped.

Airing entreaty in his voice, he asked a question instead of answering hers. "Can you give the police the information I provided?" He placed the hat back on his head, signaling wishes to leave.

Her green oval eyes ballooned with helium. "I'm not talking to any cops. I'll ask around my brother's circle and see if Wayne knew any hulks like you described."

"I'll fry in the meantime," his mind assured.

"When I find him," she foretold, "there's going to be another murder." Vivian Allard whacked one staircase spindle using a clenched fist. The wood vibrated. "It's my sisterly obligation. I'll fill em' with a bunch of twenty-two slugs, then you can have the stinkin' reward money." Her face appeared apple-red.

Still sitting on the settee, disconcerted, he dug his hands into his cheeks. The visit was veering off course. Above a painting of a flapper woman—Bruce looked at the bronze flowered wallpaper near the wall's apex. He despondently thought, *"Her revenge is certainly not going to help clear me of the murder."* But in lieu said, "I'm going to work on getting you more details." He desired no such intentions.

Rising from the stairs, she flicked her dead cigarette out in an ashtray on a side table and began pacing aimlessly in front of him. Her body's fluctuations palpably displayed that she remained highly irritated. She talked and walked. "Sounds similar to what the slob who just left here said. And precisely, how can I reach you?" She stopped near his knees, bending her torso over him like an angry mother, and acerbically inquired, "At the same run-down hotel fatso is staying at?"

He took his hands off his face and opened his mouth, but no words came out.

Vivian Allard extended her arm and lightly poked a keen, pink fingernail under the brim of Bruce's hat, making it askew. "Hello.... did you hear me? Where are you staying, Mr. Wells?"

His mind spoke, *"Gotta get out of here."* Mr. Ellory hopped up and fixed his hat straight. "I told you I don't know him. I rent an apartment in town. I'll contact you again soon."

She distasted his cageyness. "Goodbye, Mr. Wells."

He unlocked the door and showed himself outside. The weather lingered cloudy; the air felt brisk. As he exited the property, he never looked back at the house with the vines, but he mysteriously sensed the eyes in between the blinds staring at him from the strange No Admittance room.

What Mr. Ellory could not perceive was the white wingtip shoes that picked up his tail as he turned right at the sidewalk and dawdled down Orms Street in the direction of the subway station.

15

MAX BECOMES INTRIGUED

FROM HIS NINTH-FLOOR OFFICE IN THE KEISER Building, Max Weatherbee studied today's *New Paris Times* headline:

> *Police Report: Still No Leads on Location of Prominent Insurance Man Wayne Palmer's Killer. Unidentified Person of Interest Remains at Large.*

He then curiously viewed the small classified ad he cut out: *A $500 reward for information that leads to the capture of Mr. Wayne Palmer's killer. Call HP7-1303.*

The private detective juxtaposed the two snippets on his steel desk—contemplating. He dialed the digits.

16

THE PURSUIT BEGINS

MR. ELLORY QUIETLY DEPARTED THE HOUSE WITH the vines and headed down the hill on Orms Street toward the subway station. The November sky above him remained cloudy as sweat pooled around the collar of his untidy white shirt. Every house he passed seemed stately to him. When Vivian Allard's house was no longer in sight, he stopped, loosened his tie, and then took out a pack of Chesterfields located in the brown suit's right inner pocket. He lit up, utilizing a match. *"I accomplished nothing there. It is either time to go to the cops,"* he thought, *"or jump off the roof of the Duncan."*

One city block behind, the tall stalker's stride outpaced Bruce's enough for the stranger to frequently pause, nonchalantly doing pointless things such as checking the time on his watch or pocket fiddling.

A wrought iron fence went right—Bruce Ellory went right with it. He found himself amid an undersized area of greenery. Between two manicured arbor-vitaes, his wife Mona's words replayed in his head. *'Bruce, when we met, you were a highly regarded engineer. Your designs…. breathtaking. Now you can't even hold a job at a department store.'* Feeling like a loser, he removed a metal flask from his left inner suit pocket and chugged desperately. The gin's taste felt succulent to his lips. He chugged again. His hands no longer shook.

The white wingtips, which were tracking Bruce, halted at the sidewalk corner of the wrought iron fence without entering the greenery.

Oblivious, Mr. Ellory diagonally cut through the bushes and was back on the sidewalk, almost approaching the hill's bottom, this being the Wickford section's bustling retail district. Soon, Bruce became engulfed in Tuesday's packed streets, consisting of lunch-breaking businessmen and elegant lady shopaholics. Pathetic Bruce Ellory, sporting his wrinkled suit and worn-out brown shoes, fit in here like a stack of religious magazines in a gentleman's club.

The crowded streets made the distance between Mr. Ellory and the tall, thin, hatless man wearing a stiff white suit plus black bow tie appear greater than the one hundred actual feet. The six-foot-four man's immaculate blonde coif stuck out like a white queen's crown on a chessboard.

Mr. Ellory adjourned to buy a pretzel from an elderly street vendor.

The white wingtips also stopped. Their occupant

sparked up a cigarette while facing a clothing store window. A young woman in a pink coat, guiding a stroller, came betwixt the man and the window. "Pardon me, miss," the tall, thin man said. His voice presented squeaky—coated with an air of sarcasm.

The woman smiled demurely, advancing to the next corner. His eyes followed her lecherously.

The man in the ivory suit lost a step due to tarrying during his temporary distraction. Mr. Ellory and his pretzel were in motion, descending the stairs under the street to the subway platform. After dropping a token in the turnstile and making it through the gate, Bruce noticed his train was already at the platform. He picked up speed.

His suave-dressed stalker, now taking giant leaps, had reached the gate. The pursuer pushed the turnstile bar before the token was fully down in the collection chamber. The gate did not open. Thrusting hard using a knee, it opened on a second attempt.

The time-lapse benefited unsuspecting Mr. Ellory, who boarded the populated subway train and took a standing position. If Mr. Ellory had not rotated his face in the opposite direction of the door's window, he would have seen a scar-faced, dirty, blonde-haired, towering man struggling to scramble onto the train. The scramble became interrupted by a fast-shutting metal door.

Frustrated with his dereliction of duty, the walking totem pole threw a lit cigarette against the train's window; it caromed and landed on the pavement. Next, he whacked the thick glass with a gangling spread-out palm.

A college-age male rider, alongside Bruce, pointed at the closed sliding door's window and imparted, "Wow, is that tall guy outside mad at someone!"

Bruce's facial expression grew incredulous, hardly nodding, as if to discard the baseball cap-wearing young man's subjective statement, not realizing it was he who had been ensconced.

The persistent lad then elbowed Mr. Ellory playfully and implored, "Come on, mister... look at this feller quick!"

Bruce finally turned around towards the glass window, but all he saw was a brick wall flickering as the subway train accelerated away from the underground platform.

PART 3

17

A PLAN FOR A BROKEN MAN

SLEEP WAS ATTEMPTED. BRUCE ELLORY'S BODY jerked side to side while sweat encased his forehead. Again, his heart pounded against his thorax wall as though it were a jackhammer. Night terror visions of a jail cell and a judge—savagely smashing down a mallet played continuously in his subconscious mind during this fragmented sleep. He unconsciously called out, "Mona!"

Wednesday at 7:00 a.m., as daylight filled room twenty-five, the eyes of the man in hiding remained shut as he reached a hand onto a bedside table next to the tarnished brass bed. Bruce's fingers crawled—like a spider—until they found the Chesterfield pack and book of matches. It was a morning routine for him to put the cigarette in his mouth and light it with his eyes still closed. Once Mr. Ellory ingested his first nicotine puff, his eyelids popped open.

He smoked right-handed and rose to the side of the

bed, putting two bony bare feet on the stained rug. His skin crawled enough for him to start scratching his lateral left forearm, using a tremulous right hand. *"Where do I go from here?"* He ruminated, *"Have to try Mona again. Warn her about the note I received in Adamsville. Will she think I killed Palmer? I need a drink."*

When the cigarette died, Bruce poured gin into a dirty glass on the bureau. He buried it quick and did it again.

At 8 a.m., Mr. Ellory's call was placed from the lone phone booth in the Hotel Duncan's rear lobby. As the receiver gave its initial ring, Bruce leaned out of the booth, warily gazing through the distant front door's glass window at a small group of old men who were conversing outside. On the second ring, he swiveled to the right, observing the short, stout female clerk possessing a high-pitched foreign accent. She appeared to be reviewing charges with a middle-aged man who seemed confused by what she was showing him. Everything in his environment made Mr. Ellory suspicious.

On the third ring, Mona answered, "Hello."

"Mona, it's me," stated Bruce as he shut the phone booth's glass door utilizing his free hand.

"Bruce, are you on the run?" questioned Mona Ellory's fuchsia-polished lips. She spoke close to the mouthpiece. Her tone grew somber. "You only left me fifty dollars in the bank."

"I'm still in the city, staying at a hotel." He ignored

the complaint; just hearing her voice sounded eupho-
nious to his ears. Mr. Ellory slowly lowered his wimp-
ish frame onto the wooden bench.

"Do not give me the name of it, and do not go to
the police. They will interrogate, break you, and force
a confession," she deterred.

"I didn't.... I didn't kill him," he stammered. His
body became fidgety, teetering between sitting and
half standing in the tight phone booth.

"You're not capable of murder, Bruce; you are too
weak. But a police detective named McGann has come
by the house three times asking questions." Her voice
aired splendidly articulate, as usual, during her narrative. She went on, "This McGann told me, Mrs. Kerns,
our neighbor across the hall, phoned the police when
she read the story in the newspaper and reported your
Wayne Palmer threat to them. She remembered word
for word what you said in the hallway about wishing
to make Wayne 'pay dearly.' And a young couple saw a
man of your description on Wayne's street right after
the killing. The man said he bumped right into you.
Explain this, Bruce. Are you involved somehow? Tell
me you aren't."

"I only witnessed the murder, Mona," he disclosed
gravely. "I just wanted to take another look at the guy
who ruined my life. I didn't know he was going to be
murdered. It happened so quickly."

Her polished lips briskly retorted, "You made your
life the way it is." She took in some air, and resumed,
"The detective is aware of the affair," she cautioned,

then added, "Wayne and I always kept things very private."

"Why did you tell the police detective?" he asked bleakly.

"I had to explain why you said what you said in the hallway."

There was silence.

She spoke first. "It doesn't look good for you, Bruce."

"I have no idea what I'm going to do," he replied.

"Listen, I think Wayne might have been involved with some bad people," she divulged. "I know he had a predilection towards gambling."

Bruce's respirations increased. "His sister told me he had gangster associates."

"You went to see her?" she asked, puzzled.

"Yes."

Mona narrated. "Bruce, I told this police detective that Wayne made frequent private phone calls while we were out, which he called 'urgent.' He was often late when we met and always blamed it on his insurance business. Sometimes, he looked back over his shoulder as we walked along the street. I told Detective McGann these facts, and he snarled, stating Wayne fared as 'an outstanding citizen who has been generous to the Boy's Club of New Paris.' Sorry, Bruce, I tried."

"Outstanding? He ruined my life."

"Stop saying Wayne ruined your life. You ruined your life, Bruce," she chided, "because of the drinking."

"I'm going to quit drinking once I clear this up," he foretold.

"Bruce, it will never be fully cleared up. I was in love with Wayne, and now he's gone." She sniffled for a mere second, then swiftly regained composure. "I do hope you can save yourself."

He got to the reason he called. "Mona, I have been attempting to reach you. You're not safe in that apartment."

"What?"

"The killer took a bus to Adamsville following the murder. I traveled up there Monday trying to find him, and someone hit me over the head with a bar stool. They went in my wallet. They can find the address to the apartment."

"You're going to get yourself killed too, Bruce."

"I know," he muttered.

"I guess you couldn't have killed Wayne," she said, "the one thing you are not is a malevolent person."

His eyes were wet. "Mona, I ......" He attempted to find words but broke down sobbing.

"I'm leaving the apartment for good this afternoon," she imparted, "I'll be staying at my parent's house in Freeport." Her tone was stoic.

"You'll be safe there," he wept.

"My father will find me a job."

"Okay."

"Contact me when you are no longer on the run," she prospectively stated, "and I'll arrange the divorce papers for you to sign."

"Divorce, please no," he begged.

"Don't make it difficult, Bruce."

"Mona, what should I do now?" he whimpered.

"I discovered a private detective's ad inside a free newspaper at the supermarket and cut it out in case you called. His office is in Old Downtown. Write it down, Bruce—you need help."

"I'm desperate, Mona. Give me the information." Bruce blinked vigorously to air-dry his eyes. Next, he grabbed the pencil from his shirt pocket, stood up, removed his dilapidated wallet stored in his right pants pocket, and found an old receipt. He flipped it over, placed it at eye level on the wall, and said, "I'm ready."

Mona Ellory picked up a neatly cutout piece of newspaper from the table beside the telephone and read what she saw:

Max Weatherbee
Private Detective for Hire
No Case Too Small
Privacy Assured
505 10th Ave Suite #312
Phone HP1-2314
After Hours Answering Service HP1-6090

"Bruce, please tell this private detective, Mr. Weatherbee, the things about Wayne Palmer that I confided to you."

"Okay, but how will I pay for the services?"

"Do what you always do when you're in a money jam... ask your sister Susan."

The comment hurt like a judo punch to the belly. Bruce sucked it up and pleaded, "Can't you meet me at Mr. Weatherbee's office?"

"No. I have to get packing now for Freeport."

He tossed in a desperate, "I love you."

Mona's fuchsia-painted lips replied, devoid of emotion, "Please spare me of the platitudes. Goodbye, Bruce." The relationship became undeniably forlorn.

18

HOWARD STANFORD HITS THE PAVEMENT

HOWARD STANFORD EXITED THE CHADWICK Hotel's expansive lobby in the Queens Row section of New Paris. It was a day after he visited the house with the vines, briefly encountering Bruce Ellory along the walkway. Mr. Stanford had a carton wedged deep into a spacious armpit. He wore a big, fat, plaid suit and an immense gold fedora above his soft forehead. A torpedo-sized cigar hung out of the left side of his mouth between wet lips. November's cool weather, accompanied by a blue sky overhead, greeted him. Standing on the mid-size, uptown hotel's curb, he fetched a cab. While keeping the cigar from being spit out of his trap, Mr. Stanford authoritatively told a scruffy-faced driver, "Roosevelt Heights, Empire, and 18th Street!"

The cabby drove fast bearing taut triceps bulging. His loose yellow cap jiggled in all directions atop a full head of dark hair. Howard Stanford's stomach grew queasy as he pressed into his oval spectacles using two sausage fingers and felt his wide rump slide on the rear bench seat with each wheel turn. Mr. Stanford made no verbal complaints; there existed somewhere he wanted to be, and the quicker, the better.

As they approached Roosevelt Heights, the taxi driver remarked, "They sure got some nice homes up here, bud." His tone sounded cheerful.

Howard Stanford briskly retorted, "And mine's not one of 'em." Still chomping on the thick cigar, he ordered hoarsely, "Pull over... right here!"

The driver obeyed. Once stopped, he looked back over the front seat, grinned, and politely requested, "One dollar and fifty cents for the fare." Shadows existed on his Mediterranean facial skin.

Howard Stanford grabbed the carton, pushed his body out of the cab, then stood with the rear door above the curb and his buttocks holding it open. After sluggishly digging into his pockets, he reached across the front passenger's seat and, using a hefty, sweaty palm, handed the driver a crumpled dollar bill containing two quarters wrapped inside of it. Mr. Stanford shut the rear door and slapped the metal roof of the taxi, rudely announcing, "I'll tip ya next time... when I gots some money."

The driver floored it in aggrievement, propelling the cab away down Empire Ave.

Amid a sea of grandiose dwellings, Mr. Stanford opened the carton. He removed a hammer, two lengthy

roofing nails, and a thin cardboard sign, and dropped
the box of remaining articles to the pavement at his fat
feet. He hammered two nails through the twenty by
twenty-inch sign's outer borders—deeply into the pole.
The wannabe sleuth glanced up at his work and read:

> *INFORMATION   WANTED   ON*
> *RECENT NEIGHBORHOOD MURDER*
> *of MR. WAYNE PALMER, please con-*
> *tact Howard Stanford at the Chadwick*
> *Hotel HP7-7500 and request room 707.*

Mr. Stanford continued to the adjacent pole.

After finishing his fourth pole, he leaned against
it with the hammer in his right hand and caught his
breath by way of red, puffy cheeks. Escorting a leashed
black poodle, a man in his sixties, owning an all-white
mustache, sporting a round black derby waltzed up to
the pole. "Precisely what are you posting in our neighborhood, sir?" he questioned snobbishly.

"Offering my services, attempting to solve a case,
and disseminating awareness," Mr. Stanford replied.
The burning cigar was short now.

The older man peered up at the newly placed sign.
His tone became alarmed, "Oh boy, that has us all
locking our doors."

Howard Stanford pried as he unstuck himself off
the pole. "Do you know anything?"

The man shrugged. "Nobody does; it's still the talk
of our coffee shop." The elder's draw turned pessimis-

tic. "The police have done a fair reconnaissance, don't think your signs will assist much. Well, good luck anyway." The man strolled onwards, ending any future dialogue.

Howard Stanford located a pole at the next corner and affixed another sign. He stretched his torso and retrieved his accouterments from the ground. A very tall man came from the other side of nowhere and loomed inches behind Mr. Stanford's bent buttocks.

Mr. Stanford returned to an erect position. Recognizing the encroachment, he gazed way up and exclaimed, "Hey!" The eyes he perceived were stone cold.

"Hay is for horses," sarcastically stated the blonde-headed man carrying a two-inch pink scar on his right cheek, a full head above Mr. Stanford. He stood tall enough to be at eye level alongside the posted sign. The towering man's blonde hair seemed perfectly parted in the center, lacking a hair out of place. The bow tie-wearing stranger mimicked the sign's capital letter words, "Information wanted... on recent neighborhood murder... of Mr. Wayne Palmer." It was presented loud and slow in a high-pitched, provoking tone.

Mr. Stanford's cheeks still appeared red from his minor exertion of picking the box up off the ground. He plodded away beyond the pole, utterly ignoring the annoying man, causing him such vexation. The gangly man took several elongated strides and then inescapably blocked Howard Stanford's path on the city sidewalk. He extended vast arms, supinating his palms laterally, and mordantly said, "I was only trying to be of help, pal."

A flummoxed Stanford thought the tall man with arms stretched out from his white suit looked like a cross that had fallen off a church. "What do you want, Mister?" barked the ponderous unlicensed investigator. Expressing irritation, Stanford abruptly discarded a little stump, which remained of his cigar, on the pavement.

"Oh, just one of those signs to hang up at my apartment." He pointed a long index finger in the north direction and imparted, "It's merely up the street."

Mr. Stanford obliged, reducing his own exasperation. "Okay, fine, but now I have work to do. People like you keep interrupting me." He fished into the box and gave the man what he requested.

The six-foot-four, lanky, scar-faced man furled the flimsy sign tightly and stuck it in one inner pocket of a starched white suit. His white wingtip shoes retreated down the opposite path from where he claimed his apartment was situated.

19

MAX TAKES OVER

3 P.M. WEDNESDAY, BRUCE ELLORY ENTERED THE lobby of the forty-year-old Keiser Building in Old Downtown. His brown fedora's rim was bent downwards on an angle that covered most of his forehead. He wore a red tie and a galaxy blue suit, which he acquired from the Hotel Duncan's lost and found. It did not fit snugly and was hand-pressed as best as Duncan's iron allowed. Even with his scuffed brown shoes, he looked better than in previous days. However, beneath his skin, he felt fasciculations. On floor nine, he exited the elevator right, and to the left, he read a black metal elongated sign that hung above the doorframe: *Max Weatherbee Private Detective for Hire.*

Following his conversation with Mona earlier this morning, Bruce called his sister, Susan, who arranged the appointment. The wooden door propped open by a rubber stopper seemed welcoming enough to Bruce.

Mr. Ellory stood hunched forward in the doorway, appearing older than his thirty-seven years. Dashing Darlene sat preoccupied at her desk, filing French manicured fingernails with her brown hair fixed in a bun. The bare pink neck below it was tender—so tender a vampire would have been licking his lips.

"Hello," he announced, still at the threshold.

Darlene's lengthy brown eyes greeted him. "Hi, are you my three o'clock, Mr. Ellory?" she asked as if the agency were busy.

Bruce's stomach churned because he was not using an alias. "Yes," he mumbled.

Darlene—donned in a snug, low-cut, gray sweater with a turquoise cross necklace superimposing over its apex—introduced herself, displaying youthful animation. "I'm Darlene, Mr. Weatherbee's intern," she said. "Please have a seat."

The college student directed a slim index finger towards three mangy, non-matching, armless chairs five feet in front of her desk.

Mr. Ellory selected the chair on the right with an orange padded seat. Settled, he stared at a cardboard—1947 Rexall calendar above Darlene's head—while she loudly snapped gum and returned to her nails. Mr. Ellory observed X's pen marked on the days before today's date, Wednesday, November 19th. He removed his fedora and started spinning it on his index finger in a clockwise motion. *"What if this guy calls the cops?"* he pondered.

Darlene pushed the red buzzer on the intercom

box. "Mr. Ellory is here to see you," she broadcasted enthusiastically.

Max Weatherbee peeked through the off-white vertical blinds that covered a rectangular window on the wall separating his office from the waiting room. He viewed Darlene's innocent neck, then watched Mr. Ellory pointlessly spinning his hat. Beyond the window, Mr. Ellory's initial impression came across as a waiflike, nervous Nellie to the private detective. He knew the type, certainly not his cup of tea. Using his gut instinct, Max eliminated his first murder suspect, internally reflecting, *"He's too spongy."*

Max's office door swung open. "Max Weatherbee," he publicized professionally, causing Bruce to stand. Max, who had a good five inches on Bruce's five-foot-eight frame, sported a powder blue dress shirt over his square shoulders. His tie sagged loosely. The private detective extended a powerful right hand. The handshake grip was nearly crushing around Ellory's phalanges.

Max released the unintentional, tenacious grip. "Follow me, take a seat in my office," he urged. Darlene closed the door behind the two men.

"Let's do a smoke," Max suggested nonjudgmentally, once both men were seated facing one another.

Max's dark black hair with gray speckles looked waxy under the buzzing fluorescent lights. He slid a cigarette pack atop the metal desktop at his client. They were not Chesterfields, but Ellory offered no complaints.

The duo lit up.

The investigator took his first puff and spoke through a chiseled face, "Your sister Susan has hired me for two weeks; the retainer is paid. She wants me to deal directly with you and only call her if it is extremely urgent." He moved some saliva up from his pharynx and swallowed it. "Excuse me." He coughed and elaborated, "I hear cigarette smoke can paralyze the cilia in your throat."

Ellory's chin assented, doing a slight nod, unsure of what that had to do with anything relevant. He placed his fedora on the desk and picked at one meatless earlobe, conspicuously showing his tense mood.

"Okay, let's get to you." Max grinned cleverly. "Your sister didn't seem to know much, so tell me everything from the beginning. I'm aware of the Wayne Palmer murder, but the newspaper gave few details. I assume you are this primary suspect." He squeezed his square jaw with his left index finger and thumb, waiting for Ellory's response.

"Are you talking to the cops?" Mr. Ellory inquired, exhibiting tense eyes.

"No cops!" Max promised.

"I... I would hang myself if I'm put in a cell," Bruce Ellory revealed gravely.

Max's face became concerned. Mr. Ellory's fingers were now tapping the front of the metal desk.

Max heard Bruce's dancing fingers. The PI gazed down at the distal edge of the desk and disclosed, "Your sister stated that you have a drinking problem." As he said it, he pointed at Bruce with his middle finger.

Mr. Ellory did not mind how Max pointed his finger, but the drinking query caused his pale face to turn rose color. "I drink.... I drink," he stammered, "when... when I'm nervous." Bruce continued, "It relaxes me, but... but often I pass out instead. I usually drink... drink alone or in quiet bar rooms."

"I need you to loosen up," Max advised. "Start with a little about yourself." The tone was sympathetic.

"I... I grew up here in New Paris, went to college for engineering, graduated, and then worked a high-pressure job. Between stress and the inability to please my wife, I... I began drinking. It... It was sufficient to get me fired from my engineering job. Recently, it became so bad I couldn't hold a job at a department store." Bruce sat sweating profusely; his partially balding scalp was soaked.

"Do you fancy a drink now?" Max spoke benignantly—as if he were the doctor and Bruce Ellory was a patient. "One drink to calm your nerves and open up?"

"Yes," Bruce said sheepishly as he broke eye contact, focusing on the pack of cigarettes still on the desk in front of him.

"Gin and tonic? Scotch and water?"

"Just gin. Tonic not necessary," Bruce replied.

Max rose, took a few steps to the mini bar, and poured the gin into a clear highball glass. Bruce buried it, taking one swig. Max poured the next, and Bruce buried another.

Mr. Ellory sucked a breath through hollow cheeks, and the five-minute sequential oration began—the gin erased the stammering. Bruce's narrative started with the affair he discovered between his wife Mona and Wayne Palmer. He explained the threat he made in the hallway overheard by his elderly neighbor, followed by witnessing the gruesome murder in Roosevelt Heights from the alley two days later while suicidal. Next came the young couple that saw him on the street of the killing, the burning barrel, encountering the murderer in the park, and the gorilla getting on an Adamsville bus. He also told of his temporary residence at the Hotel Duncan under the alias of Mr. Cecil Wallace, his physical attack up in Adamsville trying to play detective, and including his visit to the house of the vines with Vivian Allard and her reward money. Mr. Ellory provided Max with the threatening note he received in Adamsville. He finished by telling of his wife Mona's and Vivian Allard's suspicions of Wayne Palmer possibly being involved with unscrupulous people, such as racketeers.

"See, the lump on my head?" asked Bruce

"I see it." Max's empathetic eyes acknowledged Ellory's trauma. "How are you holding up after all this?" Sincerity existed in his cadence. The PI commenced the examination of the hostile handwritten note from Adamsville.

Ellory's reaction was frank. "Honestly, I don't care if I live or die, Mona's not coming back." His recessed eyes were sad.

"Let's go with live," Max replied seriously.

"It's sort of on hold. I wanted to kill myself before the murder, but now I can't because it would make me appear guilty. I don't want to be remembered as a murderer."

"You would look guilty," Max agreed.

Mr. Ellory changed the morbid dialogue and asked, "Ever hear of a fat fellow named Howard Stanford?"

Max roared, "The reward sleuth!"

"He was at that house with the vines poking around because of the reward offered," Ellory informed.

"He couldn't find a tornado in Kansas," Max assured, applying a jocular tone.

Bruce smirked a painful smirk.

Max resumed, "The lummox, Mr. Howard Stanford, has been bumbling near my cases for years, going back to when I was working for my Uncle Harry. He's a two-bit wannabe dick operating without a license. He primarily attempts to solve cases involving reward money. When he can't fetch a reward, Howard suddenly becomes a freelance true crime writer and tries selling the story to local newspapers instead."

"I see."

"Hey, I tried getting through to that phone number on the five-hundred dollar reward classified advertisement myself," Max said. "Figured I could take it on as a case. Hours later, a chemist finally picked up and told me, 'Our reward has been rescinded,' with no explanation. Within two seconds, the man abruptly hung up the receiver."

"Mrs. Allard, the chemist's wife, Wayne Palmer's sister, probably pulled it," Bruce theorized, "because I told her what the killer looks like."

"Oh."

"Mrs. Allard implied she would handle this gorilla herself," Bruce divulged. "Tough lady."

"Well, it sounds bad for you if she does."

"I know. I went there hoping she would take my information to the cops for me."

The private detective imparted, "I'll be doing the legwork from now on."

Bruce bobbed his head.

"Do you really know your wife, Mona?"

"Oh, gee. I... I never considered such." Bruce did not repudiate the idea, adding, "She did leave town pretty fast."

"Where?"

"Her parents in Freeport."

"Everyone is a suspect. From this point, I don't want you snooping," Max directed, "or making any more excursions." He puffed. "Call me daily at the office regarding updates, and I'll come see you on Sunday evening at your hotel." He further instructed, "No venturing out of that joint except for food."

"Are you familiar with the Hotel Duncan?" Bruce asked.

"Sure... in Webster Hills, borders Chinatown. The Duncan is a place where someone down on their luck comes into a few bucks and rents a room for a week. Be careful in that section of town."

Bruce impassively nodded in agreement.

Max continued with certainty, "I should have your case solved in the next ten to fourteen days."

Bruce's eyes widened.

"We'll hand deliver this gorilla to the cops," Max envisaged, "getting you off the hook." The private detective exuberantly slapped his desk. "Palmer's execution was not a random attack. It was a revenge killing, and somebody out there knows something."

"Why can't real cops solve it so fast?" Ellory questioned.

"Firstly, our New Paris police are not looking at every piece of salient evidence because they are searching for you. Number two, they think it is a clearcut case. Number three, people on the streets aren't going to talk with cops. For starters, I'm going up to Adamsville right now."

Max Weatherbee's confidence eased Bruce Ellory's anxiety. Both men stood and shook hands again.

The gumshoe gentlemanly opened the door.

Walking past Darlene, Bruce said, "Goodbye, miss."

Max poked his head in the anteroom at Darlene, who was now reading a college textbook, and winked. "Hey, he never looked at my pictures on the wall."

She gave a whimsical smile and remarked, "I understand… that's how you like to 'break the ice,' I think you mentioned."

Max moseyed back to his desk and unfolded today's folded newspaper he had sitting on top. The headline read: *Police to release suspect's name in the Wayne Palmer murder on Friday afternoon, if not captured sooner. Suspect is not currently felt to be a public threat.*

20

NO ANSWER

ONE HUNDRED MILES WEST OF NEW PARIS, A black desk phone sitting on top of a rectangular, mahogany bedside table started to ring. Wedged under the vibrating phone sat a white crocheted doily that made it look like it was floating on a piece of ice. The Bakelite device rang and rang. It stopped.

Three hours later, the jangling returned amidst the dark, empty room. Next to it, the small, simple bed, lacking a footboard, was unmade. The ringing ceased.

21

HAMBURGERS

LATE IN THE AFTERNOON, FOLLOWING HIS MEET-
ing with Max, Bruce Ellory came moping into the
Hotel Duncan through the unmarked rear entrance.
He carried a small white paper bag. Immediately, the
clamorous lobby startled Bruce's perpetual anxiety,
increasing his exhalations. He minced to the opened
caged office and glimpsed left, becoming alarmed by a
group of men much older than himself playing a dice
game. The men were acting rowdy, while one sixty-ish
fellow was standing on the red couch hooting. Clouds
of cigar smoke seemed ubiquitous. Timid Mr. Ellory
did not care for any of it.

"Good afternoon, three packs of Chesterfields.
Add the cigarettes to my bill, please," he said, gently
through gin breath. His words were aimed at the short
and stout, gray-haired female clerk who never introduced herself and appeared to cover the caged office
every minute of daylight hours.

"All clients must be paid in full for the week on Friday," she informed, broadcasting her piercing foreign accent.

"That gives me two days," he countered politely.

"It's Just a reminder." She dropped the cigarettes in front of him, using her chubby fingers.

To Ellory's right, a white, handmade sign hanging on the external side of the cage, not present the previous day, caught his attention. He glanced at it employing bewildered eyes: NO HOOKERS.

The clerk astutely noticed Mr. Ellory's moment of bewilderment. "Mr. Duncan is trying to clean the place up." Her melodious voice was as high-pitched as ever.

Mr. Ellory thought, *You can start by clearing out the old geezers in the lobby.* Instead, he said, "That's nice of Mr. Duncan. Does he visit his hotel much?" His visage of staidness hid a dark, deep depression.

"Not too often," she replied, "walks with a cane these days, poor old soul." She looked at him with soft eyes. "Mr. Wallace, do you require housekeeping today?" Bruce's alias remained intact.

"No, but I do need laundry and dry cleaning."

"We send it a few blocks down the street to Chinatown, takes three hours." She handed him a discolored white robe to temporarily wear and a canvas bag. "Put the clothes in here and leave them outside your door," she directed colloquially.

He nodded in agreement.

She questioned, "What smells delightful in your paper bag?"

"Hamburgers," he responded bluntly.

She laughed. "Do you eat anything else?"

"Not really." Bruce almost grinned, having no idea how his hamburger runs would soon prolong his misery.

22

NEXT ORDER OF BUSINESS

IN A ROOM OF SOLITUDE, ONE HUNDRED MILES west of New Paris, a black desk phone that rested atop a rectangular mahogany bedside table jangled. A goliath-sized hand reached for it.

The lonely gorilla of a man sat at the bed's edge, facing the table. He buried the receiver in a bushel of dark hair and answered, "Hullo."

The mammoth killer listened.

"I've been out havin' fun. Whadda ya think I'm doin'?" The killer's voice aired gruff.

The killer listened.

"Uh huh," the Gorilla replied. "Did you say two more loose ends?"

The killer listened.

"When do I get my cash for clubbin' pretty boy Palmer?"

The killer listened.

"Okay, I'll start headin' to Adamsville tomorrow,"

he muttered. "And I'm not takin' any more buses after I rub out these next two pansies. You're gonna give me a ride back to your place from each bloodbath yourself."

The receiver was slammed hard enough to kill a mouse.

23

MAX HITS THE PAVEMENT

THURSDAY MORNING AT 11 A.M., FROM THE HOTEL Duncan's solo phone booth, Bruce Ellory phoned Max Weatherbee's office. Darlene, dressed in red, put him through.

"Hello, Max Weatherbee." The PI's tone seemed chipper.

"Mr. Weatherbee, it's Bruce Ellory. I... I wanted to inquire about how you made out in Adamsville last evening." The tone was solemn.

"Call me Max."

"Okay."

"Couldn't make much progress up there. I spoke to Charlie, the bartender at Sam's Pool and Drink. Ole Red Face told me you went in the place stumbling drunk, fell, and hit your head. He's not going to flip for a twenty-dollar payoff or anything else in our budget."

"Max, you... you saw the note the young fisherman gave me."

"Nobody in the joint confessed to knowing your uncanny note passer. But one thing is for certain, this gorilla, as you call him, who killed Palmer does not live in Adamsville. I asked everywhere. I think the whole post-murder bus ride was a decoy."

"What... what do we do now?" Bruce questioned apprehensively.

Max became stern, making known his feelings towards Mr. Ellory's ineptitude in his recent amateur detective work. "There's no 'we.' You are to stay put. Got it?"

"Sure but—"

The sleuth cut him off as if he knew the rest of the sentence. "I'm not giving up on Adamsville," Max imparted, "someone in that city knows something, which is why you got attacked. I'm sending an associate up there to hang around town. Adamsville is thirty miles from my office, and it's better to send him up there so I can concentrate on people who knew Wayne Palmer here in New Paris."

"Okay," Bruce said, but grimly thought, "*My time is running out.*"

"I also snooped all over the crime scene this morning," Max reported. "Nothing there either." The private detective glanced at the electric clock on the wall and then resumed, "That city park burning barrel you talked about has been suspiciously removed. Don't abandon hope, I'll solve this case, but soon, it is going to get dangerous."

"Thank you, Max," Bruce replied, nervously thinking to himself, *"Dangerous? I need a drink."*

"Bruce, call me tomorrow." Max terminated the call.

———————

Max Weatherbee, adhering to the belief that time is money, stayed busy after updating his client, Mr. Ellory. After two hours of phone calls, Max appeared ready to burn some shoe leather. He enthusiastically grabbed his gray suit jacket and hat off the hanger, then opened the door dividing his office from the waiting room.

Max buoyantly told Dashing Darlene, "You look fabulous."

She attentively lifted her head out of the textbook. The intern's hair presented shoulder length again—the bun was yesterday's news. "And why is Mr. Weatherbee so cheerful?" she queried in a playful tone.

"My dear, Wayne Palmer's father passed away five years ago, but… his mother is alive, living at Saint Elizabeth's Home for the Aged!"

"You're off to the races!" she exclaimed.

"Please leave any messages on your desk. I'll return later tonight," he directed cordially.

"Sure thing, Mr. Weatherbee." Her tone bore obedience.

"Stop calling me Mr. Weatherbee." He pointed using his middle finger, holding his hat and jacket in the other arm.

"Okay... Max. Stop pointing with your middle finger, and I will," she coyly negotiated.

"Can't help you there... been doing it since I was a kid," he disclosed, heading for the open hallway door. "At least I point it downwards, not upwards."

"I'll see you later, Mr. W," she joked through bright red lips, just catching him beyond the threshold.

With his back to the waiting room, Max rotated his neck towards her, winked a left eye, and questioned, "Mr. W?" He quickly added, "I'm not your father's age, you do realize?"

24

SAINT ELIZABETH'S HOME

SAINT ELIZABETH'S HOME STOOD IN THE NORTH-
ern section of New Paris, known as Lafayette Gar-
dens. The M line served as the only subway that could
transport you there from the Keiser building in Old
Downtown. However, Max Weatherbee felt fortunate
to own a car. The secondhand 1941 Ford he purchased
when he came home after the war served as a valuable
transportation tool for his trade.

The vehicle was a simple black, V8, two-door, standard coupe. Max's quick corner-taking ability with the
Ford became a sequel to his driving of military jeeps.
In the service, peers nicknamed him 'Crazy Turns.' His
ride to the northern outskirts of New Paris would have
taken most twenty minutes; Max arrived at Saint Elizabeth's home in a keen fourteen.

Amid the twilight, Max parked his Ford coupe par-
allel to the curb, out front of the elongated two-story,
metal, and concrete structure featuring a plethora

of uniform windows. In his gray suit plus matching fedora, he confidently swaggered up the concrete stairs, passed by a large red cross stuck to the outer façade on the right. He then opened an all-glass door.

There were two women standing behind the counter-style reception desk. One was a nun dressed in black and white—old enough to be Woodrow Wilson's mother. The other happened to be a curvy, red-headed nurse in her late twenties. Max chose red.

The private detective removed his hat. "Hi, I'd like to visit Mrs. Judith Palmer," he said, showcasing a steady gaze.

"Visiting hours are not until 6 p.m.," the red-headed nurse replied delicately through orderly teeth. Her vast doe eyes were hazel in color. Meanwhile, the prehistoric nun egressed the nurse's station.

Being accustomed to this situation, Max's chestnut brown eyes magnified, hypnotically, penetrating her own. "I'll know next time; I'm a friend of the family and haven't had a chance to see Mrs. Palmer since her son's passing," he fibbed convincingly.

"Oh, it is so tragic. Mr. Palmer stopped by just about every day." Her pulchritudinous face showed sympathy. "My name is Cindy; I work here as a nurse most evenings."

"Can you make an exception just once, Cindy?" he requested.

Gazing at his rugged, handsome face, Nurse Cindy's eager eyes answered the question. Max followed

Cindy down the hall. The nurse pointed to the last door and stepped aside.

Seeing the elderly woman in bed, Max halted to avoid frightening her as he got near the open door. "Hi, Mrs. Palmer," he said softly from ten feet away. "I need to ask you a few questions regarding your son. May I come in?" The sleuth edged closer, and his face turned disappointed.

Mrs. Judith Palmer's lost eyes stared into space. Her color ominously loomed sallow. The debilitated, white-haired lady's frail body let out a constant, non-sensical moan via a never closing mouth. Nurse Cindy entered the room and pulled down Mrs. Palmer's blanket to her abdomen, further exposing the geriatric lady's enfeeblement. Max Weatherbee's inquiries would be of no use. Mrs. Palmer rested on her side; all four extremities remained contracted.

Max tarried dumbstruck before the invalid.

Cindy returned the blanket to its original position.

"How old is she?" he asked poignantly. "What happened to her?"

"Only seventy-one. She acquired some kind of neurological disorder that caused early senility."

"I'm sad to see this," disclosed Max.

"So, just who are you?" Her big eyes grew bigger. "Obviously, not a close family friend."

"I'm a private investigator, Max Weatherbee, hired to find Mr. Palmer's killer."

"Do you think you can?" She probed, interestedly.

"Yes." He utilized the opportunity. "Did you get to know her son, Mr. Wayne Palmer?"

Her tone became flirtatious. "I take a break in thirty minutes."

———————

Nurse Cindy sat under the stars on the Ford's hood smoking a cigarette—togged out in a crimson candy-striped uniform and white nursing shoes. The nasolabial lines beneath her rosy cheeks appeared deep, making them prominent. She wore minimal makeup, which she explained, "I wear more makeup when I'm not working... the nuns, you understand."

"Sure." Max doffed his suit jacket, then tossed it through the half-open passenger window and proceeded to business. "What can you tell me about Wayne Palmer?" he inquired, squeezing his square jaw solemnly, using a thumb and index finger. "Anything suspicious?"

Before Cindy spoke, she twirled her red hair between thin fingers, and her doe eyes admired Max's masculinity. "Mr. Palmer visited his mother alone, often late, after normal hours. We all let him in... so good-looking," she giggled.

When her lips were serious again, she continued. "Sometimes Mr. Palmer would receive phone calls while here, often from his wife. Sister Jean, the old nun you saw, usually took the calls and made Mr. Palmer call back on our pay phone."

"Don't stop." He stood attentively on the curb like a gossip hound.

"One time, maybe a month ago, I answered an incoming call for him, and the voice sounded different. See, I knew it couldn't have been his wife, Mrs. Palmer, because she visited occasionally with him and acted so rude, very cocky. The woman who called that night was younger and presented as extremely nervous. She seemed in distress."

Max asked sharply, "Is there any possibility her name was Mona?

"No. He identified her as Pearl in a subsequent call."

"Very interesting." He pried, "Subsequent call?"

Nurse Cindy resumed, "Around a week later, I saw Mr. Palmer sitting in our lobby's telephone booth, keeping the door partially ajar. This really wasn't out of the ordinary, but I heard him say, 'Pearl, calm down!' and scolding her like a child."

"Please go on." His tone grew ardent; he loved the hunt.

She stopped to puff, then recommenced the short story. "Naturally, I became curious and pretended to be organizing magazines in the lobby. I merely overheard a fragment of the conversation. I heard Mr. Palmer mention her working at a 'nightclub,' but he didn't say which one. He told Pearl to 'stay put, I'll handle it,' and that's all I remembered, Mister Private Detective."

"You were helpful." He leaned his backside against the coupe's passenger door, lighting up a cigarette. The crisp November air caused Max to point toward the half-opened window. "Can I offer you my jacket?" he asked.

"No, I must go in soon."

The PI nearly pleaded, "One more question. What about Wayne Palmer's sister? He paused and puffed. "Mrs. Vivian Allard, I believe."

"She's a handful. Gives us all a hard time, always speaks with discourtesy."

"Did Mrs. Allard ever call on her mother accompanied by her brother Wayne?"

"Come to think of it," she imparted, "I've never seen them here together." The caregiver glanced at her ginormous timepiece, which made her hand look bitty. "Hey, I have to be getting back. I guess I won't see you again."

"Is this what you want?" he pitched smoothly.

It proved good enough for Nurse Cindy, still sitting on the Ford's hood, to fish into her alligator pocket-book beside her. She found a ballpoint pen, followed by an unused napkin, and jotted down two letters and five digits. The redhead removed a small bottle of perfume and then gave the napkin two squirts.

The napkin was his now. He took it and placed it in the front pocket of his dress shirt. Max opted for a circuitous route to linger in the reverie on his evening return drive to Old Downtown. He could smell Nurse Cindy. It was a good smell.

"*Gotta find this Pearl dame,*" he pondered.

25

THE FLIGHT

AT 11 P.M., HOWARD STANFORD SAT ON A GOLD fabric Ethan Allen armchair in room 707 of the Chadwick Hotel in the Queens Row section of New Paris. He had a big white hotel robe—featuring an embroidered capital C in cursive—wrapped around his planetary body. Mr. Stanford could be described as a crude intellectual. He had just finished the nightly routine of reading to induce somnolence. A yawning Mr. Stanford placed his oval spectacles and a Raymond Chandler novel on the table next to him. His extra-large frame sitting in the armchair gave the appearance of an oversized doll propped on doll furniture, which was of the wrong scale.

Suddenly, a knock echoed off the door.

"Hold on… I'm comin," Mr. Stanford announced to the unknown someone beyond the closed door as he ambled to it at a snail's pace, maintaining complacency. "Who is it?" he questioned with arrogance.

"Package." The voice presented gruff.

"At this hour?" he growled. "Why couldn't you just leave it downstairs at the damn desk?"

"Too big."

Mr. Stanford opened the door as far as the chain-link lock would permit. His head, with its receding hairline and gray temples, peeped through the crack before the door blasted him in the kisser.

Mr. Stanford remained erect, holding his bleeding face, when a gorilla of a man barreled inside the hotel suite, shut the door, and grabbed him by the back of the head. The Gorilla pressed humongous fingers into Mr. Stanford's scalp, causing him to scream. Next, the hulking beast pushed the fat man to the floor face first.

The Gorilla laughed forcefully out of his mango-sized mouth as Mr. Stanford rose from all fours to an unsteady standing position.

Mr. Stanford's respirations were tachypneic, inducing temporary aphasia as he wobbled, trying to get near the door.

The Gorilla, in his big black suit, bent low, exhibiting a three-point defensive football stance. "Gra-ah," he bellowed, ramming Stanford, flooring him again. Mr. Stanford only inertly got to his knees this time. The powerful Gorilla's subsequent charge seemed unabated, accompanied by remarkably deft leg movement and precision in striking his target.

After the latest thrust, Mr. Stanford was on his stomach, all the way across the room, in front of a multi-pane picture window. He barely pulled himself up by the sill's wooden frame while wheezing through his oral cavity.

The Gorilla's unshaven face, dark eyes, and evil grin enjoyed the torment. Wayne Palmer's killer returned to the previous tackle stance, now facing the paned window and Mr. Stanford. "Gra-ah," he howled once more, intimidatingly. In their locked position, his legs garbed in dark dress pants resembled tree trunks.

"No... no....," desperately gasped an apple-faced Howard Stanford, who had his backside to the square paned window. The fake sleuth teetered on his hind legs aimlessly in that spot for a few seconds prior to caterwauling.

If one were gazing up from the sidewalk, one would have seen glass shatter and wooden window panes splinter down into the night below. For the encore, at no extra charge, they would have perceived Mr. Stanford's white robe-swathed body descend seven stories, splatting in the center of the street.

A cab driver stopped his unoccupied vehicle and reluctantly plodded up to the homicide victim's body, obstructing the taxi's path. When he became within arm's length, the young cabby's disturbed eyes witnessed Mr. Stanford's head looking like a deflated football. Lying supine on the pavement, one meaty dead man's mouth hung open. Blood trickled out of both sides.

Notable Characters Introduced in Parts 1-3

Wayne Palmer: Murdered insurance man, first appearance Chapter 1

The Gorilla: 300-plus-pound murderer of Wayne Palmer, first appearance Chapter 1

Bruce Ellory: Witness to Wayne Palmer's murder, first appearance Chapter 2

Max Weatherbee: Private Detective, first appearance Chapter 3

Mona Ellory: Unfaithful wife of Bruce Ellory, first appearance Chapter 5

Mr. Gray: Hotel Duncan night manager, first appearance Chapter 7

Yet to be identified Scar-Faced Tall Man wearing white wingtip shoes and a white suit, first appearance Chapter 10

Dashing Darlene: Student intern to Max Weatherbee, first appearance Chapter 11

Red-Headed Fisherman: Note passer and customer at Sam's Pool and Drink, first appearance Chapter 12

Howard Stanford: Obese man Bruce Ellory met outside the house with the vines, who was also inquiring about the Palmer murder. First appearance Chapter 13

Professor Allard: Brother-in-law of Wayne Palmer, first appearance Chapter 13

Vivian Allard: Sister of Wayne Palmer, first appearance Chapter 14

Mrs. Judith Palmer: Wayne Palmer's debilitated mother, resides at Saint Elizabeth home, first appearance Chapter 24

Nurse Cindy: Works at Saint Elizabeth's Home, provides care for Wayne Palmer's mother, Judith Palmer, first appearance Chapter 24

PART 4

26

FRIDAY MORNING

THE TRIP TO SAINT ELIZABETH'S HOME FOR THE
Aged provided Max Weatherbee with more intel about
Wayne Palmer than when he walked into the place.
Feeling temporarily satisfied on a Thursday evening,
The gumshoe grabbed a bite to eat before heading back
to the office. Around the same time Howard Stanford
took his last breath, Max found a prime spot and
stalled the Ford in front of the Keiser Building. The
ninth-floor hallway appeared bright but desolate as he
unlocked the office door. Dashing Darlene, now having
her own key, had locked up and was long gone. The
private detective peered down at the handwritten note
on a yellow piece of paper, torn out from a notebook,
on Darlene's desk. The note read:

> *Johnny Knuckles called, saying he felt
> sorry he missed your call earlier. He
> will call you at 11 a.m. sharp tomorrow*

*morning. Mr. Knuckles sounded eagerly
available to help... And just who is this
Johnny Knuckles?? And is that really his
name?? Why did he ask me what I look
like?*

*Your favorite intern, "Dashing" Darlene.
PS: See you tomorrow!*

The cute note brought a genuine smile to his face.

Friday morning at 8 a.m., a round, black, metal West-clox alarm rang. Its resonance blared amongst the tight studio apartment like a fire alarm in a sleeping station. A bare-chested Max Weatherbee sprang up, lifted the clock off the nightstand, and pressed a button on its reverse side. The annoying sound stopped.

He plopped his head back on the pillow and pleasured himself below the waist for a moment, devoid of ejaculation. Today's sensual thoughts were mostly of Nurse Cindy, the flaming redhead he met briefly early yesterday evening.

Max's morning routine in his underdrawers began. He made the bed, pushed it up soundly against the wall, and slid the kitchen table over five feet from the opposite wall. He showered in the miniature bathroom and then stood in front of the mirror, wearing only a towel around his waist. Belly fat was null. His abdomen to upper sternum looked similar to a forest of soft black trees.

He shaved a craggy face and sarcastically mused privately, "*A girl who works at a nightclub and calls herself Pearl should be easy to find in a city housing millions of people... As easy as getting Humphrey Bogart's autograph. Pearl isn't even her real name, a stage name... that's it.*"

Mr. Weatherbee donned a royal blue bathrobe and brown slippers. He turned off the bathroom light, then proceeded to the kitchen table, currently sitting in the spot where the edge of the wall bed had occupied earlier. Sunlight beaming through the half-drawn shades of the studio apartment's only two windows brightened the narrow room enough for him to see what he was doing without putting on the overhead light. He fixed his favorite breakfast—eggs, toast, bacon, and black coffee.

At 10:30 a.m., decked in a brown suit and blue tie, carrying today's newspaper folded under one arm, Max strolled into his detective agency. Darlene was already at her compact desk in the waiting room, reading a textbook. She wore a radiant burgundy dress, which made her long eyes more stunning.

"How's school?" he asked.

"It's okay." She straightened up in the chair. "Hey, when is there going to be some action around here?" she questioned naively, almost like an adolescent.

"Soon enough, Darlene." His tone seemed shorter

and more serious than usual. Business monopolized his mind, and the new case desperately needed his ministration. A poor soul's life depended on it.

"So, who is this Johnny Knuckles?"

He lowered his head down stoically, and fiddled with the key to open the rear office door. "Nobody you want to know," he divulged. "Our relationship certainly lacks camaraderie."

"You didn't even notice my dress!" she cried out as he rotated the handle.

"Very nice," he said, but conveying a stolid cadence.

Her eyes were resigned. She felt insufficient.

He placed the New Paris Times newspaper on his enormous metal desk. The front page had a headline about a city scandal he previously saw when purchasing it. As he got to page two, his spine went numb.

> *Howard Standford, 48, amateur sleuth and freelance writer, plunged seven stories to his death. Police will release more information.*

———————

The minute hand on Max's gold Hamilton wristwatch displayed five past eleven. *"Come on, Johnny, you're late."* The investigator stared at his suit jacket and hat hanging nearby on the oak, stand-up coat rack featuring an umbrella slot towards the base. He loathed working in his suit jacket. The PI preferred rolling up his sleeves proximally above his Popeye forearms.

Darlene transferred a call.

"Johnny, I need your help," Max supplicated mildly. "I'll get to the point. I'm looking for a dancer named Pearl. All I have is that she works at a nightclub somewhere in the city, and she had some sort of relationship with this guy Wayne Palmer, who had been bludgeoned in Roosevelt Heights last weekend."

Max leaned back in his red oak bendable chair—listening to the other end of the line.

When it became his turn to speak, Max directed. "Start with the middle-class establishments; I doubt Mr. Palmer trekked into any dives sporting the kind of jewelry he probably wore. Talk to dancers, bartenders, and patrons who might know this Pearl dame. I'll hit the joints downtown by Loews Square and Cornell Park."

The receiver trumpeted.

"Yes... Pearl is her name or stage name," he reiterated.

Max listened, surveying the gloomy green paint on the walls through squinted eyes.

"Yeah... yeah, Johnny, you'll be compensated," Max assured. "Call my new intern, Darlene, once you got something. After hours, phone the answering service... same number."

Max's eyes hardened with exasperation as he listened to Johnny Knuckles on the other end of the line. "No, Johnny," Max lied flatly, "she's not attractive. Keep it professional with her if you get my drift." It was a friendly warning.

The line on the other end went dead.

27

MONA

LATE FRIDAY—MORNING, SIXTY MILES—FROM
New Paris, amid the hallway of a modest single-family house in Freeport, a thin white-haired man heard a muffled voice through his bedroom door. The man, Mr. Winthrop, knew Mrs. Winthrop was out playing bingo. This meant the only other person, possibly using their bedroom phone, could be his daughter Mona.

He passed a cauliflower ear to the wooden door, but the voice remained muffled. Next, the plaid shirt-wearing, elderly man staggered ten feet and carefully picked up the black hallway phone that hung at eye level on the wall. He listened. Under white eyebrows, his eyes became alarmed. Thirty seconds later, Mr. Winthrop gently returned the receiver.

The bedroom door popped ajar. Sandy brown-haired Mona Ellory poked a charming, made-up face betwixt the space. A pearl necklace hung above the nadir of her low-cut lime green dress. Via fuchsia lips, she archly chided, "I'm on the phone, Daddy!"

"That doesn't sound like Bruce," Mr. Winthrop imparted in a croaky old man's voice.

"It wasn't, and why were you eavesdropping Daddy?" The wily woman snapped.

"I lacked cognizance of who was in my bedroom."

"Well, put a phone in my room, Daddy." The heartless woman pitched it with a beguiling tone.

28

A SEARCH FOR A PEARL

MAX GRABBED A SANDWICH FROM THE SHOP IN the Keiser Building's lobby and ate it ravenously in the Ford coupe. His Smith & Wesson pistol was tucked neatly in its holster, sitting on the seat to his right. The private detective understood his excursion, starting at noon, would last deep into the night. Sleuthing was his vocation—he cherished every minute of it.

Loews Square, the financial district, is where Max Weatherbee began snooping. These seedy establishments were open early and at lunchtime, catered to affluent, white-collar stock brokers who had to be home pitching a squeaky-clean smile, plus roses for their wives by five. Max ordered a scotch at the third joint through a floozy bartender offering nothing helpful as he sat with a lit cigarette in his hand on a wooden back bar stool. He loitered, hours away from being frustrated. Part of 'expense money,' his agency charged clients, was for enticing stooges who coughed up information. This afternoon, such money stayed in his pocket.

The November weather stayed cool, without precipitation. At 4:45 p.m., squeezed inside a sidewalk phone booth, Max dropped a nickel and buzzed Darlene before she left. Johnny Knuckles had not called again. Somewhere around 10 p.m., he stopped at a pharmacy lunch counter, bought the *New Paris Evening Bulletin*, and requested a roast beef sandwich from a scruffy waitress who did not stimulate his zeal. The bottom of page one publicized the expected news.

> *Police Release Suspect's Name in the*
> *Wayne Palmer Killing: Mr. Bruce Ellory.*
> *Alleged Love Triangle.*

The photo, used by the newspaper, looked like it had been taken ten years ago when Bruce possessed a full head of hair, a thick mustache, and possibly a life. Max mused, "*This aged photo could buy us some time.*"

He entered one of the pharmacy's three vacant phone booths and dialed the Hotel Duncan.

Following the second ring, out the earpiece, Mr. Gray drawled, "Hel... lo Ho... tel... Duncan."

Max had the phone booth's door closed. "I need to speak with Mr. Wallace, room twenty-five." He hoped Mr. Ellory's alias, Mr. Wallace, remained secure.

"You'll have to... leave your instructions. I'll... buzz his room. Gray's tone was as flat as the world in 1491.

Max had been aware there were no phones in the

rooms at the Hotel Duncan, so he complied, kicked open the booth door, and waited for Bruce's return call.

In the barren room, numbered twenty-five, Bruce Ellory sat on the bed playing solitaire for the thousandth time today. A gin bottle, showing half its contents untouched, perched on a dresser. Alongside it, the rolled-up white paper bag served as the single vestige of his three-hamburger supper. Mr. Ellory's temporary confinement felt comforting. He did not care to be bothered by the rest of the world. But his room buzzer buzzed.

Anxiety returned. He partially filled a dirty glass with straight gin and guzzled till it emptied, then plodded down the stairs toward Mr. Gray's cage.

Mr. Gray's morbid, bloodshot eyes met him at the bottom of the stairs. "Here you are... Mr. Wallace," he said apathetically to Mr. Ellory who approached the caged office. Bruce took the index card wedged between Mr. Gray's bizarrely curved first two fingers, avoiding contact with the desk clerk's sharp talons.

The card contained an unfamiliar phone number, plus the initials M.W. Mr. Ellory's recessed eyes showed relief. *"It came from Max,"* he internally theorized. Utilizing the Hotel Duncan's sole phone booth, the recluse deposited a nickel and called the number.

The investigator picked up at a pharmacy phone booth across town. "It's Max."

"It's Bruce."

"How are you holding yourself, Bruce?" Max seemed genuinely concerned for his client.

"I'm still here," the fugitive's tone sounded desperate.

"There are no phones in the rooms, correct?" Max inquired.

"Correct. If a guest receives a phone call, they'll buzz your room—"

Max finished Bruce's sentence. "And if the client isn't passed out inebriated, he can come down to the desk and receive the message."

"Yes, but the occupants here receive few incoming calls."

"Sadly, Bruce, nobody really cares about the Hotel Duncan's derelict residents or their depleted life savings."

"True," agreed Bruce.

Max changed the topic. He asked, exuding supervision, "Are you staying put?" To ease any offense taken, he innocuously added, "I will solve your case if you don't do anything conspicuous."

"When the creep is here at night, I go out for a few hamburgers and come right back. I... I play cards by myself in my room to pass the time. I can hang on like this, maybe for another week."

Bruce Ellory's tone seemed woeful, yet Max noticed decreased stammering in his voice and thought, *"Bruce is less nervous. Maybe he'll hold out a bit longer."* He then asked, "Does the guy, you call, a creep, suspect anything?"

"I don't think so. And he is a creep," Bruce assured.

Max laughed wryly on his end but subsequently turned serious. "Your name's been released in the evening newspaper. However, the picture appears really old."

Bruce grew wide-eyed inside his phone booth. "Yes, I picked up the evening edition on my way here, after the hamburger joint. That was a work-issued photo from my last engineering job several years back. There weren't any recent photos at the apartment for them to use."

Considering Bruce's failed marriage, Max thought to himself, *"I'm not surprised."* Next, he scolded, "Stop buying damn newspapers!"

"Okay... no more unnecessary stops, I promise," Mr. Ellory agreed with Max's dissuasion.

Max informed, "Listen, if the night guy at your hotel gives you any inklings he is on to you, I can lube him to keep him quiet."

"Lube?" questioned Bruce.

"Lubricate. You know, grease his palm."

"Gotcha."

Max paused and inwardly reflected, knowing Bruce must not have purchased a morning paper because he would have certainly been spooked by Howard Stanford's unmentioned death. *"He's not in imminent danger using the aliases,"* Max thought, *"so I'll omit the fat man's swan dive for now."*

The rest of the conversation aired colloquially. Max ended with, "I'll be stopping by the hotel Sunday night for a briefing."

Max Weatherbee's long night of exploring the bowels under several neon cocktail signs terminated at 3 a.m. At every establishment, people shook their heads when the name Pearl became pitched. Parked outside the Kitty Kat Club, Max's chestnut brown eyes lingered halfway closed as he languidly slumped his head against the Ford's steering wheel. Multiple pours of scotch started wearing off. His head pounded like a gong.

At an uninhabited intersection, Max found a corner phone booth. Once inside, he held the receiver to his ear, utilizing a shoulder, pressed one palm into a throbbing frontal lobe, and dialed the answering service he shared with other assorted professionals.

An all-night receptionist energetically reported, "Mr. Weatherbee, you have a telegram sent by a JK sitting at the Westgate Hotel."

The fire in Max's eyes was fiercely reborn. *"Johnny Knuckles had something!"*

Max Weatherbee did not trust the answering service with personal details. He instead had associates call the after-hours answering service and simply notify them that a telegram had been sent somewhere. They were further instructed to provide only their initials on all correspondences. The Westgate Hotel, two blocks from Max's studio apartment, happened to be used most frequently. The night manager knew to forward these telegrams to Max Weatherbee exclusively.

Max went to the Westgate, retrieved Johnny's telegram, and opened it on the counter.

Meet me down by the water tomorrow
(Saturday) at noon at the usual spot. J.K.

29

JOHNNY KNUCKLES

SATURDAY MORNING, FORCEFUL RAIN AND INDIA ink clouds gave way to a new November day in New Paris. In the Keiser Building's lobby, Max collapsed the wet umbrella, which dripped, making a trail on the marble floor all the way up to his ninth-floor office. Darlene, the student intern, had the weekend off for her studies.

Going back to the few years he understudied his doting Uncle Harry, Max fully comprehended all the drawbacks of being self-employed. When he took on a case, seven-day work weeks and sixteen-hour days were part of the game. However, according to Max Weatherbee, one cannot consider work doing something you love. There was not a place on earth that he would rather be right now than his office in Old Downtown reviewing his case before getting ready to hit the streets. He felt invigorated from head to toe.

The PI locked the hallway door behind him, passed

through the waiting room, and then opened his office. He stuck the wet umbrella in the coat rack stand and hung up his dribbling raincoat. He presented decked in Saturday casual: a red dual pocket button-down shirt plus gray trousers. Mr. Weatherbee's shirt sleeves were already rolled up when he phoned the answering service. His number of messages equaled a goose egg.

Inside an almost empty pack on the desk, he fished for a Lucky Strike cigarette and lit it. Also, on the metal desk, sat Wayne Palmer's photo, cut out of last weekend's newspaper. He pinned it to the center of a corkboard hanging in the rear of the office. Never removing the burning cigarette between his lips, a stack of index cards was taken from the desk. Max scrawled Pearl in large letters on one white card in black marker. His Mr. Wayne Palmer detective corkboard began its infancy.

Max egressed the Keiser Building at 11:30 a.m., hopped into his Ford coupe, and headed for the shipyard area, located in New Paris's lower south side. High-rise office buildings soon yielded to three-story flat roof tenements; this morning's rain seemed less intense.

Close to the water, in between immense union-operated ships, amidst dingy bars and pool halls is where degenerate gamblers and roughnecks associated. If you wore a suit around here, you would stand out like a steak dinner in a coffee shop. Even Max's Saturday casual appeared a tad overdressed in this neck of the woods.

His relationship with Johnny Knuckles dated back

to the pre-war days under Max's Uncle Harry's detective agency. Then Max went into combat—Johnny slithered in and out of the slammer.

Max parked his Ford on the long road, which lacked traffic lights, adjacent to the massive ships that had been Saturday deserted. His gold Hamilton watch told him he was on time for his meeting alongside the once laddish, now permanent hood dubbed Johnny Knuckles, whose street smarts were imbued in him at a young age.

Legally, in police documents, he was referred to as John Severoni, but no one called him such. Without ever having to punch a time clock, Johnny Knuckles earned a fair living hustling pool, doing odd jobs, and serving as a jack of illegal trades. On any given day, Johnny could manipulate like a grafter or furtively play the role of tipster. If he could obtain impunity from a charge, he would indeed serve as a stoolie, or rat, as some would call it.

Johnny loomed in his usual shipyard spot, the Pool Palace; however, Hoodlum Palace would have been a better fitting name for where Johnny managed his bailiwick. Johnny's leather jacket dangled off the pool table, and in one of those jacket pockets existed his weapon of choice, brass knuckles—hence, an outlaw's asphalt jungle tag became born.

Max purposefully walked along the right side of the one-story building. The ubiquitous stench of harbor aroma struck his olfactory nerves like someone else's bowel movement. For such a macho stop, he wisely ditched one accoutrement—the umbrella. Raindrops speckled the top of his fedora. When he entered Pool Palace, his brawny frame hovered in the doorway—resembling a Roman statue. It was a familiar spot, but he needed an acute visual of his surroundings.

The grungy joint housed a small vacant bar to the right and one open room consisting of a dozen or so billiard tables. Four were occupied. During the day, three large commercial windows overlooking the avenue kept the place bright enough for the suspended lights over each table to remain unlit. Through one window, Max could vigilantly see his Ford coupe amidst the drizzle, and he fancied that.

The private detective looked to the far left. Thirty feet away, he saw Johnny Knuckles leaning over a pool table near the last window, about to hustle a stout opponent out of yesterday's wages.

Close to thirty in age, Johnny wore a crumpled pork pie hat rearwards above a rough face, appearing dark for a Caucasian. He sported a gold chain, white tank-tee shirt, cream-colored cotton pants, and brown work boots. The outcast's homemade tattoos caused his tight-skinned arms to seem more muscular than they really were. Still slanted over the table, he paused his shot, creating eye contact with the operative before sinking the red three-ball.

Max casually approached Johnny Knuckles, who now stood erect. Johnny's wiry body frame made him a good twenty pounds lighter but two inches shorter than Max.

Johnny's quick, streetwise tongue spoke first, "What's up, Mr. Bee?" This being his personal moniker for Max. In Johnny's world, everyone had a nickname.

Johnny's stout pool opponent guffawed but verbalized nothing.

"Let's talk alone," said Max, meaning to be inaudible to Johnny's victim of the pool hustle.

"Step inta my office, Mr. Bee." Johnny picked the hat off his head using his left hand and applied it to direct. His slick hair was combed back, the color of coal.

Both men unobtrusively ambulated towards an unoccupied corner. Max set the wet beige raincoat on a stool and then placed his right arm overhead, leaning a square palm into the brick wall. He gazed hard, infiltrating Johnny's dark eyes. "What you got on Pearl?"

"Man, dat took a lot of pokin' around," complained the abysmally articulate Johnny Knuckles. His deliberately squashed hat returned to its natural resting place.

Using his right fingertips, Max beckoned a zippy, come on talk, kind of motion and ordered as if he was the law, "Let's have it, Johnny."

Johnny's narration began. "There wuz a dame named Pearl who worked, months back, at a gentlemen's club in Dogtown known as Lucky Shamrock. One of duh guys who owes me dough used ta get wit her in a private box. And dig dis... so did your Wayne Palmer cat." Johnny engaged in a breath and finished. "My guy got tossed outta there for good last spring for bein disorderly. He said he heard she ain't workin' at duh joint no more. He also told me, 'Go there and see a dame called Evelyn,' I guess she would know more."

"I like it." Max always found Johnny's work unerring.

Johnny pressed his back against the brick wall and smiled around a few gold-capped teeth, as if he knew Max would ask for more.

Max did. "This one should require less legwork. I saved it for in-person. How bout... a three-hundred-pound gorilla possessing a bushel of black hair... a murder-for-hire guy."

Johnny's response came rapidly. "Duh hair ain't right, but sounds like Ice Box Collins." Johnny's response came rapidly.

"I've heard of him," Max affirmed. "Maybe he wore a wig."

"Yeah, okay, still nobody you wanna meet in an alley." Johnny warned, "Be careful he's connected ta duh outfit." The hood's dark eyebrows curled. "And I'm not tailin' em for yuh. He kills people... very dangerous. Dat's way above my head."

Max asked, "If Collins is the guy I'm looking for, where could I find him?"

"If you're askin' around... he'll probably find yuh. How many pieces yuh carryin'? Johnny's tone aired sardonic.

"Two. One is strapped to my ankle."

Max handed Johnny a twenty-dollar bill. The sclera around Johnny's dark eyes turned incandescent. Next, the hood gave a mini bow of his chin, expressing agreement for the compensation, and stuffed the bill in his right pants pocket.

"Hey, I heard about Howie duh Hippo," Johnny imparted.

"Howard Stanford?" Max questioned, not humored by the sobriquet.

"Dat's what yuh call 'em," Johnny snickered.

Max's tone remained serious. "I don't know if Stanford connects to Palmer. I can think of a lot of people who would have wanted to chuck Howard out a window."

"Uh-huh," muttered Johnny, displaying incredulous eyes.

"I'm serious," Max countered.

"His guts probably made a mess when day hit duh sidewalk," the hood chuckled. "Glad I'm not cleanin' it up."

Max altered the conversation. "Johnny, I need you to go up to Adamsville for me. Our killer boarded a bus there after he was done playing baseball with Dapper Darling Palmer's cranium. I've already been up there. This gorilla definitely does not live there; I even asked at all the restaurants. But someone up there knows something because my client got attacked at a place called Sam's. Look for a young red-headed fisherman. He passed my client a threatening note."

Johnny put both palms up towards Max. "Cops have a warrant out on me in Adamsville. Can't go up there, man, but I'll send my pal Rico from Puerto Rico ta snoop aroun' for a fee."

Max's grin showed sarcasm. "Rico from Puerto Rico? Hey Johnny, that almost rhymes."

"You can tell 'em, Mr. Bee, but watch out for duh box cutta he carries in his pocket." It was playful banter.

"Thanks for being on board, Johnny; we'll talk soon," Max concluded and left Pool Palace.

30

THE CHADWICK HOTEL

SUCCEEDING HIS EGRESSION FROM THE POOL PAL-
ace, it was officially afternoon when Max Weatherbee
hopped back into the Ford coupe. He tossed his raincoat and damp fedora on the bench seat next to him.
He got on the expressway north. Drizzling rain persisted; the wipers creaked languidly. Saturday, November 22nd, 1947, aired as dark and dreary. The kind of
day that could induce somnolence.

At 1:35 p.m., he pulled into the half-circle driveway
out front of the fifteen-story Chadwick Hotel in the
Queens Row section of New Paris. The same Chadwick Hotel where Howard Stanford met death.

He immediately became encroached upon by a
young bellhop dressed in red as he killed the engine.
"Valet, sir?"

"I'll only be ten minutes," Max assured, leaving his
raincoat and hat behind but taking his keys.

"Hey, Mista!" The bellhop pursued him through the revolving doors.

Unlike the Hotel Duncan, the Chadwick Hotel accommodated both tourists and locals alike. It featured a generous lobby, including an abundance of spread-out seating, a tavern, a cozy fireplace in the corner, and its own house detective for security. The security part was somehow excluded for Howard Stanford.

The bellhop terminated his hounding three-quarters of the way to the front desk when Max shook hands with the manager, Leroy Burton.

Mr. Burton presented as a scrawny, elderly man who had not had a full head of hair since automobiles used cranks. His white mustache looked thick, and he smiled graciously under it. "Hi, Max," greeted Burton.

A hatless Max appeared curt. "Leroy, I need to see the guest register for Wednesday and Thursday nights."

"Are you here to pay Mr. Stanford's bill?" Leroy Burton joked.

Max winked. "Not if it includes all his room service deliveries from the kitchen."

"My boy, you haven't changed." The old man grinned.

The cordial temperature at the front desk was about to drop. Across the lobby, charging like a rhino, came a burly man Max recognized as Bronc, the hotel detective. Emeryk Broniewski had been called Bronc ever since his third-grade teacher could not pronounce his name. Max had hoped he did not work on Saturdays, for he knew Mr. Broniewski, aka Bronc, lived deep in the pocket of the roguish, New Paris underworld.

Bronc, in his forties, possessed a big nose, and wore a cream suit accompanied by a matching, extensive brim hat over his yellow hair. The house dick's face grew inordinately red, bearing rage.

Leroy, the manager, addressed a raging Bronc first. "Mr. Weatherbee is requesting to view the register." His tone drawled so courtly that Max sensed it as dubious.

Bronc's flaming face spoke directly to Max. "Plenty of people would want to see ole tons of fun Stanford dead, not just the guests on the register." Indignant about Max's casual attire, he imperiously warned, "And don't come in here again without a tie."

Max kept his composure. "Okey-dokey... I was just in the area."

"Good idea to sit this one out, Weatherbee! Besides, it's my territory," Bronc growled pugnaciously.

Max's stoic face remained unfazed by the house detective's aggressive delivery. He stretched his arms laterally like an airplane. "Any guys this wide walking around here Thursday night?"

"Just me!" Bronc's tone remained supercilious, pointing his chunky thumb to his own chest while Leroy Burton, the aged manager, stood idle on the sidelines like a football coach losing 49 to 0.

"How bout Ice Box Collins?" Max inquired.

"Heard he fell on hard times," Bronc disclosed, widening his baby blues. "If I bump into him, I'll tell him you said hello."

Max puckered his chiseled face and sized up Bronc by way of his own eyes. *"Maybe we'll meet again in a not-so-populated place,"* he internally reflected.

Mr. Burton, who took a taciturn position once Bronc arrived, offered Max the register book. It lacked signatures with the last name of Collins or any other local thugs that stood out to the private detective. Max thought, *"It was worth a check; some criminals have been known to be dumb as dumpsters."*

Max Weatherbee exited the Chadwick's lobby, the same way he came in. Whatever happened to Howard Stanford seemed to be a dead end. The walls did not talk here.

31

MRS. WAYNE PALMER

FROM HIS OFFICE, EARLIER SATURDAY MORNING, prior to visiting Johnny Knuckles at Pool Palace or going to the Chadwick Hotel, Max Weatherbee dialed ST1-9054, the telephone number on the business card Bruce Ellory gave him for Wayne Palmer. The insurance agent's home number and company contact were the same. As he hoped, Mrs. Wayne Palmer answered his call. The reception he received on the other end of the line seemed cool and uninviting, but he still arranged for a 3 p.m. meeting at her house.

_____

After leaving Bronc and the Chadwick Hotel in the dust, Max headed back to his studio apartment, checked the mail, and made two quick baloney sandwiches. He ditched the casual attire for a navy-blue pinstripe suit, not because Bronc told him to wear a tie, but because he had three women to call upon.

The Ford coupe took him to the pricey upper westside Roosevelt Heights neighborhood for visit number one. The rain departed, but the sky lingered dolphin gray. Max arrived at 475 8th Ave and parked five feet past where, a week earlier, Wayne Palmer lay dead on the sidewalk. Near the sidewalk's edge, he exited his coupe and dodged a sand pile absorbing the bleach underneath—the bleach used to clean Mr. Palmer's macabre bloodbath by the city maintenance department.

Cars whizzing down nearby Empire Ave were plentiful in his ear. A fedora-garbed Max stood rigidly on the steps of the third luxury brick dwelling in a row of five, all connected and identical except for each owner's own individual exterior designs. The Palmer house had piles of cardboard boxes on its tight porch to the left. An attached cardboard sign read: *Good Sisters Pickup. "Getting rid of his stuff pretty quick,"* thought Max as he rang the doorbell.

The inner wooden door gaped briskly. Through the outer door's screen, Max saw a plump woman with short, black, flat hair, chubby cheeks, gorgeous eyes, and not much makeup. Next, she kicked the screen door ajar hard against his own foot. He delicately grabbed the handle and opened the rest of it.

Using lardy fingers, she beckoned him inside, and he edged into the vestibule. By what he could see, her home appeared immaculate and elegantly decorated.

For looks, the forty-year-old Mrs. Palmer's shelf life expired at least ten years ago during the Dirty Thirties.

Her belly was soft with love handles. The green dress she answered the door wearing made her body look like a Christmas tree missing its ornaments.

Max carefully broke the thin ice, remembering that Nurse Cindy regarded the woman as 'rude.' "You must be Mrs. Wayne Palmer," he said, "thank you for agreeing to see me on short notice."

She backed up five feet beyond the vestibule, intentionally blocking him from advancing any further, then spoke brusquely. "So, you mentioned on the telephone you're a private detective. What's this concerning, Mr.... I forgot your name?" One would perceive her pitch as smug.

He humbly announced, "It's Weatherbee, Ma'am, but you can call me Max." In her flats, the sleuth towered over her.

"Don't call me Ma'am, and I'm not calling you Max," Mrs. Palmer snapped.

Max removed his hat, expressing condolences, "I'm sorry about your husband. I'm really here to help." His tone aired genuine, coated with staidness.

The round-faced woman stayed hostile. "Don't bother removing your hat; you won't be staying long." Her eyes were now ice-cold blue.

Mrs. Palmer acted impervious to Max's strong sex appeal, which usually benefited him in such situations. The conversation became a standing one, confined to the foyer. The private detective was not offered a seat and definitely not a refreshment. He attempted to ask the routine questions.

"Did Mr. Palmer have any enemies?

"Nope."

"Recent altercations?"

"Nope."

"Gambling debts?"

"Nope."

Displaying a flush face, she chose to present cagey, shaking her head indolently to each question of the cordial interrogation.

He continued, "Affairs?"

She didn't shake her head this time but acerbically imparted, "The real cops were already here asking the same stupid inquiries." Then she added, "And the better answer to all your nitwit questions is… he wouldn't tell me if he did."

For an alternate approach, Max tried silence, adding a visage of doubtfulness, and stared fixedly within her eyes.

It worked. Mrs. Wayne Palmer engaged a deep breath, placed two puffy hands over her mouth, and pushed both pudgy index fingers into the medial corners of her eye sockets, trying to contain tears.

"So… there existed affairs?"

The evocative subject triggered Mrs. Palmer's teary eyes to narrow. "Listen, a woman knows when her man is cheating. That gigolo ran around with multiple women while I sat alone like a sap in our house answering his business phone calls," she angrily divulged. "Maybe some jealous boyfriend clipped him."

"Is there more you can share?" Max's eyes became easy.

She opened up further. "How about constant lipstick on the clothes I brought to the dry cleaners." Her rosy face soon amplified ashen, as if she needed air. "I married him because he served as my meal ticket. "I grew up dirt poor, you know, way uptown." She pointed northwards.

Max's face shifted to confidence; she seemed to be falling all over herself. The ball bounced in his court. He figured now was the time to break her down completely. The PI asked the one quintessential question. "Seeing your husband Wayne earned a living in the indemnity business, I gather he left you plenty of life insurance?"

The comment aggrieved Mrs. Palmer, and a firm impromptu slap came to Max's right cheek. He took two steps back towards the vestibule's opening, moved his right hand to the tender cheek, and thought humorously, *"A leftie, didn't even see that one coming."*

The irascible woman leered. "You bet, and I'm checking my mail every day for payment for my suffering."

Max cautioned, "I've been hired privately to solve your husband's murder case."

"I couldn't care less, Sherlock, and who exactly implemented the hiring, my lovely sister-in-law Vivian Allard?"

"I can't disclose such information," Max informed frankly.

Mrs. Palmer's derision intensified. "The police already searched the residence and found nothing. You're a sucker!" She raised her left hand up again.

Max kept his chestnut brown eyes focused and judiciously retreated farther hindward to the screen door. He wasn't going to take another slap from the woman exhibiting such enmity in response to his visit. Without spinning around, he tactilely felt the door handle behind him and let himself out, avoiding turning his rear on the unsavory woman. He calmly shut the screen door and headed toward the street.

"And you'll find nothing, absolutely nothing. Sucker!" She yelled at his posterior side through the screen.

Max walked down the grandiose steps. *"She's insane,"* he unambivalently thought. *"I cannot rule her out."* The investigator meant ruled out in the murder of her husband.

32

FRANK

SATURDAY AFTERNOON, MAX WEATHERBEE paraded around town playing private detective. Paradoxically, Bruce Ellory remained in his gloomy, ill-lit cell—room twenty-five of the Hotel Duncan. The fugitive's attire consisted of brown pants, an unbuttoned white shirt, black socks, and no shoes.

Bruce Ellory sat on a hard Windsor chair adjacent to the shabby desk, creating engineering sketches in pencil. His drawings consisted of circles, rectangles, and mathematical symbols, which would be confusing to most folks. The noisy vagrant guests, hooting and hollering while playing lobby dice games during the day, no longer bothered Bruce. By late evening, most of them were in a comatose state and were redirected to their rooms by Mr. Gray, so sleep for the other guests became reachable. Bruce sensed content inner feelings, as some incarcerated inmates claim when separated from society.

It was too early to run for hamburgers. Two Hershey bar wrappers, plus a half-eaten bag of peanuts rested on an unmade bed. On the dresser and all throughout the floor were unique playing card houses, some being as tall as four stories. When construction almost finished, Mr. Ellory relished putting aces at the apexes of each one. Amid Bruce's newfound peace, building card houses evoked his childhood. In the last twenty-four hours, he drank less than any time in the past few years.

The radiator felt cold and hence was the room. Mr. Gray only turned up the heat in the evening. Bruce's torso arched over the diminutive desk while guiding a black-bodied pencil that advertised the Hotel Duncan in red block letters near the eraser. As he sketched on white paper, the unlocked hallway door opened gradually. An unkempt, undernourished man in his sixties, bearing a purplish face and attenuated gray hair, stood in the threshold—swaying. He wore a white undershirt with short sleeves, and his posterior arm skin hung pendulously. The man's intentions appeared to be desultory.

Bruce indolently rotated his head toward the doorway. "Oh, hi, Frank," he greeted composedly.

33

THE HOUSE WITH THE VINES
PART 2

6 P.M. SATURDAY EVENING, MAX'S FORD COUPE arrived in the graceful Wickford section of New Paris. He stopped at the Wickford Pharmacy to use a phone booth and call another phone booth across town. Max's instincts told him the case was starting off well. His call was answered on the third ring. An unfamiliar voice to Max took the call. "Hello."

"I wish to speak to Johnny. Tell him it is MW."

Luckily for Max, Johnny Knuckles still loomed at Pool Palace. Johnny left his crumpled hat on the pool table and moseyed toward the phone booth. "Hey, wuz up, Mr. Bee? I wuz about ta head out inta duh night and spend your twenty."

"Johnny, I need you to tail someone starting Monday morning." Max enjoined gravely.

"Hey, dat's gonna be new money." Johnny's tone aired leery.

"You'll get paid," Max guaranteed. "Yesterday, I checked with my contact down at Motor Vehicles. The woman doesn't drive, but she might take cabs."

"No prob. I just scored a hot box carryin' a full tank of gas," Johnny blithely confided. "And dig dis, nobody's gonna be lookin' for it."

"Why is that, Johnny?" Max questioned dryly—as if he really cared.

"Because duh cat who owns duh Buick is sittin' in duh can, doin' a six-month bid."

"Clever. Okay, back to business. Find a pencil, write this down."

Johnny fished behind his ear for a yellow one containing an eraser. "Go head."

Max dictated, "The house is located in Roosevelt Heights, 475 18th St., the third house in a row of five, just off Empire Ave. Our woman's name is Mrs. Wayne Palmer. She's short, plump, and has short dark hair."

"I'll be on her like white on rice," the hood foretold as he finished drawing diagrams and numbers, knowing he had trouble writing words. He then spread his fingers wide, creating a comb, and ran them through slick black hair.

"Johnny, I need her daily schedule." What Max meant was he needed to get into her house. "And her every move, who she meets, where she goes."

"Got It, Boss Man!" Johnny responded eagerly.

Max warned, "Johnny, one more thing. Don't get

too white on rice. She slaps." The telephone conversation terminated.

———————————

The economical Ford, parked in front of the splendid house, certainly looked like hired help. A fedora-wearing Max walked manly up the damp, cobblestone walkway. His navy blue pinstripe suit seemed flawless. Saturday's sky beyond him projected ebony now.

In the darkness, the green vines wrapping around the majestic, burgundy brick dwelling could tickle one's imagination towards dreaming ominously that it was being devoured by a green spider's web. It all presented as Bruce Ellory had aforementioned—eerie.

The slamming of Max's car door caused a silhouette of a human shadow to appear behind the horizontal blinds in the window to the left. The door gaped before he got to the doorbell. The same slim man who greeted Bruce Ellory on Tuesday, possessing combed forward, jet-black hair and bunny eyes, waited in the doorway. Max ascended the steps and found he had him by a good three inches.

The man gazed up and intoned in a demeaning manner, "Sorry, there are no walk-in appointments; the lab is closed for today." He straightened a lapel of his white lab coat as if no further explanation was necessary.

Max glanced at the weather-peeled, white, wooden *Allard Chemists* sign. "Oh, I'm not here for the lab. My name is Max Weatherbee; I'm a private detective investigating the Wayne Palmer case," he humbly affirmed.

The man announced pompously, "I... am Professor Allard, Wayne's brother-in-law." His eyes were piercing. "The reward has been rescinded. You could have called first."

"I'm aware; I was told this on the telephone a few days ago." Next, Max pitched one of his favorite lines, "But... I was in the neighborhood. May I speak to your wife, professor?" Max stood erect and widened his broad shoulders as if he was not leaving anytime soon.

"I'm finishing up my work. We are on the way out for dinner," the chemist countered.

The private detective kept his ground and foretold, "It will only take a minute of her time." Max's rectangular lips simpered as he told the chemist the fib.

Allard shrugged, "I'll see if my wife is available; wait here." Which meant outside.

The windowless door closed anteriorly to him. "*I'd gladly pay ten bucks to give this guy one punch to the jaw,*" Max reflected internally.

The overhead exterior lamp became illuminated. From the top of the steps, Max stared at the chevron motif of the etched glass transom window. Soon, the thick, archaic wooden door, which would have fared well in a Robin Hood movie, reopened slowly. "My wife will see you now," Professor Allard announced obsequiously like he was the butler.

Max entered the well-heated, sumptuous foyer. His eyes alertly followed the chemist as he slid the door that read *No Admittance* to the left ajar, stepped in, reversed it, and then was gone. Funeral flowers occupied the house visually and olfactorily. The sleuth removed his hat.

The sound of a boisterous voice and clacking of high heels emerged prior to her body. "When are you clowns going to stop showing up here?"

The door to the rear of the spiral staircase swung open. Vivian Allard wore a high-collared, knee-length, mauve-colored sarong dress tied at its waist, accompanied by gray high-heeled pumps. The knot made an almost perfect hourglass. Her blonde hair sat tucked in a round, silver-colored, turned-up brim ladies hat.

Her red face cooled instantly as she laid eyes upon the handsome structure of Max's own face. Mrs. Allard's need for confrontation, Bruce Ellory experienced, suddenly abated. For a second, their two bodies squared off in front of one another. She appeared exquisitely dressed to go out to dinner—and Max wished it was alongside him.

He clutched his fedora hat in his hand. Max's signature full head of dark black hair, featuring a right-side sweep parted to the scalp, shined like a black diamond under the chandelier's beam.

"Max Weatherbee, ma'am. I am sorry about what happened to your brother," he said, "and waited until after the burial to come see you." He supinated his free hand. "I'm trying to catch his killer."

With her inner fire extinguished, she extended a

purple-gloved right hand for him to shake, and he willingly did, but would have preferred to kiss it.

"Nice to meet you. I'm Vivian Allard." She continued, "Ignore my husband's demeanor; he's a real stiff." Her green, oval, egg-shaped eyes were divine.

"He's certainly not as charming as you."

"I keep him around because he's my OBP."

"OBP?" he questioned.

"Official bill payer."

Max smirked and then acknowledged admiringly, "This is a lovely house, such decor." His head moved in all directions, appreciating the art deco pieces in the grand foyer.

She placed her gloved hands on her hips. "I guess if you favor the Roaring Twenties. It's the house I grew up in; we kept it as is." She seemed polite, but her voice still sounded rough as sandpaper.

"Can I ask you why you stopped posting the reward in the newspaper?" Max queried.

She pointed a purple-gloved finger to the gold settee bearing its flowered brocade pattern. "Please sit." He did, keeping his hat on his lap. "What can I offer you to drink, Mr. Weatherbee."

She now stood over him.

"Scotch on the rocks," Max requested, "if you have it."

There was a black cherry antique bar on wheels at the posterior end of the foyer. He watched fastidiously as she removed her gloves, scooped up ice, and then poured scotch. She fixed herself a scotch, copying his, and put a cigarette, stuck in an amber Bakelite holder, between curved lips. Vivian's fingernails were painted identical to her violet lipstick.

For now, she stood, he sat. He reached high, gentlemanly lighting her cigarette.

"Okay, back to your question. We pulled the reward because several delusional people kept calling us saying they saw the murder." She moistened her lips using a tongue. "Also, one fat guy, Mr. Stanford, who had been snooping around, ended up dead just two days after he came here. So, it is probably too dangerous to get involved in my late brother's affairs."

Max nodded. "Sounds reasonable."

An enchanted Vivian Allard lowered herself and sat next to him on the settee. She enjoyed the cigarette, and they, blithe to the dinner plans with her husband, sipped scotch as if they were on a date. He dug it—he dug her. He did not fancy how her husband lurked on the other side of the uncanny door, which read 'no admittance.'

She crossed her legs, dangled a spiked-heel shoe, and buried an additional swig before resuming. "All these coo coos who contacted us had different descriptions of my brother's killer. I can't deal with such loonies. How could there be so many people on his deserted street that night?"

Max laughed. Then he said, "I'm sorry I laughed," apologizing for the levity.

She sighed, giving a half-smile; her violet lipstick stained the Bakelite holder the same color. "It's okay.

The police say they have a suspect anyway. They'll find him."

He gazed at her, displaying understanding eyes, not leading on the suspect, Bruce Ellory, was indeed his client. Max could handle her, and she behaved accordingly, resembling a lion who instantly transformed into a kitten. He wondered what happened to the capriciousness that his client reported.

Vivian Allard disclosed, "My brother and I weren't too close, but he is my blood; it's why I offered a reward. I hope the murderer is caught. Do you have any clues, Mr. Weatherbee?" She seemed to abandon the malediction from Bruce Ellory's visit about 'filling the killer with slugs.'

"Please call me Max," he urged. "Unfortunately, nothing concrete, as of yet." He leaned rearwards against the settee, extended his legs, crossed them, and internally reflected, *"Funny, Mrs. Allard, you know what the killer looks like because Bruce Ellory gave you a vivid description. But you won't tell me. Let me guess, you want to ice this gorilla yourself."*

"Max, may I ask who hired you?" She spoke through white teeth, straight as a picket fence.

The private detective heard this question during his first home visit and was not sure if the same response would trigger her mercurial disposition as well. "I really can't disclose such information."

A tough-looking but attractive face happened to be a trait they both shared. Hers turned deadpan.

He figured it was time to pull out the big gun and

asked, "By chance, did your brother have a life insurance policy listing you as beneficiary?" After delivering it, he thought humorously, *"What the hell...just how many times can a man get slapped in one day?"*

Her rainbow-arched eyebrows elevated, showing reticence, but her tone stayed subdued. "No. Definitely not."

"I see. Can you think of anyone who would want to hurt your brother?"

"No. Wayne was a nice guy; my temper hindered our relationship. He was seven years older than me, and I always wrongly felt he looked down on me." Her mascara eyes were soulful. "Being our parents' only two children, my mother wished Wayne and I would grow closer as we aged. To make matters worse, Wayne's wife, my sister-in-law, became a difficult pill to swallow. A former beauty queen who turned into a blimp and grew mad at the world." She paused, exhaled smoke towards the chandelier, and then resumed answering Max's probing prior to going astray. "I don't know anything of his dealings or the people in his circle, but somebody seemed to be very angry at him."

"Anything else you can think of that will help me catch his executioner?"

"I can't... but you're easily the best-looking one who has inquired." Exhibiting scotch on her breath, she ogled deep into his chestnut-brown eyes. "Will you at least call me if you find the killer?"

"I'd love to call you for other reasons," he mused privately. But instead answered, "Yes." He handed her

his empty tumbler, rubbed his facial stubble using two fingers, then took one more glimpse of what he perceived to be a wondrous, wine-glass-shaped face—her neck serving as the stem. Arising from the settee, he cordially concluded, "Thank you for your time, Mrs. Allard."

When Max reached the cobblestone walkway over his right shoulder, he sensed a shadow behind the blinds in the chemist's office and said to himself, *"I know you're there, buddy... If I had a dame like that, I'd be jealous too."*

As the private detective headed down the remaining cobblestone, he fantasized about Vivian, the good-looking dame, possessing a rough voice and the harmony they discerned. Sadly, for his swashbuckling zeal, this would be the last time Max Weatherbee ever saw Vivian Allard again.

34

EVELYN

IN THE DARKNESS, MAX DROVE THE FORD COUPE away from the house with the vines and down a hill to the commercial center of New Paris's Wickford section. He returned to the same pharmacy phone booth where he called Johnny Knuckles an hour earlier. He fished into his wallet—the napkin containing Nurse Cindy's phone number was what he was fishing for. Spotted ink had been flecked about the napkin due to being furled, but the digits were legible.

She answered cheerfully on the third ring through glossy lips. "Hello."

"Hi Red. It's Max," he informed through thick lips.

"I wasn't sure if you would call."

"I'm busy on Mr. Palmer's case but free tomorrow around noon," he pitched, slouching in the phone booth.

"How's 11 a.m.?" she negotiated. "I work at three."

"Okay, eleven. Do you know the Temple of Music, City Park?"

"Oh, yes," she responded, glowing.

"See you then, Red."

———————

At nearly 9 p.m., Max Weatherbee arrived at the final destination of this intricate Saturday. The rigmarole started with morning work at the office, followed by meeting Johnny Knuckles at Pool Palace, irritating Bronc at the Chadwick Hotel, getting slapped by Mrs. Wayne Palmer, and sitting on the settee alongside one lovely, hardnosed Vivian Allard.

Like Amelia Earhart, today's rain was long gone. Debonair Max, still donned in the navy-blue pin-stripe suit and fedora, exited his coupe three blocks from Lucky Shamrock. It was a club in the Dogtown neighborhood of New Paris, a tough, impregnable Irish community east of mid-town. Its green neon shamrock sign illuminated the entire city block. An abundance of hooligans existed, mostly congregating on car hoods against the curb to his right. As he strutted past, over the sidewalk's concrete squares, Max inwardly reflected, *"Why would a money guy such as Palmer come here?"*

He walked into the Lucky Shamrock and was instantly greeted by a rugged, fully shaved, bald-headed man in a cranberry suit, who Max thought resembled *"a thug trying to go good."* The gentrified greeter's nose, which seemed like it got busted years ago, happened to be his most prominent feature. The forehead of little scars would get an honorable mention. He wore a gold chain bearing a Jesus crucifix outside his white dress shirt and tucked his pot belly in as if he were still in shape.

Max requested, "A table for one."

The moon-headed man began the sentence using a street tone he could not shake in the business world but finished it polished. "Upstairs is topless… or you can sit down here." He pointed a sausage finger to a dim, half-filled, smoky room of small round tables that could accommodate one to four male patrons. Only the unoccupied stage area remained reasonably lit.

"Whatever room Evelyn is working in is fine," Max replied.

"She's downstairs tonight. Take any open table," granted the flat-nose ex-thug gone good. And Max dubiously wondered, *"Just how good?"*

Conversation voices were prominent, and the house ensemble was on break. The humming of ceiling fans could be heard overhead, attempting to serve as some kind of exhaust for the plethora of tobacco smoke that filled the air—eddying underneath the ceiling. Dozens of lit cigars gave the impression of being the house favorite.

Max found a vacant table in the room's center and soon became solicited by a cute blonde-haired girl with double braids carrying a box of tobacco products. The sleuth purchased one Lucky Strike pack and asked, "Can I see Evelyn?"

"She'll be up on stage dancing in about fifteen minutes." Her accent sounded Gaelic.

Max lit up a Lucky Strike, flipped his fedora onto the round table in front of him, ordered a scotch on the rocks via an unsmiling waitress, and then made it last the fifteen minutes.

The returning five-piece band played soft. Over the speaker, Max heard, "Let's hear it for Evelyn!" A minuscule applause followed. The buxom, thick-waisted, bleach blonde's black pumps and stockings danced around a chair on stage. A snug, two-piece, white lingerie outfit unveiled the adult dancer's tummy as flabby. Her fluffy hair appeared not very long. She gave everything she had into the dance. When it ended, the ovation blared thunderously.

After Evelyn descended the stage, she was approached by the cute cigarette girl who said, "A well-dressed man is asking for you."

Evelyn's hooded eyes reacted unsurprised. She knew it had to be the handsome, perceptible stranger in the middle of the room, the one who did not applaud.

Max kicked out a chair opposite him. She sat. Once her elbows met the table, he steadily studied her dark lipstick, pasty skin, pudgy arms, fleshy cheeks, and a costume jewelry necklace consisting of a string of triangles. In his self-assured mind, Max rated her a five.

"You asked for me by name." Her damaged smoker's voice sounded bad enough for one to think she smoked more than she breathed the earth's free air.

"I don't know you. Are you an entertainment agent?" she inquired, pointing a chunky polished finger at him.

He giggled, "Hardly."

"What's so funny? You a cop?" Evelyn accusatorially squawked. Her buttocks started rising off the chair.

He placed a ten-dollar bill on the table proximal to her.

Her cowled eyes goggled. "Okay," she said, "you're not a cop." Evelyn's bum returned to the seat. "You've got fifteen minutes." Her tone presented coarse, like limestone. "Can't sit with customers longer than that," she imparted, "unless you want to go into a private box downstairs."

"Fifteen minutes is more than enough." Max did not need to go into any private box.

Her full face appeared disappointed. "Uh-huh," she replied. The ten remained in front of her.

Max confided, "I'm looking for a dame named Pearl who used to work here."

"It's going to require more than ten," she haggled, "to answer your question." The dancer had control.

He put an additional ten over the previous ten still on the table. By the front door, Max's '*thug gone good*' surreptitiously took notice of their conversation at the center table.

The Buxom bleach blonde stuck Max's two tens in her bra, then relayed, exhibiting alacrity, "She quit here a good six months ago. That big yellow apartment building across the street from Moon's Oriental Laundry in Chinatown is where she was living, maybe still does."

"Did she work elsewhere after she left here?" Max probed, displaying alert, upright posture.

"The Eldorado."

He clarified, "The private club?"

"Yes… owned by Joe Martinelli."

Max already knew who owned it and comprehended these were noxious waters he seemed to be insidiously treading into. "Have you seen her since?"

"She came in here once," the dancer divulged, "looking like she was full of dope."

Max's chestnut brown eyes grew curious. "Did she come alone?"

"No. She pranced in clinging to that dead guy who is in the newspapers," Evelyn disclosed. "Wayne… Wayne Palmer."

Notable Characters Introduced in Part 4

Mr. Winthrop: Elderly Father of Mona Ellory, first appearance Chapter 27

Johnny Knuckles: Hoodlum associate of Max Weatherbee, first appearance Chapter 29

Bronc: House detective at the Chadwick Hotel, first appearance Chapter 30

Mrs. Wayne Palmer: Pugnacious wife of the deceased Wayne Palmer, first appearance Chapter 31

Frank: Derelict residing at the Hotel Duncan, first appearance Chapter 32

Evelyn: Dancer at the Lucky Shamrock Club, friend of Pearl, first appearance Chapter 34

PART 5

35

CINDY

SUNDAY MORNING, MAX WEATHERBEE DROPPED his mother off at her house after church and arrived at his destination by 11:10 a.m. The November weather was brisk at fifty-two degrees; breathing in the cool air felt good to him. The PI masculinely entered City Park wearing a black suit, black hat, and black dress shoes and carried a bag of Wonder Bread. Max happened to be the kind of guy who would only wear a long winter coat if icebergs were present.

The smell of roasted peanuts pervaded the air. He could see her from a hundred yards away on the cement, leaning against a pond's railing, pretending to be organizing her makeup in a pink flamingo handbag. It pleased him.

Nurse Cindy stood dressed in a lengthy, red wool coat over her candy-striped uniform. Her small white cap sat atop her red pompadour—blazing side curls ran down to the base of her neck.

The bag of bread was intentionally bumped into her curvy backside by the virile private detective. Nurse Cindy's hazel-doe eyes blinked. She looked up and cupped her hands around the rear of his thick neck, sending his hat askew. It turned into a hug, their first.

"You made it!" she exclaimed with ardor.

"Yeah. In my business, you never know." He winked.

Her face brightened like a Christmas bulb. "You smell so good," she opined. "What are you wearing?"

"Courtley Gold."

It became a simple first date. They fed ducks in the pond, held hands, and then he bought hot chocolate and two bags of peanuts. At 1:30 p.m., exhibiting regret, she said, "I have to get the train to work."

Preserving his gentlemanly repute, Max gave her a ride. Cindy pecked his right cheek and got out of the Ford coupe at Saint Elizabeth's Home. While keeping the passenger's door ajar, she inquired, "So, where are you going from here?"

"Going back to my mom's. I go there every Sunday afternoon." His smile was strong enough to pucker his forehead.

36

SUZY

CHINATOWN, 6 P.M. SUNDAY EVENING, MAX Weatherbee cruised by two colossal golden dragons, which mimicked guardians, on each side of Duke Street. Within sixty seconds, amid the shadows, he parked his Ford coupe close to a curb, below the lights of a green, yellow, and red neon sign reading: *Suzy's Chopsticks. Dine In or Take Out, Free Local Delivery.*

Max fleetly pushed open a glass door and saw his petite friend. The under-five feet, attractive, early-forties, lithe Chinese American possessed short black hair. Suzy, garbed all in red, stood behind the cash register, perched on top of a display case consisting of Chinese souvenirs such as pocket fans and miniature Buddha statues. Suzy's compact establishment featured eight red vinyl booths—seven of which were empty.

Being American-born, Suzy's English was perfect. "Max, so good to see you," she warmly enunciated warmly as if he was family. "But why do you only come to see me when you want something?"

The private detective coolly grinned. "How do you know I want something?"

She looked way up at him. "Because you're here."

Max shrugged. "I'm here for a bowl of that Chinese soup."

"And I know you already ate," Suzy said, "at your mother's house; it's Sunday!"

They both laughed.

"Suzy, there is a Caucasian woman who calls herself Pearl and lives somewhere in the big yellow brick apartment building across from Moon's Oriental Laundry," Max disclosed, then requested, "I need the apartment number."

Suzy furtively whispered to a Chinese youth about fifteen who absconded out the back door. Next, she disappeared beyond the display case, returning swiftly, carrying a dragon motif bowl of steaming hot soup.

Twenty minutes later, Max sat finishing his piquant soup in a booth near the window. Suzy came over, sat across from him, and informed, "Apartment three hundred and one. She lives alone."

37

SUBORNING MR. GRAY

SUNDAY, 7:30 P.M., STILL IN HIS BLACK SUIT AND
hat, Max Weatherbee passed through the glass double doors and set foot in the arid lobby of the Hotel
Duncan, a mere seven blocks north from Suzy's Chopsticks. A stale cigar smell filled the air. Two old timers
were playing a card game on one cracked red leather
couch, and on the other, a middle-aged male vagrant
was curled up in dreamland. Mr. Gray's radio played
loud and staticky. It made the choppy jazz music coming out of its speaker as annoying to Max as a bunch of
holy jumpers pitching brochures against your bread-
basket while you walk through downtown.

Ghost-white Mr. Gray skulked in his dimly lit
caged office. His protuberant bat ears tardily rose from
a sitting position. "Can I... interest you... in a room,
sir?" he drawled slower than molasses, aiming his diamond-shaped chin at Max.

"What's up with him?" Max asked, concerned,

pointing his right thumb over his shoulder at the vagrant snoozing on the couch.

"He can… only afford… the lobby," Mr. Gray said stolidly.

"He better not be a war veteran," Max warned, displaying indignation and blazing eyes, towering over the frail Mr. Gray on the other side of the half door with the caged portion above it closed. Mr. Gray attentively stood donned in his usual wrinkled, tieless, white dress shirt. Max announced, "I'm here to see Mr. Wallace, room twenty-five."

There were a few seconds of silence. "Is that… his real name?" Mr. Gray contended, exhibiting morbid bloodshot eyes.

"Did you have another in mind?" Max questioned sharply, putting his elbow on the wooden half door's sill, and pointed through the aperture at Gray. Max idiosyncratically pointed, as usual, using his middle finger.

Mr. Gray reached to his tiny desk, unfolded a newspaper, and held it up to the cage. "How about… Mr. Ellory?" He smiled crookedly with thin lips. The hotel clerk's harbinger was assumed to warrant a bribe. Max quivered his head incredulously, then propped a ten atop the sill inside the cage door's aperture.

"Thank you… sir… but my wife… who covers the desk… on the day shift has to eat… as well"

Max's chestnut brown eyes resigned, perceiving Mr. Gray as rapacious. He added a ten to the payout, experiencing Déjà vu thoughts. *"Didn't this happen with Evelyn last night? I guess a sawbuck doesn't make people jump anymore. And his wife works the day shift? They can't even see each other; I guess she digs it that way."*

The eerie, dyed, black clumps of side hair around Mr. Gray's chrome dome and his bent first two fingers featuring long nails made him look like he belonged in a Bela Lugosi movie. He had a business card lodged between those first two bent talons, which he stuck into the aperture. "Somebody... left a calling card," Mr. Gray entrusted.

Max pulled the card rapidly from Gray's tortuous fingers and silently read the top line: DETECTIVE Dan McGann Homicide Division.

"Worry not... our client's privacy is... assured," Mr. Gray guaranteed. "Your associate ... is in room... twenty-five... up those stairs... to the right."

Max dropped a five-dollar bill on the sill, then instructed benevolently, "Get this guy on your couch a room, will ya?"

38

SUNDAY EVENING BRIEFING

WITH HIS ALCOHOL DEPENDENCY SLIGHTLY EBB-
ing, Bruce Ellory sat working on engineering drawings.
For the moment, his inner feelings were content. He
heard the hallway floorboards creak as they usually did,
below someone's feet, under the hallway's decrepit red
runner carpet. It amplified louder than the occasional
creaking the derelict denizens or Mr. Gray made. Next,
a soft knock sounded on the old wooden door of room
twenty-five. "It's Max," came a gentle tone from the
other side of it.

"It's open!" Bruce sanctioned. Max wondered why.

Max walked into the room illuminated by a cop-
per-framed overhead ceiling light dating back to the
Benjamin Harrison administration. He tossed his
fedora on the made brass bed, then directed an index
finger towards the floor, meaning downstairs. Further-
more, he puffed out the sides of his black hair with his
fingers, bulged his eyes, and curved his hands—resem-

bling claws—make-believing to be choking Bruce Ellory, who was still sitting in the chair. As he did it, Max hooted, "I am... Mr. Clumps and Claws. Do you need a room?"

For the first time in his recent memory—Bruce Ellory laughed. His face turned red, and he roared like hell at Max's Mr. Gray imitation.

When the laughter died, Max peered interestingly at the sketches.

"Some engineering patterns, I'm working on," Bruce revealed.

Max noticed the stammering seemed to be gone from Bruce's articulation. "Wow! I can see you doing this again," he forecasted. The PI supinated his right palm and complimented, "And neat card houses... showing the aces on top."

Max dragged one lopsided green chair over to the desk near Bruce, careful enough not to knock down any card houses he had just admired. The floor screeched as he did it.

Mr. Ellory, tieless, dressed in blue suit pants, no jacket, and a white dress shirt, listened attentively as Max took charge, recapitulating events since their last meeting: "Wayne Palmer's mother was no use; unfortunately, she is an invalid. However, thanks to a cute nurse there, I discovered another fling of Mr. Palmer's, an adult dancer and escort named Pearl. If I hadn't gone to Saint Elizabeth's Home, I would never have found this out." Max placed a pack of Lucky Strike on the desk and subsequently jammed one in his mouth. He nonverbally offered one to Bruce, who shook his head no, tapping his finger at his own box of Chesterfields.

Max continued, "One of my associates is sending his best man up to Adamsville tomorrow. The oversized killer you saw might be a hired guy called Ice Box Collins."

The name meant nothing to Bruce Ellory, who shrugged his bony shoulders and expanded his pale cheeks.

"At some time soon," Max foretold, "I'll call on you to identify or rule out Ice Box Collins as your gorilla. It's not wise to get too close; I'm trying to get a photo of him."

Bruce nodded.

"If he is the guy," Max informed, "we'll go to Detective McGann at the police department." Max exhaled and talked beyond the smoke. "I sat with Wayne Palmer's sister, Vivian Allard. Her anger appears subdued; she's just been through a lot. Mrs. Allard pulled the reward and seemed concerned for her own safety." Max coughed, then went on, "Mrs. Wayne Palmer is the first one I'm going to tail. She is responding inordinately to her husband's death and excitingly waiting on a life insurance payment."

The door gaped. The man entering could be conservatively described as frowzy. His purple face swayed in the doorway like a docked motorboat during high tide. Bruce Ellory greeted, "Hi, Frank."

Frank did not walk; he teetered, making it to the brass bed. The old derelict aimlessly rested his behind on the edge of the mattress, missing Max's fedora by inches, and stared straight ahead in a complete torpor. He wore a red-checkered shirt accompanied by unmatching green pants. Max figured Frank's body odor could certainly paralyze a cloud of flies.

Bruce Ellory ran his hand through what remained of his straggled hair and explained in detail. "That's Frank. His room is across the hall. Sometimes, he comes into my room, especially when I return from my hamburger run late at night. He thinks this is his room." Bruce inhaled some air and resumed, "He had it before me, then he left for a few days and returned. We play cards often. Right now, besides you, he's my only friend in the world."

Max's eyes expressed empathy. "He looks harmless." He waved one hand to the puny, gray-haired man sitting on Bruce's bed. "Hi, Frank."

Frank asked, exhibiting confusion, "What are you doing in my room?"

Mr. Ellory redirected the wino. "Frank, we'll play some cards later."

Bruce's soulful, recessed eyes gazed at Max. "My father was an alcoholic. I used to occupy so much of my childhood in my room building card houses. He played a mean drunk."

Max's face went numb. "Sorry to hear such joylessness." His cadence shifted woefully. He puffed.

"My old man left home when I turned fifteen. I heard a few years later, he got hit by a car and died," Bruce gravely imparted.

"Is your mom still living?" Max asked dolorously.

"Yes. She remarried. Her new husband has an awful disposition. I only see them at my sister's house on holidays."

"Mona and you don't have children?" Max questioned.

"No, we tried years ago."

"Speaking of holidays," Max said, "Thanksgiving is Thursday. You must stay put." Max pointed using his middle finger again.

"I can't survive much longer." Bruce Ellory's tone transformed into hopelessness.

"You wanna go to the cops?" Max knew the answer to his question.

Mr. Ellory shook his head no.

"Detective McGann was here recently; nothing happened. He left his calling card with odious Mr. Gray."

Bruce's face looked like it just saw a ghost. "Oh, Jeez. If I spend one night in a cell, I'll hang myself. That's why I don't call a lawyer; they will still make me turn myself in. And I can't ask my sister to cover the bail."

Max put his elbow on the desk and rubbed his fingers into his temple. "Let me figure this out."

Just then, Frank slowly raised his body off the bed and muttered, "I don't think this is my room." He tottered away into the hallway.

The two men lingering in room twenty-five were impassive to Frank's exit. Mr. Ellory quickly recommenced the conversation. "What is your view of the outcome of where we are heading?"

"My thoughts are revenge killing versus Mrs. Palmer's life insurance claim." Max's tone seemed encouraging. "I'm trying to dabble in both directions. Your wife, Mona, suggested to you that Wayne Palmer became involved with unscrupulous people, so it could be simply a revenge killing. This dancer, Pearl, works at the Eldorado club and might hold the key to our mystery." Max flicked his ashes in the Hotel Duncan glass ashtray on the desk. "Besides your wife, Wayne Palmer was seeing this Pearl. Pearl probably lurked on Palmer's dark side. I need to find that dark side. The bigger problem is the club is run by Mr. Joe Martinelli, the leader of the most sophisticated outfit in New Paris."

"I've seen his name in the papers," Bruce acknowledged.

"Yeah, I doubt I can penetrate Martinelli's inner circle, but I'm hoping our dancer Pearl talks. If she cared for Palmer, she might. She's my next stop tonight, lives in Chinatown."

"Why would she live there?" Bruce questioned.

Max shrugged broad shoulders. "Possibly another thing I ought to find out."

Bruce lit up a Chesterfield.

Max blew his own smoke and resumed, "Bruce, I can't rule out your wife Mona as being involved."

Bruce's skin crawled.

"Freeport, being sixty miles away, is too far to monitor daily," Max said, "but I plan on digging deep into her Wayne Palmer relationship."

"Please don't tell me what you discover."

"While we are on Mona, I need to see a picture of her."

Bruce fished in his wallet, unfolded the face shot he carried around with him, and dropped it on the desk. The paper photo showed visible deterioration.

The private detective examined the pretty lady possessing sculpted cheekbones plus shoulder-length hair. "Tough loss," Max remarked. Next, he went into his own pocket, retrieving a small camera. He took two snapshots of the woman's faded image and slid it back to Bruce."

"Huh?" Bruce said, motioning his hands as if confused.

"I just need to know what she looks like."

"Okay."

Next, Max proposed another theory. "I've even entertained one idea, thinking Mrs. Palmer and the outfit are in cahoots splitting the life insurance money."

Bruce Ellory's recessed eyes widened as he blew smoke.

"Have you been buying newspapers?" Max queried.

"I have not," Bruce Ellory affirmed, "since we last spoke."

Max, dipped into his suit jacket, unfolded a ripped-out page three of Sunday morning's newspaper.

> *Wayne Palmer Murder Suspect, Bruce Ellory, Last Seen in Adamsville. Thought to be heading north.*

"I think your trip up to Adamsville earlier in the week threw them off," Max hypothesized. "Might be a good thing."

"Okay."

"I also must inform you, Howard Stanford could've been murdered," Max disclosed. "Thrown out a window."

Bruce Ellory's eyes became aghast.

"Listen, you're safe as long as nobody realizes you are here. If they did, their trespass would already be known," Max assured. "There are a hundred of these dive hotels throughout the city. They are not going to find you if you don't venture out," he apprised. "Where is your hamburger joint?

"Two blocks south, just before you get into Chinatown. They are German immigrants, hardly speak English. The photo the cops put in the newspaper looks nothing like me; I doubt they even saw it."

Max cautioned, "The night creep knows who you are by way of the newspaper's old photo. He probably did not decipher it until Detective McGann came calling. He still didn't sell you out to McGann. But I had to lube him plus a little extra for his wife, who works days."

Bruce Ellory's heart rate bounced from seventy to one hundred twenty. Following the acceleration, he confirmed, "Mr. Gray knows who I am?"

"Yes, he won't talk. I'll lube him again if necessary."

Bruce bobbed his head and asked, "So, the foreign crone is his wife?"

"Foreign crone?" Max questioned the question.

"Never mind," said Bruce.

"Bruce, with all our lubricating of flunkies, we are running low on expense money. I'm required to call your sister Susan."

"Please don't take much more out of her. I'm really not worth it. I'll pay her back once I'm on my feet."

"I fancy that, Bruce. I'm going to take off now," Max said. "I'll visit again Wednesday evening before Thanksgiving. You can phone the office or leave a message with the answering service if you need anything. And in the meantime, I formulated an exit plan if you ought to bolt the Hotel Duncan."

"What would that be?" Bruce's tone unfurled, worried by the oblique danger warning.

Max milled the cig, rose out of the dilapidated chair, and picked his hat up off the bed. "You'll run south to Chinatown and find a little joint—Suzy's Chopsticks. Here's her address." Max fished into his wallet and handed Bruce a torn Yellow Pages section. "I helped Suzy earlier this year when her son was murdered. We couldn't bring him back, but we caught his killer, who is rotting in a cell for the rest of his life. If you ever must run from here, run there. She will hide you until I arrive."

39

APARTMENT 301

SUNDAY NIGHT, BACK IN CHINATOWN, JUST before 9 p.m., Max strolled unswervingly into the eight-by-six entranceway of the ten-story yellow brick apartment building across from Moon's Oriental Laundry. He was surprised to find nobody at the shabby reception desk. *"Piece of cake,"* his mind told him.

He utilized the center stairs to get to a bite-size, luminous lobby on floor number three. He found a comfy chair, keeping apartment 301 in sight.

Max's gold Hamilton watch on his left wrist read 9:27 p.m. when apartment 301's lock unfastened. She presented as voluptuous, sultry, regal, sylphlike, and any other word you can use to describe a woman who you could never have unless you lived as a thug owning a bankroll like King Midas. The lollapalooza's necklace and flaxen hair sparkled in sync. Her red heels were sharp, and a black sequin dress shined under a short fur coat.

"I knew you wouldn't stay home," Max thought, now standing in the hallway. He slid a black pantleg twelve inches to the right. That leg and his broad shoulders intercepted her path to the elevator. He removed the fedora. "Pearl, I'm Max Weatherbee. I'm trying to find out who killed Wayne Palmer. Can I sit and chat with you?" Her dark, upturned eyes showcased as enchanting below crescent moon-shaped brows.

"How do you know my name? I don't talk to cops. Excuse me."

He moved like a sliding door to let her pass. She got into the elevator, then pushed the L button using a claret, polished finger. His own elevator ingression caused her to sigh, not cherishing the encroachment.

The elevator descended.

Before the steel door reopened, he beseeched, "If you really cared about Mr. Palmer, you'll talk to me."

She opted not to reply, exited the elevator, strutted through the lobby, and headed past a glass door into the Chinatown night. When she reached the sidewalk, Max, following behind like a puppy, breezily yanked at her coat sleeve. "Did you hear me?"

The lady called Pearl hurriedly said, "I must run over to Moon's Laundry; please wait in front of my building." Her magnificent nyloned legs crossed Duke Street, and entered the Chinese laundromat. The private detective, decked in the black suit, stayed put.

Max inanely became friendly with a cement wall,

accommodating his backside, in front of the yellow brick apartment complex. He waited forty-five minutes, smoking as the glare of red neon signs reflected off his face. He thought in between drags, *"How can it take this long to pick up laundry?"* His lips simpered, realizing the rakish woman had cleverly eluded him. He had been hoaxed for now.

40

A NIGHT AT MICKEY'S

SUNDAY 11 P.M. BRUCE ELLORY'S HEAD HIT THE pillow, but sleep became nonexistent. The racing thoughts and anxiety—that had recently attenuated— reverted. *"Detective McGann has been here... Howard Stanford was murdered... Can Mr. Gray be trusted?"*

Bruce sat on the bed in underwear; the bureau's cast shadow darkened his pallid face. He could see one empty gin bottle through an illumination entering room twenty-five from the remaining lit bulbs of the Hotel Duncan sign hanging outside on the façade.

He ascended to a standing position, flicked the toggle switch up, returned to the bed's edge, and counted, then recounted the lingering ninety-four dollars in his wallet, satisfied knowing his Hotel Duncan bill was not in arrears. With dejected brown eyes, Mr. Ellory stared bleakly at a print of Whistler's Mother in an old varnished frame on the wall. *"I gotta get out of this room,"* an inner self told him. His blue suit and wrinkled white dress shirt hung flaccidly on the desk's Windsor chair. He donned them without a tie, picked up his light gray fedora, and slithered out of room twenty-five. Ties were certainly not in fashion where he planned on going.

The wooden stairs creaked below an old red runner carpet as Mr. Ellory dawdled his way down to the lobby like an inmate heading to the gas chamber. Beyond his cage, ghastly, Mr. Gray glared at him, exhibiting dilated black pupils and red sclera bulging out of their sockets. The two men did not exchange words. Mr. Ellory exited the hotel via its back entrance, traveling east. He knew his destination but just forgot its name.

Bruce Ellory lowered the brim of his hat and set foot in a dimly lit Mickey's Lounge at 11:30 p.m. This establishment stood just blocks from the Hotel Duncan, still in the run-down Webster Hills section of New Paris. A hardwood bar in the narrow room curved right after the tenth stool. There were three unassociated male patrons spread laterally along the bar and a small group of men playing cards at a round table in the seedy establishment's left rear. Bruce Ellory chose a bar stool proximal to the entrance.

The white-haired, toothless bartender served a glass of beer to a full-bellied man in a beige sweater, sporting a double chin, who sat at the far end of the bar. Bruce Ellory thought this weighty patron looked similar to some dog he remembered from a cinema short cartoon. The full-bellied man responded in a boisterous tone, "Thanks... Mick!"

White-haired, beady-eyed Mickey approached the bar space adjacent to Mr. Ellory. The voice sounded hoarse. "What'll it be, stranger?" An old chin jutted out of his skull like a wooden spoon handle, and a red scar on the left side of his maxilla dominated an ancient face.

Bruce had one elbow on the bar, and a cupped palm supported his jaw. "Gin and Tonic," he said solemnly while his recessed eyes morosely focused on Mickey's filthy white apron.

Out of Mr. Ellory's left ear, he perceived drunken voices laughing, howling, and airing incivility. Anxiously, he turned his head slightly that way, visualizing five men sitting about a round table in the rear of the joint. They were amusing themselves, wagering poker and smoking cigars. The group's leader was an extremely rotund man in an expansively enormous white suit and western bolo tie. He sat facing the front door, pointing his meaty buttocks to the back wall at the table's twelve o'clock position. His white cowboy hat appeared so massive it could have covered an adult armadillo.

The big man possessing the big cowboy hat growled, "Holy crap!" as a skinny man owning a weathered face seated at the two o'clock position of the table flipped over his cards. More laughter filled the air.

"He got ya. Huh Butch?" Mickey yelled and guided his spoon handle chin playfully over to the noisy table.

A younger man, bearing a boyish face, sat at the hefty urban cowboy's right, at the table's nine o'clock position. He ordered humorously through a lisp, "Another round here! Pronto Mickey... before Butch is out of dough."

"Ha ha ha!" the table roared because his lisp made the way he said it even funnier.

Directly across from Butch at the table, a tall older man owning a putty face in a black suit and hat, who had his hind to the bar, stood up, then announced, "I'm low on loot, and I gotta piss."

"Jeez, whatta ya gonna tell your wife?" quipped red-faced Butch, in his twenty-gallon hat with cigar intact. His tone projected truculent.

The older putty-faced man in the black suit and hat said nothing, leaving his space and creating a gap in the table as he opened a door cautioning *restroom for patrons only.*

The bar stayed quiet for a minute while Mickey swiftly prepared and placed drinks atop a black round metal beer tray. Red-faced Butch's wide-set eyes suddenly became riveted on Bruce Ellory, who stared straight ahead on the barstool. Bruce inwardly sensed the fat man's eyes covering him like a blanket. The immense man, called Butch, reached for a pile of peanuts, took his cigar out of his mouth, chomped into the pile, and aggressively blurted as some pieces of chewed nuts drifted to the floor instead of his esophagus, "Hey pal, we need a substitute player!"

Mr. Ellory abstractedly murmured a confession, "I'm not really a good one." He remained oblivious to the latent trouble that lay yonder.

A burst of tumultuous laughter resonantly pervaded the air again. "Just the kind of player we relish," the idiosyncratic fat man named Butch disparagingly snickered.

A red-haired man who had not yet spoken, having slitted eyes and a frozen face, at the round table's four o'clock position, pulled out the vacant chair next to him. Frozen Face's fingers balefully beckoned to Mr. Ellory, "Sit down, Pally!" It wasn't a choice the shill offered.

Too scared to run, Mr. Ellory mumbled grudgingly, "Okay." He then plodded over in his tieless, wrinkled suit to the chair that faced both the back wall and Butch, providing no view of the rest of the bar. On the wall above Butch's head, Bruce Ellory saw sports photographs, which meant nil to him as he would not have known a baseball from a field hockey stick.

The urban cowboy grunted through his half-chewed peanuts, "Hey Mickey, get newbie here another round."

Mickey comically saluted, pretending he was still in the service. "Yes, sir, Butch!"

Mr. Ellory drank a second gin and tonic, holding his cards loosely. He felt like a shrunken man. Within thirty minutes, the twenty dollars he laid down on the table was gone like the flapper era. As the game continued, the fat man in the cowboy hat displayed menacing brown eyes across the table at a shuddering Bruce Ellory, who presented intimidated enough to only gaze at his own cards. While Mr. Ellory nervously analyzed his poker hand, the fat man looked past him to the burly, cartoon-looking canine man in the beige sweater, sitting at the bar's end, who pitched hand signals behind Mr. Ellory to Butch. Butch knew Bruce's hand, so did the other players. Mr. Ellory did not stand a chance.

The tall, older, putty-faced man in the black suit, who occupied Bruce Ellory's seat prior to him joining the game, had vamoosed the restroom and found a stool in the middle of the bar. Two of the three other bar patrons soon departed. The cartoon canine-looking man and the tall, putty-faced man in the black suit were now the only patrons positioned on bar stools. The tall man reached beyond the bar with his belly over it and grabbed a neatly folded Sunday evening bulletin newspaper.

"What the hell ya doin'?" cried Mickey, who was hand-drying a tumbler. "I'm gonna' read that on the throne after you punks leave." The bar owner teasingly flexed an anchor tattoo on his wizened right arm.

"Oh shit," the putty-faced man whispered to Mickey and shared what he saw in the newspaper while Butch's rigged game at the rearmost table stayed in progress.

Mickey peeked at Bruce Ellory's posterior side, then returned the whisper. "Might be him."

Putty Face refolded the newspaper, stuck it under his right arm, and walked over to red-faced Butch.

Mickey crept around the oak bar and locked the front door.

41

NIGHT VISITOR

11:45 P.M. SUNDAY EVENING, AFTER LEAVING Bruce Ellory, Max buried a few stiff drinks at Perry's Jazz Club in mid-town. Despite this section being the omphalos of New Paris, there was a lack of action tonight. He drank solo, choosing to be alone as his mind began recapitulating the events since Wayne Palmer's murder. When he could think no more, a weary Max Weatherbee and the 1941 black Ford coupe headed back to his bachelor pad.

At the same instant, unbeknownst to him, a very big man maneuvered a rusty flatbed truck up to a fire escape in an alley—the alley in the rear of Max's apartment building. In the darkness, the hatless, colossal brute fiercely climbed the ladder attached to the building like he was looking for Fay Wray.

Ten minutes later, Max entered the sixth-floor, compact studio apartment. A hanging light above the kitchen portion remained lit just as he left it. His Smith

& Wesson pistol and holster were taken out of his right pocket and placed on the table. The fedora, suit jacket, and tie followed. Subsequently, he hastily dragged the kitchen table over a few feet, not noticing a few folded papers on its top, before pulling the bed down off the wall.

Suddenly a startling sound to a lone man in an apartment was heard: a toilet flushing.

Max could have jetted out past the front threshold, but instead, he moved with lightning speed behind the closed bathroom door to the studio's distal end. A giant man wearing a red aloha shirt finished his private business and slowly made the door ajar. Max startled him by grabbing the door knob utilizing his left hand, swinging it fully open, and delivering a right-handed judo strike deep into the Hawaiian shirt, settling in the huge man's ribs. The huge man stridently grunted, before putting Max in a smothering headlock, cutting off his ability to breathe.

Max did what his Uncle Harry showed him to do. He delivered two dual-hand, potent dukes one after the next, using the big man's abdominal meat as a punching bag. The strength of the headlock lost intensity. Max's instinct foretold choosing hand-to-hand combat would be insuperable, so deftness kicked in. He broke free and leaped onto the bed. Ending up on his knees as he rolled over, he yanked out his Colt from an ankle strap, then aimed.

"Whoa! I'm not armed," the intruder calmly enunciated through mammoth teeth, evidently unfazed by Max's knuckle strikes. He raised a pair of gigantic hands above his head as a non-verbal plea for life. When he raised those two meat hooks, his aloha shirt also elevated, exposing an island of belly flab.

"Yeah, and I never hit anyone so hard that didn't fall down," Max divulged, expressing a dignified tone.

The snub-nosed, spacious-faced oversized man's full head of ebony hair looked reasonably cut and parted to the left. "Folks call me Ice Box Collins," the enforcer egotistically disclosed. "I heard you been askin' around for me." The introduction was not necessary—Max knew who had come calling.

Max, still kneeling on the bed, kept his firearm on the target, displaying alert eyes. "I made a few calls."

"Before you pull that trigga," Ice Box said, "I left some papers on the table for ya." The underworld soldier widened his dark eyes with pupils resembling buttons on a trench coat.

Max got off the bed, slid sideways to the kitchen table, still pointing the revolver, and warned, "Stay where you are."

The private detective unfolded the papers, inspected them, and said to himself, "*These are jail release papers following a thirty-day bid. The incarceration ended last Tuesday, two nights after the Palmer murder.*" One thing Max was now certain of—Ice Box Collins could not be Ellory's gorilla.

Max firmly kept the Colt on Ice Box Collins and concluded, "Okay, big fella, no hard feelings... but you'll need to leave the same way you came in."

42

BUTCH AND HIS CRONIES

AFTER MIDNIGHT, WITHIN THE WALLS OF A DIMLY lit Mickey's lounge, the tall, older man owning the black suit plus putty face walked over to the fat, red-faced Butch in the cowboy hat. He publicized through decayed teeth, "Hey, Butch, check it out!" Putty Face unfurled the *New Paris Sunday Evening Bulletin* on the poker game table in the lounge's rear.

The fat man Butch, sitting at the table's twelve o'clock position, squinted his eyes, making the skin underneath puff outwards. He internally read the headline and what was showcased below it.

The newspaper became passed to the right and left of the portly man in the white suit for the other card players, except Bruce Ellory. Each inspected its contents and then coldly began staring straight into Ellory's aghast eyes. The newspaper was finally abruptly dropped in front of Bruce Ellory, sitting at the table's six o'clock position, by the standing, putty face man in the black suit.

Skittish Bruce Ellory read what had been placed before him: *Mr. Bruce Ellory, the Prime Suspect in the Wayne Palmer Murder Still at Large. Last seen in Adamsville.* The shocker was not its headline but a police sketch of Mr. Ellory replacing an outdated picture previously used in the morning edition. The paper further stated, "This is what the murder suspect may look like now." The man in the sketch had thin hair, a receding hairline, hollow cheeks, recessed eyes, no mustache, and an oval-shaped head.

Bruce's face turned deadpan; it was certainly him. He thought, *"Max must not have seen it before his visit a few hours ago."* Mr. Ellory could feel his bones rattle.

"Well... how bout them apples!" big Butch exclaimed provocatively to his entourage as he blew an enormous cloud of cigar smoke into Bruce's face. The reflecting shadow of Butch's cowboy hat behind him filled half the wall.

The urban cowboy rotated his head down on a triple chin, then arrogantly gloated, "Calling the cops won't put any dough in my pocket, don't see any reward under your picture." He blew more smoke, giving Bruce a seething glare. "Tell ya what... two hundred bucks will buy ya a get out of jail tic."

The big man chomped more peanuts; several wet pieces gauchely landed on the table's edge.

Bruce Ellory's cheeks turned chalk white. He mumbled timidly, "I don't... I don't have anything near that."

The now pathetic man, once an engineer, was already down over twenty dollars due to Butch's rigged poker game, which could be subtracted from the ninety-four he had left the Hotel Duncan with just a little over an hour ago.

Holding up one pudgy index finger, Butch granted brusquely, "We'll give you one phone call." The big man closed his fist and then bellicosely pounded the round table so hard it bounced off the floor. "If not, your next spot is going to be face down on the carpet with one of our knees in your back until a prowl car gets here."

The skinny, weathered-faced man still at the round table ordered through holey teeth, "Mickey, bring the phone over here."

It was an older candlestick phone, the kind you could not dial directly, featuring a cord long enough to wrap around San Diego. Max's words replayed in Bruce's mind, 'stay put.' The fugitive mused, "*Max can't find out.*" Bruce waited for the operator. Soon, his brother-in-law Walter Kazarian picked up on the other end after four rings. Into the mouthpiece, Bruce abashedly beseeched, "Walter, I need two hundred dollars cash. And I need it right now."

––––––––––––––

Thirty minutes later, Walter Kazarian, a successful, local Oriental rug dealer dressed in a crisp burgundy suit, banged on the locked metal door of Mickey's Lounge. Mickey opened the door, let him pass, devoid of saying anything, and locked the door again.

Mr. Kazarian possessed a high forehead, a dark Middle-Eastern complexion with a thick black mustache, and a pair of eyebrows that could have been siblings to that mustache. His facial stubble appeared inky.

His concerned mocha eyes observed his brother-in-law Bruce Ellory perched introspectively with his hands pressed into a pale face at the last bar stool bordering the restroom. The burly, canine cartoon man and the four poker players, except for Butch, who was sitting alone playing solitaire, occupied the barstools in front of Ellory.

The red-haired, slit-eyed, frozen-faced man curtly spoke first, "Sit." He pointed to the first bar stool near the door, stymieing the Armenian man from entering any further. Next, he added maliciously, "You got something for us?"

Walter Kazarian ceded to the frozen-faced racketeer and sat as instructed—like a boy in a dunce cap. Twenty feet away, at the other end of the bar, Bruce passively nodded to Walter Kazarian to give the envelope to the villainous red-headed man. Walter did, showing aggrieved eyes.

Ole Frozen Face moseyed to the poker table and delivered the envelope to the obese, urban cowboy Butch, who ripped it open and then counted ten twenty-dollar bills.

Satisfied with his blackmail loot, Butch motioned to Ellory using his cigar and growled, "Now get the fuck outta here!"

The younger boyish-faced man added comically,

bearing his lisp, "But do come back... if you got some more money for us."

Shrill laughter erupted in the bar created by Butch and his cronies.

Walter Kazarian bit his tongue, refrained from comment, stood up, and ambulated to the door exhibiting forbearance. He could not overpower the evil aggregate in the room, plus a well-off businessman knew he did not want to ever see Butch and his goons again, especially at his rug company.

Mickey, the beady-eyed geezer, possessing a spoon handle-shaped chin, presented an evil grin as he unlocked the door, swung it open, and flipped his palm supine sarcastically—meaning, this way out, please. The two unwanted guests treaded cautiously to the sidewalk.

In the darkness, Walter Kazarian and Bruce Ellory climbed into Walter's shiny ebony Cadillac. Walter sparked the ignition, faced Bruce, and asked disapprovingly, "Bruce, how much more of this can your sister Susan and I take?"

———————

Back inside of Mickey's Lounge, Butch reached for the candlestick phone still on the round table and gave an operator some digits. He squeezed a pound of chin fat as the phone rang at least three times before the call went answered. When it was, the urban cowboy announced, "Hey Slick, sorry to wake ya. It's Butch."

Silence pervaded the air at Mickey's as Butch listened.

Butch replied, "Yeah... Yeah. It's fat Butch." Butch's eyes were blazing as he sank his cigar into the ashtray and milled the tip, killing the smoke. Butch resumed tranquilly with a reticence to the insult, "Listen, that Ellory weakling you've been looking all over town for just left Mickey's Lounge in Webster Hills."

The fat man listened via the earpiece.

Butch spoke again, disclosing, "I think the wimp is staying close by. He walked here but left as a passenger in a late-model black Cadillac."

Butch listened to the earpiece one more time and severed the chat by directing, "Hey, once you get your mitts on 'em leave that fifty-dollar reward you promised in an envelope with Mickey."

43

FREEPORT

6 A.M. SHARP, MAX WEATHERBEE, DRESSED IN A white starched shirt, blue suit, and blue tie, briskly exited the photography darkroom at the rear of his office. The photo dried overnight: a copy of the head-shot he took of Bruce Ellory's wife Mona last night when the two men had met at the Hotel Duncan. He slid it into a large envelope, locked his office, and made it to the train station by 6:30 a.m. The express train arrived at its destination in ninety minutes, plenty of time for Max to grab eggs, bacon, plus coffee in the dining car.

Amongst a small crowd, Max vamoosed his train at the dainty Freeport station, then barreled to its ticket booth like a gambler trying to place a last-minute, horse racing bet. When it became his turn in line, he dropped Mona's snapshot on the sill of the glass window's aperture.

"Huh?" uttered an extra short man with a pointy head and butterfly-shaped ears—which Max thought resembled a Billiken statue.

"Do you know this dame?" the sleuth inquired tersely, then internally reflected, *"Some men should always wear a cap."*

The Billiken looked way up uninterestedly and shrugged. "Can't recall her." His pitch contained treble.

Max squinted and thought archly, *"Sounds like someone down there is squeezing your balls every time you talk, buddy."* Next, the private detective stuck a five-dollar bill through the aperture. "How about now?"

Money talked. The now acquisitive ticket agent more closely examined the black and white photo of the comely woman, called Mona, possessing sculpted cheekbones. "Sure. I've seen her. Who wouldn't notice such a frail."

"Has she traveled in the past week?"

"I think she boarded a train to New Paris last Friday. Central Station was the destination. I remember because I was going on break and she kept fishing in her wallet for change."

Using a dead serious tone, Max requested, "Can you call me the next time she boards another train?" This time, he put a ten in the aperture along with a business card.

"I can do that," replied the dwarf, expressing eager, bulbous eyes.

"What's your name?"

"Hank."

Max glanced at his watch, bought a ticket back to New Paris, and said, "Talk to you soon, Hank." Heading to the train tracks, the PI inwardly pondered, *"I'll get you, Mona."*

44

THE CONVERSATION

MONDAY MORNING AT 9 A.M., WAYNE PALMER'S sister, Vivian Allard, sat at a small table near the large glass storefront window inside Bortone's Coffee Shop on 16th Street in the gracious Roosevelt Heights section of New Paris. This was just two blocks south of where Wayne Palmer became a homicide victim. The shop's owner, Mr. Bortone, a middle-aged man possessing a potato nose and very little hair on the apex of his cranium, was engaging pleasantly amongst patrons.

The shop consisted of a medium-sized counter with stools plus about ten or so small tables featuring ice cream-style chairs. Monday morning traffic filled the place to seventy percent capacity—aromas of sweet loaves of bread permeated the air.

Hatless Vivian Allard wore a gray checkered skirt pleated from the hips down, a pink sweater, nylons, and black stiletto pumps showcasing ankle straps. Her sable knee-length wool jacket was folded on the backrest of her chair. She sat erect; her legs were crossed. Mrs. Allard glanced at her silver watch every minute in between sips. Her impatience could be ascribed to her utter dislike for the woman who set up this meeting, coupling these two quarrelsome souls.

Vivian Allard's sister-in-law, Mrs. Wayne Palmer, walked into the café wearing very little makeup. Her big, beautiful blue eyes found where she was supposed to be.

Mr. Bortone yelled above patron gossip, "Buongiorno… Signora Palma!"

The forty-year-old chunky Mrs. Palmer sported a blue dress under a mink coat and on her head a blue Stetson hat that looked like an upside-down flower pot over her short black hair. She wore flat shoes which snapped loudly on the linoleum floor.

Outside the coffee shop lurked one hood, Johnny Knuckles, garbed in his usual leather jacket and muscle tee shirt. As instructed, he had been tailing Mrs. Wayne Palmer and now stood across the street leaning leisurely against a telephone pole as if he was doing the utility company a favor. He deliberately left his crumpled hat in his hot box on wheels—a 1936 Buick parked around the corner near the Palmer residence. Ten minutes prior, Mrs. Palmer had egressed her dwelling and strolled to the beanery on this cool, clear November day with the hired hoodlum not too far behind.

Inside, Mrs. Wayne Palmer sat while Vivian Allard's tough voice promptly started the conversation. "Why did you ask to see me?" Vivian's rouged-up, crimson kisser appeared already huffy as she continued, "I'm piqued; what's our conference regarding?" Vivian reached into a purse for a pack of cigarettes. Her tone remained indignant. "You opted not to speak to me at the funeral."

Mrs. Wayne Palmer's blue eyes became disdainful as her temper disgorged. "I'll make it brief 'cause I can't stomach much of you." She sneered using unpainted lips, then pressed, "I want to know why you hired a private detective and sent him to my house?"

"Huh?" Vivian exhibited, puzzled, wide eyes below rainbow-arched brows. The rough beauty lit up a cigarette, stuck it between red lips, took a drag, and remarked ardently, "Oh... I know who you're talking about." Vivian wistfully added, "He's so handsome... that tough guy face. He understands how to protect a gal."

Mrs. Allard ran her nails through brown streaks at the base of her meticulously peek-a-boo-styled blonde hair with her left hand, showing infatuation for Max Weatherbee. She smoked utilizing her right hand.

Mrs. Wayne Palmer's pitch stayed bitter and briskly retorted, "You're married, but I forgot there's no rules for you."

Vivian countered in a quick tone, "A girl can look."

"Ha... I slapped that face." Mrs. Wayne Palmer disclosed her previous pugnacious behavior and went on. "He's too proud. And asks a lot of questions. He needs to let sleeping dogs lie."

Mrs. Allard blew smoke towards the ceiling, her high cheekbones elevated. "What do you have to hide?" Vivian's sharp tone seemed accusatory.

Mr. Bortone approached the table and interrupted. "The usual Signora Palmer?"

"Yes, Vito, thank you."

Vivian Allard, lover of confrontation, hit underneath the belt with the java joint owner still hovering over their table. "What's 'the usual' a dozen donuts?" She laughed jocularly—no one else did.

Mr. Bortone withdrew. The eight-years-older Mrs. Wayne Palmer stared at Vivian Allard, displaying penetrating eyes. "I'd fancy to see you in ten years; your face will look like it belongs on Mount Rushmore."

Mrs. Allard's long, attractive visage showed deprecation from the comment.

Words ceased for thirty seconds, both staring in other directions. Mr. Bortone quietly delivered one croissant, a piece of Italian Bundt cake, and black coffee in front of Mrs. Palmer, who put a temporary stopgap on her mocking tone. "You didn't answer my original question concerning the dick." Before Vivian could speak, Mrs. Palmer added, "I saw your spot in the newspaper offering a reward."

"His visit was not my doing, never hired the dick," Vivian Allard answered. "And I offered reward money because I wanted to find my brother's killer. Money talks, you realize?"

"Even when you don't have any?" contested Mrs. Wayne Palmer.

Mrs. Allard inappropriately flicked cigarette ashes in the air. "My husband does alright for a chemist."

"Yeah, and he can't afford to buy his own house, so you live in my mother-in-law Judy's house." Her tone aired as disparaging. "My husband... your older brother wasn't happy about it, you know."

Vivian Allard stuck the one-third-smoked cigarette in the ashtray, stood up facing Mrs. Wayne Palmer, and pointed a long right index finger across the table. "And you couldn't control your man! Which is why he's dead, you squab." Her voice's truculence fared equal to that of a drill sergeant.

The stocky Mrs. Wayne Palmer also jumped up, ready to fight. Mr. Bortone and his coffee cup motif apron quickly barreled around the counter, carrying a glass pot of coffee. "Signoras, hav-a some more coffee," he said in broken English. "Fightin'... no good."

Vivian Allard softened her mercurial mood and acquiesced first, turning to the small business owner. "Okay, for the sake of your cute nook, I'll be good. But I would fancy a fresh pot, please."

Mr. Bortone gladly agreed, "Sì, Signora... un minuto."

Tensions ebbed—both ladies returned to a sitting position at the same time.

Out of the bistro's rear exit, a Mexican dishwasher in his mid-twenties with dark, obsidian hair went outside and took his break. Johnny Knuckles crossed the street and entered the alley towards the man.

Back inside, Mrs. Wayne Palmer resumed the conversation. "I see your ad is no longer in the paper."

"I only ran it a few days."

"Any leads?" Mrs. Wayne Palmer queried, fixing
her posture.

"Nothing solid," Vivian Allard informed, remaining
cordial for the moment. "But from this point on, I'll
leave it up to the police."

Outside, on the other side of the wall, Johnny
Knuckles had been conversing with the dishwasher
when a very tall, hatless, dapper man donned in a
white suit and matching wingtip shoes ambled by the
alleyway entrance. Johnny thought the tall man flaunting the blonde hair parted in the center was someone
he had seen somewhere before in his life, so he hustled
to the sidewalk.

The six-foot-four man peered into the window and
then strode away without entering the establishment.
Johnny shook it off as an unrelated coincidence of little
importance and returned to the alley.

Inside Bortone's, the discussion seemed to become
reheated. "Come to think of it, if you didn't summon
that private detective to my house, how do you know
what he looks like?" Mrs. Wayne Palmer accused, plus
upbraided, "You're such a liar."

Vivian Allard's countenance once again became
incensed, bearing rage. She slammed her chair rearward, making contact against the person's chair behind
her, got up, and taunted, "You're a fat bitch!"

This time, Mrs. Wayne Palmer remained seated

and smugly divulged from below, "People resembling you are exactly why I'm selling my home and getting out of town."

Vivian Allard spoke from above. "I'm sure you won't leave until you get your life insurance money." Her oval eyes hardened as she threatened vindictively, "In the meantime, if I find out you killed my brother, you're going to be eating dirt in the cemetery." Mrs. Allard egressed Bortone's Coffee Shop, flustered. She deeply despised the woman whose company she just departed.

Mrs. Wayne Palmer sipped coffee—displaying an old-fashioned smirk on her pudgy face. Her mind wished illness on Mrs. Allard. It would be the last conversation these two cantankerous sisters-in-law would ever share with one another.

Notable Characters Introduced in Part 5

Suzy: Friend of Max Weatherbee, owner of Suzy's Chopsticks, first appearance Chapter 36

Pearl: Dancer, hipster, and fling of Wayne Palmer, first appearance Chapter 39

Butch and his Cronies: Hefty cowboy and his band of unscrupulous poker players at Mickey's Lounge, first appearance Chapter 40

Ice Box Collins: New Paris Outfit enforcer. Originally thought by Max to be the Gorilla. First appearance Chapter 41

Walter Kazarian: Armenian rug dealer, brother-in-law of Bruce Ellory, first appearance Chapter 42

Hank: Ticket agent at the Freeport Train Station, verbally promised Max to keep his eye on Mona, first appearance Chapter 43

PART 6

45

DETECTIVE MCGANN

11 A.M., MONDAY MORNING, A TIELESS MAX Weatherbee was back at work, still dressed in a white dress shirt and blue pants. His tie and matching suit jacket dangled in the corner of the room. The private detective stood in the rear of the office gazing at his Wayne Palmer Case detective corkboard. He had just finished reviewing it alongside his protégé, intern Dashing Darlene. She returned to her desk in the anteroom; the door separating them was now closed.

Through the horizontal blinds of the window between his office and the waiting room, Max spied Dashing Darlene's brown mid-length hair dancing on her shoulders. *"If she were only a little older."* He egotistically thought.

Darlene sat with her perfect face stuck in a textbook. Her French-manicured nails turned the pages. She sported a dark blue and white houndstooth dress featuring a white collar plus a cute red belt. Two men

wearing suits and hats entered the waiting room. Darlene's long brown eyes lifted off the page. She animatedly said, "Hi, can I help you?"

The late-forties, taller man in the black suit
removed his hat and then gave Darlene hard eyes. He
had a rectangular head and flat cheeks. "Time for you
to go on a coffee break," The towering stranger directed
authoritatively as if it was second nature.

"Yeah, go powder your nose somewhere," rudely
insinuated the shorter, round-faced man in the dark
gray suit.

Max's keen ears heard the commotion from the
other side of the wall. He again gazed beyond the
horizontal blinds and recognized the taller man as
Detective Dan McGann, an understudy of his Uncle
Harry. Max swiftly pulled the chalkboard off the wall
and rested it face down on the table. He internally perceived what was coming next—a loud bare-knuckle
knock on his office door.

Max opened the office door for the two police
detectives. The men initially said nothing as they hung
their hats on a tall wooden coat rack. Detective Dan
McGann presented about two inches taller than Max.
He had thin eyebrows, a light complexion, long ears,
and a face that did not see a razor this morning. He
wore his tie loose like he slept in it.

The shorter detective accompanying McGann
appeared in his early thirties, owning a round, ruddy
face plus a belly that protruded through his cheap suit
like a Looney Tunes cat's ass sticking out of a mouse-

hole. His ruggedness made up for his lack of height. His blonde head looked half bald, and Max silently gave him another seven years to get to all bald.

Max cordially offered, "Please take some seats, gentlemen. Let's do a late morning scotch."

The taller Detective McGann, with his mostly gray buzz cut, spoke first and conducted so sharply. "Not needed, we won't be long." The men faced the sleuth in a way that they blocked his access to the door. "This is my partner, Detective Cobb," McGann added. Max knew of Skip Cobb's reputation. It was not a pleasant one, especially for suspects.

Max nodded.

Detective McGann confidently alleged, "I think you know where this Ellory cat is hiding out. You cashed a check from Walter Kazarian, Ellory's sister's husband. You're working for them."

"Yes, and I'm going to prove Bruce Ellory's innocence," Max vowed assertively.

The chubby man called Cobb, possessing the dank personality, pierced his dark piggy eyes and spoke arrogantly, "Weatherbee, I'd dunk your head in the nearest toilet bowl if McGann gives me the okay." Cobb lived for being a bully.

Max's chestnut eyes were filled with recalcitrance as he privately added Cobb to the long list of men whom he would gladly pay ten dollars to take one swing at.

Detective McGann solemnly assured, "We're going to be fair towards you, Weatherbee, out of respect for your Uncle Harry, one of the best detectives the departments ever had." Then the senior buzz-cut detective pushed his wide index finger into Max's chest and warned, "But if you don't cooperate, I can pull your permit to carry."

Max theorized, "Bruce Ellory didn't do it; he's too feeble."

The three men stayed standing. Exhibiting intransigence, accompanied by a red face, McGann retorted, "Really? Bruce Ellory threatened to kill Mr. Palmer in the hallway of his apartment two days before the murder. An old lady there heard it loud and clear."

Max stepped back and reached into his desk for a cigarette as McGann's prominent blue eyes followed him, and then the lawman continued to rant, displaying a hot face. "Ellory had been seen on Palmer's street right after the slaying running away. We have a young couple who are one hundred percent positive of what they saw." He counted, using his big fingers, each piece of inexplicable evidence. "And we understand he had a grand motive," McGann contended, "Wayne Palmer had been pumping Ellory's wife! So, I don't even require a murder weapon on this one."

"The murder weapon, a baseball bat, was burned in a garbage barrel in the small city park near the macabre scene," Max disclosed. "It wasn't an axe handle, as stated in your report."

"So, Babe Ruth did it?" sneered Cobb, who made a right-handed pretend home-run swing.

"Where are the remains of this baseball bat?" asked the aplomb McGann.

"The metal barrel disappeared by the time I got there, days later," Max answered tactfully.

"Ha ha, sure it did," Detective McGann snickered. Listen, Weatherbee, the DA wants Ellory signed, sealed, and locked up by Thanksgiving."

"Give me till the morning after Thanksgiving to prove you have it wrong," Max refuted.

Both detectives laughed. "Now who did it... Santa Claus?" twitted Cobb.

Detective McGann orated through jagged teeth, "We know Ellory is hiding out somewhere up in Adamsville. He is a drunkard and was last seen there a week ago looking for local bar rooms. Two Adamsville hobos gave us the scoop and helped create the new police sketch."

Cobb, full of impudence, wisecracked, "You see the illustration, Weatherbum?"

Max ignored the insult and responded, "Yes... I did."

"We're gonna find him. And after the interrogation, if he tells us that you harbored him anywhere, I'm coming down hard on you, Weatherbee," McGann forewarned.

"Which is exactly why he won't turn himself in," Max replied bluntly, "interrogation and a coerced false confession."

"We don't need a confession," McGann predicted, "with what we got on him."

Max looked at the older detective and redelivered the entreaty. "Dan, give me till Friday morning."

Detective Dan McGann rotated his rectangular head to the wall as if he was deliberating in his mind and turned back, announcing reverently, "Okay, for your Uncle Harry's sake and the fact that you served your country as a stalwart soldier overseas. But we'll return Friday morning after Thanksgiving... four days from now. You better bear something for us, or you're coming downtown."

The two uninvited guests grabbed their hats and exited.

46

THE GIRL WITH THE HABIT

1 P.M. MONDAY, MAX, IN A STARCHED BLUE SUIT, returned to last evening's ten-story yellow brick apartment building across the street from Moon's Oriental Laundry in Chinatown. This dwelling housed the Caucasian woman, possessing the aesthetic quality. He walked by the same unoccupied doorman's desk, got off the elevator, and went left down the green-carpeted hallway. Detective McGann's deadline made him uneasy. He could not let Bruce know how uneasy.

The PI removed his hat and rapped vigorously on the last door. One spacious picture window in the third-floor lobby gave enough sunlight for Oedipus to see. Apartment 301 existed at the carpet's end, facing the radiant hallway.

Pearl made the entry door ajar only as much as the chain lock would allow. Max could see pieces of her flaxen hair, amethyst necklace, and angelic face. "Oh... Max, whatever your last name is, what do you want?" she asked, apparently bothered, turning up a little cube-tipped nose.

"It's Weatherbee, ma'am, and if you don't talk to me," he imparted, airing a cautionary tone, "I'm going to create a fracas plenty loud, so your neighbors complain." Max leaned against apartment 303, the adjacent door on his left.

Pearl unlocked the chain and entered the hallway, letting the door shut behind her. She sported plaid pleated pants in a camel color, a light brown button-down blouse, and brown flats, which caused her to appear much shorter than last evening when she disappeared into the night. Evidently, Pearl appeared to be on her way out—she carried a brown wool coat and matching handbag. Her golden hair was styled, showcasing several victory rolls around the sides of her neck. "Hoot all you want." She pointed at the door to room 303 using a claret polished nail. "He's not here anyway and won't return for weeks. Chinese guy only comes into town once a month, works on a ship."

Max hopped off the apartment 303 door and stood erect in the center of the hallway.

Her rear was still to her door. "So, what do you want?" she requested again; this time, the tone aired less annoyed as she slipped her coat on her slender but curved frame.

Max became frank. "To see justice for Wayne Palmer's murder... don't you?"

"Yes, surely," she replied, "but I thought they had a suspect."

"That guy Bruce Ellory, in the papers, didn't do it." Max fished into his suit pocket for a pack of Lucky Strikes. "You might know some things that are import-ant," he said, "even though you think they are insignifi-cant." The PI lit his cigarette.

Pearl solicited the private detective as if she per-haps would provide information. "Give me five dollars and wait here." She supinated her right palm, pointing a left spindly index finger at a puffy chair twenty feet away in the cozy third-floor lobby. It happened to be the same comfy chair he leisurely sat in last evening.

Max extended a thick index finger and rotated it side to side. "Whoa... you're not setting me up again!" he emphasized cynically.

She reclined her posterior torso upon the closed splintered door and subsequently raised her crescent moon eyebrows like she had a secret. "No, I have to go across the street once more to Moon's."

"You're going back to Moon's Oriental Laundry?" Max talked through the smoke. "How much laun-dry could you possibly possess?" he queried, bearing sarcasm.

"I must go in the basement," she divulged, lowering herself submissively against the door.

"Basement?" Max's puzzled face seemed more than interested.

Pearl explained, "Yes, there's an opium parlor down there. It's a safe haven for us hipsters who are addicts. Mr. Moon Chin's underground opium den is the only one left in the city. The parlor offers a cornucopia of delights." Max's chestnut eyes riveted incredulously as he listened. She rambled on, "I won't shoot dope, so I'm dependent on him." Her dark, upturned eyes presented troubled. "I smoke it to relax my nerves; others do as well."

"I didn't know people were still smoking opium in New Paris," Max responded naively, touching his square chin.

She restored herself to standing erect. "Moon Chin learned the trade from his grandfather."

He gazed down into Pearl's eyes staidly. "I understand Moon Chin isn't a very nice man," he cautioned as if she cared, then offered her a cigarette by showing her the package.

Pearl took one and stuck it between her magenta lips. He assiduously struck a match and lit it for her. The beauty opined, "Mr. Chin runs Chinatown. He's okay as long as you don't cross him." She puffed laggardly. "Actually... I feel very safe living here because of him. He doesn't allow vagrants to hang around this district."

"I heard he has the cops down here on his payroll. But I didn't think Chin sold opium. Thought heroin was his game."

"He doesn't sell opium... just has a following of smokers," she corrected. "You can't leave there with it. You give him five dollars, they'll pass around a pipe, and you often smoke amongst others. He has his goons sell the heroin uptown, not out of the laundromat."

She leaned once more against her door, staring at his tough-guy, handsome, rugged face.

"Hard for me to sympathize," he responded impassively.

"Look, I'm already feeling sick. I require my opium fix." She placed her left hand on her abdomen, still smoking the cig, employing her right. "If you want any information outta me, you'll need to give me that five dollars. I'll just take a few puffs. When I am fixed up, I'll talk to you."

Max's resigned eyes examined her dilated pupils; she was not lying. The detective nodded his head in agreement. He reached for his wallet but left it unopened. "Can I ask a few questions first?"

"Told you I'm not talkin' til I get my fix." She stomped her foot like a kindergartener would. "I'm nauseous, and my bones ache."

He handed her the fin. "Why would a pretty girl such as you get caught up with such stuff?"

"It carries me away, makes life feel surreal."

————————————

Max sat alone, bored, on the third-floor lobby chair. He just got done fiddling through old receipts in his wallet. Via the lobby's generous window, he could see an enormous neon sign on the opposite side of the bustling Chinatown Street that read MOON'S ORIENTAL LAUNDRY. Thirty minutes earlier, from two floors above, he vigilantly watched Pearl go into the establishment.

Appeasing his boredom, Max discovered a rolled-up Sunday *New Paris Journal* in a trash can and extracted it. He navigated to the rear of the newspaper and then began doing a crossword puzzle, losing track of time. He waited and waited in the chair. The crossword grew monotonous. When she was no longer worth the wait, he folded the paper and started to rise from his chair. Suddenly, the elevator door swished open, and a goliath of a man exited.

The lofty stranger hardly noticed Max, whose buttocks were reinstated to a seated position near the lobby window. The newcomer would irrefragably be the tallest man the gumshoe would see all day. Max gave him a height of at least six foot eight. He had a pockmarked face with a crater-sized dimple on the base of his chin. He wore a black wrinkly pinstriped suit and a wizened black gangster hat.

Max knew, based on height alone, that this man could not be Ellory's gorilla. Ironically, he was not the same tall man in the white suit who pestered Howard Stanford for a flyer or secretly followed Bruce Ellory through Wickford to its subway station. The unfamiliar man Max spied presented even taller, wider, not so polished: actually, very crudely unpolished.

As Max suspected, the giant headed straight for apartment number 301. His massive knuckles pounded on Pearl's door. After several truculent knocks went unanswered, the man growled, "I know you're in there. Bitch!" He thumped the door again, displaying rage, and balefully exhorted, "Open up. Bitch!"

Concerned for Pearl's safety, Max remained seated in the lobby, frantically looking beyond the window, wishing Pearl would not egress Moon's Laundry anytime soon. Furtively, the private detective put his hand in his pocket, removed a Smith & Wesson pistol out of its holster, and stuck it on his lap under the newspaper.

The behemoth stopped knocking, strode back to the elevator, then pushed the button. Next, he leered at Max, who pretended to be reading the paper, and thunderously asked, "Hey, pal, you see a dame come out of the last apartment down the hall?"

Max shrugged. "Sorry, no." He hoped their conversation was finished like Rudolph Valentino's silent movies.

The gigantic thug took a step away from the elevator door that had not slid open yet and mistrustfully interrogated, "I haven't seen you around; you're not Chinese. You live here?" His minacious, dark green eyes resembled a pair of avocados—below his bumpy forehead.

Max, with his gift of being naturally tactful, phlegmatically lied, "I'm a bill collector waiting for the guy in 307."

The elevator door opened, and the big man shrugged his shoulders at Max as if he had been satisfied and vamoosed.

"Good riddance," Max thought.

The private detective, utilizing his bird's-eye view of the sidewalk, anxiously awaited the mammoth man's withered, black hat to turn the corner. As soon as he perceived the coast as clear, Max dashed down to the street, crossed it, and entered Moon's Oriental Laundry. A diminutive elderly Chinese lady stood behind the counter. She did not look like she dealt in dope.

"I'm looking for a lady friend of mine, nice yellow hair, wearing a brown coat who came in here a while ago," Max confided, wishing he was not being led astray for two consecutive days.

The small Chinese woman dressed in black smirked and replied, "Ha, you frein pick up laundry and go out back door ten minute ago."

47

AN UPDATE FROM JOHNNY THE TAIL

MONDAY, 3:45 P.M., A CALL CAME INTO THE DETEC-tive agency from Johnny Knuckles. In his office, a flustered Max Weatherbee eagerly picked up a black desk phone and curtly asked, "Johnny, how are you making out with the Palmer tail?"

Max's white dress shirt had its sleeves rolled up and was unbuttoned a third of the way down; he lost his tie over an hour ago. The PI relaxed, reclining in the red oak office chair positioned at a forty-five-degree angle. The humming of the fluorescent light above would soon be overtaken by the street mug's crisp voice.

Originating from a phone booth, around a corner near the Palmer house in Roosevelt Heights, Johnny's oral travelogue began. "Mr. Bee, I crept behind her big ass all day. Nothin' out of duh ordinary, she went ta a coffee shop on Sixteenth Street called Bortone's in duh morning and shopped around downtown for duh rest of duh day. High-end clothin' joints... dis broad has expensive taste."

Max listened via the chunky earpiece speaker. Johnny rambled on, "Sat for lunch by herself at Leo's in Midtown. She did make some phone calls usin' pay phone booths throughout duh day and always closed duh door. She's home now," the ruffian added, "I can follow her until seven." The hoodlum removed his crumpled hat and then brushed sweat off his fore-head, utilizing one sleeve of his leather jacket. "Hey, if it means anything, she met wit another woman at duh coffee shop. A really foxy dame, younger than her." Johnny took a minute describing Vivian Allard.

When Johnny appeared finished, there existed a momentary pause as Max thought to himself, *"Vivian Allard... Mrs. Palmer's sister-in-law. Funny, they would meet at a coffee shop. I thought they didn't like each other... Maybe I'll have him tail Viv next.* Subsequently, Max pleasantly had a daydream snapshot of the last time he saw Vivian Allard in her mauve sarong dress. *"Nah... I'll do that one myself."* The private detective lecherously smirked, heading into la-la land.

Unsure of the silence, Johnny talked over Max's daydream. "Hey, Mr. Bee, yuh catch all dat?"

"I... I did, Johnny, sorry." Max would not disclose any thoughts with the mug anyway. Johnny's job was strictly a hired tail, to no degree a partner.

The hood continued his diligent summary. "When

I got back ta her house, I noticed there wuz a for-sale sign out front. It wuzn't there in duh mornin."

Max's chestnut eyes fueled with interest. "Johnny, thanks for the keen observation. Anything else I should know?"

For the time being, Johnny Knuckles carelessly omitted seeing the blonde-headed tall man in a white suit peering into the java joint's window. Instead, he offered, "Listen, Mr. Bee, duh fat Palmer dame goes ta dis coffee shop every mornin' 9 a.m. sharp. She has a table reserved near duh window. And she's there for at least an hour."

"Certainly is helpful information," Max praised, bearing enthusiasm, making a closed fist. "Johnny, how did you obtain it?" The private detective felt a step closer to getting into the Palmer house.

"There's a dishwasher who works at duh coffee shop. We were in duh joint tuhgetha," Knuckles confided. Then he added, "You owe me a buck—I put one in his pocket."

"I'll cover that buck, Johnny," Max assured dryly. "Keep the Mrs. Palmer tail going until seven tonight," he instructed, "and again tomorrow. Did your guy Rico go up to Adamsville today?"

"He went. He'll call me at Pool Palace tonight."

"Okay, I want him up there for at least two days." Max reached into his metal desk for a pack of Lucky Strike. "You and I will settle up on Friday," he affirmed. "Please call me tomorrow, same time... but call my answering service tonight if Rico finds anything up in Adamsville."

The conversation terminated.

Max left his desk carrying the lit cigarette in his mouth, opened the door, and walked into the waiting room. Darlene was sedulously reading school notes on a pad. He stood over her dark blue and white houndstooth dress, then pointed down using a middle finger and requested, "Please be here at precisely seven-thirty tomorrow morning." An inkling of suspense flickered across his handsome face. "And get ready for some action." The tone exhibited a Hollywood sleuth's vehemence.

Darlene's brown eyes were blazing, raptly displaying anticipation.

48

THE WALLS CLOSE IN

MONDAY, 4:45 P.M., THE LATE NOVEMBER NEW Paris sky grew indigo. Absolute boredom in room twenty-five started driving Mr. Ellory stir-crazy. The primary suspect in the Wayne Palmer murder case, now beyond exhaustion, wore a wrinkled white dress shirt, brown pants, and socks. Bruce's skin started crawling again as it did a million times before. He craved alcohol, his only savior. It was coming. The pathetic man internally reflected, *"When is the nightmare going to end?"*

He took apart all his card houses, then neatly placed the playing cards from dozens of decks without any order on his tidy brass bed. The silence broke as wooden floorboards under the hallway carpet creaked. A brisk knock on the door followed. "It's open," announced Bruce, standing in a room illuminated by whatever sunlight today still had to offer.

It was not his frowzy friend Frank this time, but

instead, Bruce's aloof brother-in-law, Walter Kazarian, who he had been expecting.

Wearing an olive-colored suit and narrow-brimmed hat, the Armenian rug dealer, who possessed absolutely no sense of humor, entered the shanty of a room, showcasing a grave look on his face. Mr. Kazarian indignantly dropped a bottle of gin and cold-cut sandwich, made by Bruce's sister Susan, on a mangy dresser. In Kazarian's world, a man's worthiness was based on his net worth, and he considered Bruce to be about as worthy as a box of stale potatoes.

The two brothers-in-law faced each other; Kazarian stood a few inches taller. No handshakes were exchanged. Kazarian's khaki, Middle Eastern kisser presented unsmiling. "Bruce, why do you leave your door unlocked?" Kazarian questioned.

"I... I feel trapped in this room, and locking the door makes it worse. Besides, the lock is shoddy. It would only prolong my agony."

"Bruce, please be straight with your sister and I, if you killed this Palmer guy," demanded Walter Kazarian, pitching a cold tone. His thick black mustache could have served as a toupee for a pint-sized man.

"Walter... I didn't do it!" Bruce remonstrated. His pitch sounded elevated, like a man about to snap.

"You need a lawyer. My friend Sammy Boyajian can defend you."

"A lawyer is going to advise me to turn myself in."

"Well, you'll need a lawyer once you get caught."

"No thanks. I have alternative plans for myself if that's the case." He fought his tears.

Kazarian's phiz became alarmed. "Bruce, please talk to your wife, Mona. Maybe she can make you act sensible."

"She left... she left me," Bruce stammered.

"Why don't you just leave town for now?" Kazarian advised, displaying uneasy mocha eyes, then added, "I have Armenian friends in Fresno."

"No. It's what someone guilty would do," Bruce Ellory countered. "Besides, by now, the cops are probably watching all the train stations. This private detective, Max Weatherbee, thinks he can get me off the hook soon. It's the only thing that keeps me hanging on."

"Yeah.... well, he just hit us up for more 'expense money,' as he calls it." Walter Kazarian's tone was filled with sarcasm. "I guess he tips everyone he sees."

"Walter, people around our town don't talk unless he lubes them."

"Lubes?"

Bruce Ellory disclosed, "It's what Max calls his payouts."

"Pickin' my pocket is what I call it," scoffed Mr. Kazarian like a skinflint.

"I'm going to pay you back, Walter." Bruce Ellory's humble brown eyes appeared heavy and bloodshot. He opened his palm towards the top of the desk. "Look at my engineering drawings."

"Not now, Bruce. I must return to work." Walter Kazarian's unimpassioned reaction was punctuated by pointing a manicured finger at the gin bottle on his way out. "Go easy on that, will ya."

"Can't take much more... I'm at the end now,"

thought misty-eyed Bruce Ellory, planted at the sill of the second-floor window, watching Walter's 1947 black Cadillac's taillights grow smaller and smaller.

In Webster Hills, the grandiloquent Cadillac stuck out like a Fabergé egg in a junk store. A man noticed— not a good man.

Beneath a weathered awning, across the street in the late afternoon shadows, eerily stood the six-foot-four man who detected Mr. Kazarian's sybaritic, made in Detroit, prized possession.

It happened to be the same man that the urban cowboy Butch placed a phone call to last night after blackmailing Bruce Ellory at Mickey's Lounge. It was also the same gangling man who both took a flyer from Howard Stanford one day before he perished and also inconspicuously stalked Bruce Ellory en route to the subway in Wickford after he left the house with the vines.

The human tower called Slick, showcasing his blonde hair parted perfectly in its center, removed a case out of his suit's inner pocket. The small case was popped open, exposing a pair of magnified lenses. The folding opera glasses were now positioned up to the second-floor hotel room window.

An evil grin followed the identification of the broken man he had been searching for all over town. Slick's scarred face, white suit, red bow tie, and wiry frame were soon led away from the Hotel Duncan by his white wingtip shoes into the twilight.

49

OFF THE HOOK

MONDAY 10 P.M., IN THE COZY STUDIO APARTMENT, Max sat bare-chested, wearing pajamas, while eating a bowl of Wheaties cereal at the kitchen table. The private detective was frustrated with the Pearl section of his detective corkboard on the wall, sitting back at the office. *"I don't have time to keep chasing this dame,"* he mused.

Max reached for the phone, called the answering service, and heard, "Sorry, no messages, Mr. Weatherbee."

He interpreted this as nothing good from Johnny Knuckles in regards to Rico finding anything up in Adamsville. His mind spoke, *"I'll need to go back there myself."* But no information still made his mind unrestful.

The sleuth swallowed two sleeping pills at his bedside, assuring himself he would get some shut-eye. He took the phone off the hook and got snug in bed. Max's closing eyes would need to wait until tomorrow to perceive the horrific news that certainly would have prevented sleep tonight.

50

RAMPAGE

MONDAY, 11 P.M., A WIDE-FRAME GORILLA OF A man entered the desolate Hotel Duncan's barren lobby. He wore a large white dress shirt, no tie or hat. His bushel of black hair seemed uncombed, and an inky five o'clock shadow dominated his lower face.

Staticky jazz music played schmaltzy via a small radio in Mr. Gray's caged office. Ghoulish Mr. Gray slowly arose out of his tiny chair. The hotel's owner, Mr. Duncan, had installed the cage portion a year ago as some sort of a bulwark to protect his night-owl clerk against potential Webster Hills violence. As the mountainous man approached the protective barrier, bulging, bloodshot-eyed Mr. Gray drawled, "Can I... offer you a room?"

The powerful beast's noxious grin and two-toned face, which Mr. Gray encountered, were filled with internal rage. Using a massive left hand, the Gorilla reached into the aperture above the sill of the caged office door, seized Mr. Gray by his dirty dress shirt, then tugged him into its opening. Next, deftly using a right hand, he applied a human vice grip to the posterior of Mr. Gray's puny neck. "Give me the fucking key to that room on the second floor... two windows over from the hotel sign." He shook Mr. Gray like a rag doll.

The scrawny creep caterwauled, "Ahhr."

Through the aperture, the brute continued to shake Mr. Gray. "I'll make it even easier for ya. The room where you are hiding this Ellory mug."

Mr. Gray's vocal cords uttered, "That's... room twenty-five... please... don't hurt me."

With his rear to his attacker, Mr. Gray stretched a feeble left arm towards a board holding the spare keys as the Gorilla maintained his forceful grip. Mr. Gray's crooked index finger looped the spare key to room twenty-five and slid it onto the wooden sill between the two men.

With his head still in the aperture, Mr. Gray got a second's relief as the Gorilla's grip attenuated while he grabbed something deep in his pocket. Ashen-faced Mr. Gray began hyperventilating, edging off the cage when the thick wire was clotheslined around the front of his neck.

"Oh no... please," Mr. Gray pleaded his last audible words. The night clerk's supplication fell on merciless ears as the monster strangled the anterior of Gray's neck, pulling him off the floor and pushing his left cheek firmly against the cage. Mr. Gray vainly tried to get his crooked fingers into the wire as it garroted him into lifelessness. When Mr. Gray's tongue turned purple, the Gorilla released his grip on the wire and let it fall on the other side of the aperture along with his homicide victim.

The Gorilla sauntered pleasantly upstairs and stopped in front of room twenty-five. He rotated a copper doorknob before attempting the key. The knob spun, indicating room twenty-five's door was already unlocked. The Gorilla inaudibly mumbled, "I didn't even need Ellory's room key from the toad." Regardless of requiring a key or not, this killer enjoyed putting Mr. Gray out of his misery.

In room twenty-five, the light was off; the bed's occupant snored loudly. In the darkness, the Gorilla flared his wide nostrils and yanked one pillow out from under the sleeping man's head, then pressed it vigorously on his face. The occupant's thin arms flailed, and his bony legs kicked and kicked until they thumped no more. The Gorilla sustained the intense pressure on the pillow for another minute.

Like leaving a calling card, he kept the pillow over the dead man's head as he exited the moonlit hotel room, sinisterly whispering, "Goodbye, Mr. Ellory."

51

DREAMLAND

DEEP IN SLEEP, THE PI VIVIDLY DREAMED. IN HIS mind, Max sat up high on Uncle Harry's shoulders. There were people cheering all around him. The air appeared patriotic. He was a boy back at a parade in New Paris celebrating America's end to the First World War. The dream felt very warm and comfortable.

52

HAMBURGERS
PART 2

COMING FROM HIS LATE EVENING NIGHTLY HAM-burger run, Bruce Ellory walked in the back door of the Hotel Duncan. High on his upper left, through the wooden spindles, he saw colossal legs plodding and descending the second-floor landing—colossal legs he recognized from the hellish night of nine days ago.

In a pure panic, Mr. Ellory dropped the white paper bag he had been carrying within five feet of the base of the stairs, pivoted to his right, and closed himself into the nearest place to hide, the lone phone booth. A terrified Bruce Ellory crouched down in the booth and pinned a foot against the door.

The Gorilla paused as he reached the bottom of the stairs. The white bag sitting on the floor to his right caught his attention. As a horrified Bruce Ellory looked on, the big man possessing grisly dark eyes picked up the white paper bag consisting of two uneaten hamburgers and turned to the front door, showcasing his mammoth backside to the phone booth.

Bruce Ellory's eyebrows were furrowed over two wide, frightened eyes as he stayed crouched and thought, *"He didn't see me."*

From behind in the phone booth, Mr. Ellory observed the big man grasp one warm burger out of the bag and chomp on it. It was gone on the third bite. Next, he scooped out the other burger, held it in his left hand, then rolled up the empty paper bag with his right and tossed it into the caged office's aperture for two points. The Gorilla sank the remaining hamburger into his mouth and leisurely walked toward the front door.

Mr. Ellory knew that tranquil stroll. *"He just killed somebody up there!"*

"Oh no... Frank!" Bruce Ellory screamed beyond the closed phone booth's glass, which muffled his high-pitched cry to the outside.

Shortly after running amok, the Gorilla egressed the Duncan. Bruce hastily bolted upstairs to his room numbered 25, flicked on the light, and then removed the pillow. Frank was not breathing—for once, his face did not contain any color. Bruce took his final look at his formerly frowzy friend and pondered, *"Is it my fault Frank kept coming in my room?"*

Mr. Ellory frantically ran down the stairs. "Mr. Gray! Mr. Gray!" he howled, rattling the cage wildly with his fingers. Bruce looked down through the cage's aperture and got a glimpse of Mr. Gray's extinguished body, plus the multiple red square cage impressions indented on his face. The hamburger bag, now in a ball, settled an inch from one of the deceased man's bat ears.

Bruce Ellory realized he had made a grave mistake last night by going to Mickey's Lounge. *"Max told me to stay put. I shouldn't have gone to that bar... can't tell Max I did. These two murders are on me."* Rheumy-eyed Mr. Ellory headed for the rear door and scampered south into the pitch-black night toward the vivid red lights of nearby Chinatown.

Notable Characters Introduced in Part 6

Detective McGann: New Paris Police senior detective assigned to the Wayne Palmer murder case, first appearance Chapter 45

Detective Skip Cobb: Wise-cracking, younger partner of Detective McGann, first appearance Chapter 45

Gigantic thug who knocked on Pearl's door: Not identified thus far, first appearance Chapter 46

Previously Unnamed Characters, Now Named

Slick: Tall man wearing white wingtip shoes and a white suit, first appearance Chapter 10

PART 7

53

HOUSE HUNTING

TUESDAY, 7:30 A.M., AFTER A POST-BREAKFAST workout in his studio apartment consisting of push-ups, pullups, and sit-ups, Max showered and then drove to the Keiser building without the radio on. This morning's confidential mission did not need distractions—the private detective was deep in thought. The jacket to his gray pinstripe suit and fedora sat next to him on a bench seat. The sky aired light charcoal; November rain loomed on its horizon.

In Old Downtown, Max pulled up to the curb of the dirty sidewalk at a no parking zone in front of the archaic, eleven-story, tan cement building that resembled a forgotten sand castle. Dashing Darlene stood with her lanky frame in suspense near the newspaper stand, sporting a wide-brimmed black hat, red wool coat, red flounce dress, red leather gloves, nylons, plus black pumps. Her brown hair was tucked into her hat. She carried a black clutch bag and a folded newspaper.

Darlene opened the passenger's door, leaned forward on the curb, and then her perfect face spoke animatedly through red lips, "I picked you up a newspaper. Did you hear about those two murders?" Max never told her where Bruce Ellory had been staying, so she was not trying to make a connection, just conversation.

Lacking a hair out of place, the macho PI grinned sarcastically. "Don't know anything of it, but what else is new in this metropolis?" He moved his suit jacket over closer to himself as she climbed in the Ford coupe. He went on, "Tell me later, okay? We have to get down to business."

Max tossed her folded newspaper into the backseat as though it were insignificant.

Darlene's brown eyes sparkled with verve. "So... what's my assignment?"

8:30 a.m. in the Roosevelt Heights section, Max saw Johnny Knuckles on Empire Ave, just around a corner from the Palmer House, sitting in his hot box on wheels. Max parked the Ford coupe behind it. The private detective got out and approached the stolen Buick as Johnny started rolling down its window.

A handwritten note was surreptitiously delivered to the leather jacket-wearing hoodlum—Max backtracked, devoid of saying a word. He knew Johnny could read; he just could not write. The slick-haired hood unfurled his note:

When she comes out of the coffee shop, call ST1-9054. Let it ring once, hang up, and repeat one more time. Burn this note later. Please ring me around 4 p.m. at the office.

8:35 a.m., the doorbell rang at the exquisite Palmer House. Mrs. Wayne Palmer, in a black dress, swung the screen door open. The fortyish, stout woman sharply glanced at twenty-one-year-old, stylish, Dashing Darlene up and down, then remarked, "Pretty outfit, my dear. Can I help you?"

Darlene's tone sounded buoyant as she began her fable. "Hi, Mrs. Palmer, my fiancé and I just love your house; we saw the sign. I'm Mr. Kravitz's daughter... you know, next street over." Darlene pointed a red-gloved finger beyond the Palmer house. "Can I see the home quick? I'm sure my fiancé will buy it for me."

Florid face Mrs. Palmer nodded her double chin, pretending she knew Darlene's fictitious neighbor, Mr. Kravitz. "Well, come in quick," she consented briskly in a patronizing way. "I'm really on my way out."

The two women walked around the splendid house full of alabaster busts and made small talk that became momentarily interrupted by the ringing of a telephone. "Hold on, dear," requested Mrs. Palmer, exhibiting a hint of additional smugness, heading to the foyer's alcove to answer it. Darlene innocently continued solo with her staged home inspection, staying on the first floor.

From a phone booth on nearby Empire Avenue, it was Max on the line. Putting a handkerchief over the mouthpiece, he curled his lips to alter the sound and loudly informed, "Hi, Mrs. Palmer. It's Mr. Carlson, New Paris tax office. How are you today?"

"What can I do for you, Mr. Carlson?" Mrs. Palmer curtly queried.

"I just want to make sure you are up to date with your house taxes. I understand the house is for sale."

"My husband always paid the taxes, so I guess they are not in arrears. What do your records show?"

"Oh, I'm checking now." Max cleverly stalled her on the line. "Hey, they said it's going to rain today," he inferred off-subject.

Darlene furtively tiptoed into the kitchen in the house's rear and unlocked a window facing the back porch. It gave her an adrenaline rush. The intern felt important. Soon, she heard Mrs. Wayne Palmer brusquely yell, "Stop talking about other stuff! Are my taxes paid or not?"

In the foyer, Mrs. Palmer slammed the black phone's receiver down, shaking the taboret underneath, then complained, "So annoying." Her big blue eyes looked for Darlene, who had simultaneously returned to the foyer with the call's termination. "I can't show you upstairs right now," Mrs. Palmer disclosed, "it's really a mess because of all the boxes."

"Thank you. I've seen enough." The young intern smiled demurely, exposing pristine teeth, and announced optimistically, "I love it and will come again, taking my fiancé."

"Please contact the phone number written on the

sign to make an appointment," directed the plump widow dispassionately as she grabbed her fur coat.

The women egressed the luxury two-story brick house together, descended its grandiose steps, and passed by a dirt pile on the sidewalk over the bleach that cleaned up Mr. Palmer's blood. Once they reached the corner of busy Empire Ave, like algebra and geometry—they went in separate directions.

Darlene hailed a cab, avoiding any contact with Johnny Knuckles as instructed. Johnny tailed Mrs. Palmer towards the coffee shop at fifty yards distance, leaving behind the Buick. When the house became empty, Max exited his Ford, proceeded to the Palmer house, and entered via Darlene's unlocked window on its back porch.

He started his reconnaissance upstairs in case Mrs. Palmer came home earlier than expected. If so, Johnny Knuckles would call the Palmer house using his one-ring code, which gave Max five minutes to tidy up and vamoose.

In Wayne Palmer's upstairs office, there were numerous boxes of work folders. Max spent thirty minutes digging through the office and found nothing. The master bedroom, his following stop, was filled with trinkets and Mrs. Palmer's clothing scattered everywhere. Again, nothing there. Next, Max came across a little den that had a door leading to a spare storage room. The uncanny attached spare room contained no windows or lights and floorboards on only half of the floor.

Max brought out a pocket flashlight and then began his exploration of this unfinished room where the floorboards ended. He guided his hand way underneath along the last board until he discovered a gunnysack-type bundle. *"McGann's coppers didn't search too hard,"* he thought.

Max transferred the formerly hidden bundle out of the dark room into the den. The first folder in the bundle held a letter-size envelope. Max removed it from the folder. On the exterior, *In the event of my death, give to police had been written in pen.* Max opened it. *"I'll tell McGann it wasn't sealed,"* he pondered.

There were several photos containing various fire debris scenes and a folded handwritten note. Max's curious, chestnut-brown eyes read it:

> *I was coerced by racketeer Joe Martinelli to assist in the following arson claims: Tower Storage Company, New Paris Fur Company, and Alfredo's Bistro. All companies were opened by associates of Mr. Martinelli with the intention of filing fraudulent arson claims, which did indeed happen.*
>
> *Also, Mr. Joseph Martinelli killed Lloyd Carrington in 1945 at the Eldorado club after hours. Fred Monroe and Ice Box Collins witnessed this incident.*
>
> —*Wayne Palmer*

The second folder in the bundle contained an insurance policy for the current business owned by Mr. Martinelli, the Eldorado Gentleman's Club. The document was signed by both Wayne Palmer and Joe Martinelli, the head of the outfit in New Paris. *"A future arson claim, no doubt,"* the private detective internally reflected. *"Palmer was an underworld puppet."*

Max spread out all the papers and photos on a tiny maple desk in the den, which offered adequate daylight. From his suit jacket pocket, he fished for his camera and then snapped multiple pictures of it all.

Something else remained in the bundle—a large envelope. Max slid it out. It contained a stack of hundreds—a grand worth—and an unsigned life insurance document. Mr. Wayne Palmer stood as the beneficiary on this unfinished spousal policy in the works. Max's heart galloped as he took more pictures. It was his devoir to divulge his findings to Detective McGann. He mumbled under his breath, "Wayne Palmer appeared ready to hire someone to kill his wife. But... maybe his wife had him killed instead."

The ringing of the doorbell downstairs startled Max Weatherbee even further.

54

THE VAGRANT

RAIN WAS ABOUT TO SET IN ON A COLD, SOMBER Tuesday morning in Chinatown as petite Suzy Kwong, holding two bags of groceries, climbed the stairs to the back porch behind her compact restaurant. A stench of body odor hit her nasal cavity fiercely like a garbage dump. Down on the porch's floor, she saw an effete, desultory human body curled up in a ball. The Chinese American woman placed the bags on the top step, picked up a six-quart cauldron, and banged its side with a metal spoon. It echoed loud enough to wake Rip Van Winkle.

A brown, crusty, recessed eye opened; its owner's body remained tortuous.

Using the spoon, Suzy pointed away and scolded downwards, "Hey, you get out. No vagrants around here. Go find a job!"

A shivering Bruce Ellory opened his other eye,

and with a pathetic appeal, he uttered, "Max... Max Weatherbee told me that you would help me."

The man in the crinkled clothes uncurled himself, then humbly sat on the floorboards, reaching for a squished pack of Chesterfields in his shirt pocket. The fugitive hoped what he said would assuage her harshness.

Suzy's tone turned sympathetic. "Oh. Sorry, I know you now, just didn't expect you unannounced. Come in, and I'll fix you something to eat."

55

DUTCH AND THE BOYS

AGAIN, THE DOORBELL RANG AT 475 18TH STREET.
Under the last floorboard in the upstairs spare room,
Max returned Wayne Palmer's secret bundle, but only
leaving the grand inside. A thief was something Max
Weatherbee was not. The private detective keenly
curled and stowed the insurance papers and arson
photos, along with one dead man's note, into his suit
jacket pocket. He stuffed the mini camera in another.
In Max's mind, it appeared necessary to get this stuff
to Detective Dan McGann as soon as possible.

Descending the stairs, Max saw two suits through
a window at the front door of the Palmer house. He
could not see faces, just the suits. That happened to be
enough for him to lock the back porch window Darlene had previously unlocked and covertly head out
the rear door into the small backyard.

Two additional guys in suits greeted him. "Hold it
right there, pal," assertively ordered a short and stout

pug-faced man on the right, who made a stop motion to Max. He then stuck two fingers into his oral cavity and blew out a loud whistle.

These men were not police. Max easily recognized the mid-forties taller man on his left as Dutch O'Brien, an underboss in Mr. Martinelli's criminal outfit and no stranger to newspaper headlines. Dutch's shoulders were broad; he had maybe an inch on Max.

Soon, the two guys in suits from the front arrived as reinforcements via the rear gate, outnumbering the PI by four to one. For a moment, below a pewter-colored, rain-threatening morning sky, all five men wearing fedora hats stood statuesque.

With Max surrounded, Dutch O'Brien loudly interrogated, "Where's Mrs. Palmer?" His voice sounded deep and hoarse—face rough as sandpaper.

"She stepped out," Max curtly replied.

"And who the hell are you... her cleaning lady?" growled Dutch.

"A friend."

"Hand over your wallet," dictated the short, pug-faced gangster on Max's right while beckoning pudgy hands.

Max did as he was told.

The stout, pug-faced man snatched it, looked at its contents, and made known, "His name is Weatherbee, Dutch."

Dutch raised his wide jaw and then asked, "Harry's kid?"

"Nephew."

"He was unruly on me a few times," Dutch unashamedly disclosed. "Why you snooping around here?"

Max shrugged. "A social call."

Dutch vigilantly gazed down, noticing the bulge in Max's right pants pocket, then showing authority, instructed, "Chuck here is going to reach inside your pocket and take that piece."

Pug Face, next to Dutch, drew a .38 Special revolver on Max, who leisurely placed his hands above his head. The third gangster, a thin man called Chuck with bad coffee breath, fished into the sleuth's right pants pocket, and the Smith & Wesson in holster was confiscated. The Colt strapped to his ankle remained still there, but it stood four against one, plus Max's talus bone was a long stretch away.

Dutch continued imperiously, "Now gimme your suit jacket." Meanwhile, Pug Face, to Dutch's left, kept his aim on Max's chest. The fourth racketeer, a barrel-chested man, stayed silent.

Coffee-breath Chuck and the fourth gangster, the barrel-chested man, started taking Max Weatherbee's jacket off, one on each side. Unexpectedly, Max delivered an unerring upper-cut punch toward Chuck, who was grabbing his right sleeve. The punch landed squarely into Chuck's jaw; the weak man fell to his knees, dropping Max's heater on the grass. Dutch moved quickly, helping the silent mug who was still gripping Max's left. Both men chicken-winged the PI while Pug Face, still maintaining steady aim, enjoined, "Dutch, just give me the word."

"Not here," responded Dutch. "Rough 'em up, Chuck."

With Max wiggling in the tenacious two-man chicken-wing hold, the thin man called Chuck got off his knees, pulled out a blackjack, and whipped the private detective's jaw, on the right side, three times exhibiting vengeance. Max spat out a partial molar as blood trickled down his chin.

Dutch settled his lips to Max's ear and hostilely questioned, "Any more asinine tricks? I'll ask you nice one more time... the jacket."

Both men released the chicken wing hold. Max purposely spat blood on his suit jacket as he doffed it, leering at the man called Chuck in indignation prior to handing it over. Chuck, now sporting grass stains on the knees of his suit pants, passed the jacket to Dutch, who, between its two pockets, confiscated the insurance papers, photos, the dead man's note, and Max's camera.

"Let's have a look." Dutch briefly examined the papers in front of him, then attested using an accusatory tone, "All these papers now belong to Mr. Martinelli."

"You saved us some time," sarcastically added Pug Face.

Dutch removed the camera's film and deposited the filmless Kodak back into Max's suit jacket pocket. Chuck picked up the Smith & Wesson, emptied its chamber, and put the bullets in his own pocket. The suit jacket was snappily tossed by Dutch at Max's abdomen.

Chuck returned the bare firearm to its owner, Max Weatherbee, and mockingly cautioned, "Here, don't play with toys." His voice squeaked like a box spring during intercourse.

All the men heard the adjacent dwelling's rear door open. An elderly male neighbor came out carrying a garbage bag and placed it in a can.

Bearing eminence, Dutch, the underboss of the New Paris outfit, broke up the party and announced, "Let's go, boys."

The rugged, silent racketeer exited the backyard first, utilizing a rear gate. The short and stout, pug-faced man departed last and handed Max his wallet back, offering an inimical warning. "Next time we see you, we're gonna play bumpy."

56

CASE CLOSED

LEAVING THE PALMER HOUSE UNDER AN ASH-COL-ored morning sky, Max Weatherbee dawdled to the Ford coupe as if he were walking on the moon. *"It's all over…I failed Bruce. I had and lost the evidence for Detective McGann,"* internally reflected the now somber private detective.

The moment he got into the vehicle, Max had a temper tantrum on its steering wheel and ineloquently fumed, "Fuck… fuck!" He stopped pounding when his knuckles hurt. Blood still oozed from the right side of his mouth, staining his dress shirt.

The Ford had been traveling south on Empire Ave when the radio came on. He only caught the last part of a broadcaster's announcement: "Due to unfortunate circumstances, the Hotel Duncan will remain closed until further notice… Now, a word from our sponsor."

"What the hell?" Max's heart pulsated as he abruptly pulled his coupe over to the side of the road

and reached into its back seat for Darlene's newspaper he had chucked there earlier.

> *Double Murder at the Hotel Duncan in Webster Hills. Victims are Mr. Lawrence Gray, 51, the night manager, and an unknown vagrant identified only as Mr. Wallace. Murderer at large.*

Max wailed, "Mr. Wallace! Oh my God, Bruce Ellory is dead!"

11:15 a.m., red-faced, enraged Max Weatherbee entered the ninth-floor detective agency. He tossed his hat rapidly onto Darlene's desk, which caused her to suddenly look up from her studies at his bloody shirt. Like a whirlwind, the attractive intern in her red flounce dress ascended to a standing position. "Max..." was all she could get out of her red lips.

From the waiting room next to her oak desk, Max capriciously kicked a metal waste basket through his open office door for a field goal. It landed all the way to the rear of his office, dinging against the darkroom door. Most of its contents fell out along the way.

"Max, wait. Wait," pleaded Darlene hysterically, waving her hands as if doing jumping jacks, omitting the actual jumping.

Max ignored Darlene and walked into the office—

but immediately U-turned promptly back to the waiting room. He looked at his intern with burning eyes.

"I tried to tell you," she said, pointing a polished finger. "The woman was waiting by our door when I arrived here." Max's face had cooled off just in time for Dashing Darlene to add, "And you owe me cab money for earlier."

Max widened his cheeks and half-smirked. "Take it out of the kitty." He gave her intense eyes and then whispered, "Bruce Ellory is dead."

Her pretty face became aghast and speechless.

"The vagrant, Mr. Wallace, in the Webster Hills murders, unbeknownst to the media, happens to be our Bruce Ellory using an alias," he divulged.

The private detective returned to his office. Sitting across from Max's desk, just starting to light up, was the girl possessing the flaxen, victory-rolled hair. The dame smoked the cigarette via a black plastic holder, which made the whole thing look like an arrow—an arrow that could pierce your heart. Today, her black cherry nails matched her lips. Pearl's nylon legs presented crossed; the red-spiked heels were reborn. The aforementioned, accompanied by a snug black winter skirt and sweater, showcased her as dressed to kill. Her mascaraed, upturned eyes expressed they had a story to tell.

He dug the way she looked—a lot—but he played football and recognized defeat. Max pointed toward the hallway. "Pearl, I don't have use for you anymore," he declared, "Wayne Palmer's case is closed; please leave." His tone aired impassionate.

57

EXTRA PASSENGER

DONNED IN HER BIG BLACK DRESS, CARRYING AN unopened umbrella, Mrs. Wayne Palmer left Bortone's coffee shop with a full belly. She burned off one sugar cube's worth of calories, lumbering the two blocks back to her stately home.

A sky full of ominous, dark clouds overhead foretold Johnny they were about to burst when the maroon sedan pulled up in front of the Palmer house. The four men, who earlier today ambushed Max, served as its occupants. Max's prior fiasco with the racketeers remained undisclosed to Johnny Knuckles shadowing Mrs. Palmer. The rugged, silent gangster was driving alongside sandpaper-faced Dutch O'Brien, who rode shotgun. The top of O'Brien's fedora appeared to be scraping the interior roof.

Eyes ablaze, Johnny saw it all shortly after Mrs. Palmer turned the corner. The two unscrupulous men in the posterior seat, Pug Face and Chuck, got out of the automobile near the sandpile covering the bleached sidewalk. Chuck snuck a snub-nosed pistol under Mrs. Wayne Palmer's chubby armpit and guided her into the sedan's rear seat.

Tires screeched; the abduction was quick, like a prison scuffle. Johnny Knuckles ran back to the corner toward his hot box. Unfortunately for him, two uniformed officers were going through the stolen Buick. The ruffian's panicked face peered over the corner fence, realizing a wallet containing his life's savings sat in its glove box. The flummoxed hoodlum could no longer even make change for a telephone call.

It started to rain.

58

TRADE AGREEMENT

WITH HIS BLACK HAIR METICULOUSLY PARTED BY a right-sided sweep, hatless Max Weatherbee stood erect, squeezing his jaw, exhibiting a scowl on his craggy rock face, while waiting for Pearl to leave. Next, he picked up the garbage pail he had just punted and spat out a bloody cotton ball into it.

She did not budge but alternatively conversed pleasantly through smoke, "I've been looking at all the pictures on the wall. Your life is interesting." Pearl's flaxen locks appeared silken beneath a fluorescent overhead light that persistently buzzed. "How come I don't see any pictures of a wife?"

"Don't have one," Max responded curtly. "Okay, please, no small talk. The Palmer case is closed; why are you still here?" He articulated past the pain in his mouth, talking just like she did to him yesterday evening when he encroached upon her.

"I need your help," she entreated feverishly.

"Let me guess," Max said, "you're going to hit me up to buy some more dope?"

"I don't buy dope," she retorted, "just sit in and smoke at the opium parlor." The foxy dame glowered up towards Max's chestnut brown eyes. "You left a note under my door last night concerned for my safety."

"Yeah. Looks as if some goliath wants to hurt you," he gravely warned, peering down at her while still standing beside his giant metal desk.

"That's Junior. He's harmless."

"Harmless?"

"Well, harmless to me," she said, "maybe not to others."

The phone rang in the waiting room. Their conversation paused when Dashing Darlene cutely poked her head amid the propped open office door. "Max," she announced, "a dead guy is on the line. I'm assuming it's urgent enough to interrupt."

Max briskly scuttled to the desk phone in the waiting room faster than a poor sap with a bowel problem heading toward the john. He gripped its chunky receiver and said, "Bruce, I thought..."

Bruce Ellory came in on the other line. "It was Frank, the vagrant. He happened to be sleeping in my bed again when I ran for hamburgers last night."

Darlene closed his office door, shutting out Pearl's ears.

"Oh my gosh... poor him," Max replied. "I wonder if he has family. But for now, we have to let the killers think that was you and you're dead as Mussolini."

"Oh, it's only one guy, the Gorilla. I saw him again," Bruce Ellory imparted.

"He's not working alone," Max corrected. "Where are you?"

"Chinatown, Suzy's Chopsticks," Bruce nervously confided.

"Stay put until I get there," the private detective ordered.

After Max hung up the phone, Darlene compassionately said, "I'm going to go find you some ice."

Max made a single hand thumbs-up, then returned to his office, closing the door behind him. Pearl milled her cigarette butt in the ashtray.

"Where were we? How can I help you?" he questioned; his tone seemed effervescent now, like he had reentered the game and cared again.

She recrossed her magnificent nylon legs. "I need to escape Mr. Martinelli's grasp."

He sat down on his oak chair across from her. "Well, maybe we can make a trade."

Pearl's angelic face looked puzzled. "Trade?" she queried.

"The Palmer case just got reopened," disclosed Max passionately. He continued, "I'll help you, but you must give me everything you know about Wayne Palmer, including Wayne's relationship with Joe Martinelli." Next, the PI added, "And you can't ditch me anymore, twice is enough."

"I can do that." Her tone was coated in affirmation.

"First, tell me why your friend Junior, as you call him, was so upset with you last evening?"

"Well," Pearl said, "I was supposed to entertain a roulette high roller at Mr. Martinelli's Eldorado Club on Sunday night, but I decided to get my hair done instead. Do you fancy it?" She spoke blithely like the free spirit hipster she claimed to be. "So, Mr. Martinelli sent Junior searching for me the next day."

"Why is Junior harmless to you?"

"Because he thinks he is my boyfriend or something. I use him for free meals now and then. He wouldn't hurt me."

"Talk to me regarding you and Wayne Palmer."

"Our relationship stayed professional, meaning I received cash for my escort services. It was nothing serious; he wanted an attractive lass on his arm to gallivant around town."

"Go on."

"Wayne also supported my opium habit and treated me decently till some lady Mona came around." Her face grew red around the rouge. "I read in the papers she's the wife of that suspect, Bruce Ellory. Once he started running all over town spoiling her, I got left at the doorstep."

"Sounds like you had a motive to kill Wayne Palmer yourself," Max pried.

"No. No... don't even suggest such a thing," Pearl countered sharply.

"Everyone's a suspect in ordering the hit," he said, "including good ole Junior."

"Junior wouldn't order a hit. He would do it himself."

"Keep going. Why is Palmer dead?"

"Wayne had big gambling debts to Mr. Martinelli. Even so, he tipped all the croupiers even if he was losing, always flashing greenbacks. Everybody loved him. I can't understand why anybody else, other than Mr. Martinelli, would kill him."

"If he owed Martinelli money, why would Martinelli kill him?"

"Mr. Martinelli is mean, and the only way out of his circle is death. Which is why I need your help." She dug a red spiked-heel into the floor, and abashedly avowed below wet eyes, "Mr. Martinelli got forceful with me in a smutty way. And Junior can't do anything about it."

Max's rugged face expressed sympathy and assured, "When I'm done, if Martinelli is behind these murders, he's going to be rotting in jail."

She appreciated what her ear canal perceived and then repeated, "Murders?"

Max ignored her one-word question and lit up a Lucky Strike to avert her from his slip-up. He placed the cigarette in the left corner of his mouth, the part which did not hurt as much. "Okay, big request here." He pointed, utilizing his middle finger. "If Martinelli received some important documents by way of Dutch O'Brien, where would he store them?" He paused for a second to puff. "I assume Dutch O'Brien is familiar to you?"

Pearl leaned forward, placing two elbows on the

desk, and supporting her head using piano fingers; she confirmed, "Yes, Mr. Martinelli's right-hand man. Dutch and his boys do all his dirty work." Max admiringly gazed at her sharp dark cherry nails as her matching lips further vocalized. "I gather he keeps anything valuable in his safe at the Eldorado Club. Besides Mr. Martinelli, only Wimpy and Dutch possess the combination."

"Is this Wimpy short and fat owning a pug face?" he quizzed.

"Yes, that's him."

"I know who Chuck is, but who is the hunky, quiet bird in Dutch's crew?"

"Sal. He usually drives. His nickname is Silent Sal."

"Go figure. Okay, where does your gigantic friend Junior fit in?"

"He is the muscle at the club. Mr. Martinelli never uses him outside of it because, as you saw, he is six foot eight and obviously would be easy for witnesses to identify."

"How about a fellow over three hundred pounds, wide as an army barrack, black bushy hair, mammoth lips, missing some teeth?"

"Could be a guy they call Ice Box. He comes to the club sometimes. But his hair's not bushy as you say. Not sure there's missing teeth."

"No, this brute is not Ice Box Collins." Max smirked and revealed, "I've had the pleasure of meeting him already. The individual I'm speaking of is wider... even more fierce; no one in town seems to know him."

"Jeez... I can't recall anyone resembling such."

"Are you familiar with Mrs. Wayne Palmer?"

"I never met the former beauty queen who turned fat. Under no circumstances did she stop by the club while I was working."

"Then how do you fathom she's hefty?"

"Because Wayne used to call her Oinkeypuss."

Max chuckled. "Has he ever spoken of killing her?"

"Not exactly. But he said she 'would be out of the picture soon.' I thought he meant divorce."

Max stopped briefly to process what he just heard, then asked, "Have you been acquainted with Vivian Allard, Wayne's sister?"

"Never met her. Wayne voiced very little of her," she divulged, "didn't care for her as far as I recollect."

"You mentioned Mona earlier. Mona Ellory. Can you think of a reason she'd wish harm to Mr. Palmer?" He reclined in the bendable office chair. "Did they have a breakup?"

"I recall nothing of the woman, only her name. He never brought her to the club, either. From what I heard, he only took Mona to high-class restaurants and me to cheap hotels." She puckered her dark cherry lips tartly in indignation.

"If you want me to bring Wayne's killer or killers to justice, I need to get inside Martinelli's safe by Friday morning," enjoined the wily PI. "It's my one chance."

She intently studied the desperation on his face and raised her crescent moon-shaped eyebrows from across the desk. "If you promise to free me of him, I know a way," the sultry hipster furtively revealed.

59

RICO RIVERA

A RAINY TUESDAY AFTERNOON WAS THE SECOND day of his Adamsville excursion. Puerto Rican-born Rico Rivera did what his friend Johnny Knuckles asked of him: 'Nothing too deep, just observation, talk to local hoods, find the big man, but don't confront him.' Rico, with his college boy, neatly parted dark hair, seemed more polished than Johnny but a little less street smart. He was well-tanned, hatless, and wore a white sweater plus tan trousers. In those trousers' right pocket, he carried his favorite surreptitious weapon of choice: a box cutter.

At a place called Sam's Pool and Drink by the river, Rico encountered a red-headed, laddish fisherman wearing a bucket hat and yellow raincoat who, through crooked teeth, informed, "I can give you the name of the cat you're looking for. Going to cost you a sawbuck."

Unknown to Rico, this was the same boyish fisherman who gave Bruce Ellory a note eight days ago, just after his head had been smashed like a piñata.

Rico cleverly negotiated, "Five now, five later."

"We can't chat in here. Outside," evasively said the foul-smelling lad, jutting one finger at the rear door after sticking Rico's first fin inside a blue jean pocket.

Rico walked outside into the cold rain, placing a hand in his own right pocket behind the barely adult rodman.

The freckle-faced kid's blue jeans stopped, and then he said, "Here's what I got—"

Ferocious as a hailstorm, Ellory's Gorilla, intrepidly appeared from beyond a deserted fishing boat docked on land. His grotesque face was filled with fury. "Lookin' for me?" he roared.

Rico froze for a second while the late teenage red-haired hooligan suddenly circled around and shoved his backside. Subsequently, the three-hundred-plus pound, agile killing machine possessing black, lifeless eyes grabbed Rico's neck as he withdrew the box cutter out of his pocket. Rico descended to one knee, experiencing neck pain so intense that the cutter fell on the muddy ground. The red-headed fisherman maliciously kicked it closer to the river.

Next, showcasing omnipotent strength, the Gorilla dragged Rico into the frigid, waist-deep water, submerging his head and creating a maelstrom. The youthful, handsome Puerto Rican crony of Johnny Knuckles never came up for air. By the time the Gorilla's grip was released, Rico had started doing a dead man's float.

When the execution by noyade was completed, a suave, umbrella-carrying six-foot-four-inch man in a starch white pinstripe suit, wearing white wingtip shoes, came drifting around the corner like a heavenly ghost. The gangling gangster stared at the freckle-faced fisherman, then callously directed, "Get a boat and dump this clown way south into New Paris waters. We don't need Adamsville's finest investigating."

"Got it, Slick," obediently agreed the carrot top deliverer of death.

The tall, thin man called Slick next looked at the soaking wet, massive beast of destruction, who was now back on the soil. To the Gorilla, Slick coolly instructed, "Tommy, we gotta dry you up."

Notable Characters Introduced in Part 7

Dutch O'Brien: Underworld underboss to Joe Martinelli in the New Paris outfit, first appearance Chapter 55

Dutch's Crew: Unscrupulous gangsters including Skinny Chuck, Wimpy (aka Pug Face), and Silent Sal (driver), first appearance Chapter 55

Rico Rivera: Associate of Johnny Knuckles, first appearance Chapter 59

Previously Unnamed Characters, Now Named

Junior: 6' 8", sometimes boyfriend of Pearl, an enforcer for Joe Martinelli, first appearance Chapter 46

PART 8

60

APARTMENT 303

AFTER MEETING THE GIRL WITH THE HABIT IN HIS office, Max navigated his Ford coupe betwixt the two mammoth golden dragons, checking on Bruce Ellory at Suzy's Chopsticks in Chinatown. The rain persisted, keeping the New Paris sky charcoal gray.

Upon arrival, Bruce's body odor was putrid; Suzy could not stand much more of it. They said their goodbyes, and then Max and Bruce walked north on Duke Street amidst the precipitation. The destination was nearby—Pearl's yellow brick apartment building across from Moon's Oriental Laundry.

Once again, no door attendant could be observed. When Max and Bruce reached the third floor, Max removed a small case located inside his beige raincoat pocket before rolling the wet garment into a ball and ditching it on the hallway carpet. The private detective opened his lock kit and then began picking the lock of unit number 303, the apartment next to Pearl's.

The sultry hipster, hearing Max and Bruce conversing, immediately came out of apartment 301 and amusingly asked, "Max, what are you doing?"

To gaunt Mr. Ellory—Pearl was a sight to behold. Bruce, in the center of the hallway, became wide-eyed, mesmerized, and all shook up by the delectable younger lady, like a bobby soxer at a Frank Sinatra concert. Bruce, hyperventilating, tried to say hello, but he only nonsensically stuttered out a few h's.

She looked him up and down, then pinched her petite, cube-tipped nose skyward, showing superiority. He was not worth a second of her time.

The sleuth stopped his lock-picking. "Favor Pearl… a huge one," Max enjoined. "I must put my pal up here for three days. Need you to keep quiet. I have nowhere else to hide him." Max shrugged broad shoulders and added, "You stated that this tenant won't be back for weeks."

She responded, "You don't need to break in… I carry a key. I get his mail." Pearl, who retained her voguish fashion threads from earlier today, announced gullibly, "I don't think he would care if it is a friend of mine." She disappeared but fleetly reappeared in the corridor, offering a key. Pearl aimed a long, dark cherry nail at the handsome PI. "Come to my apartment later, alone."

Max turned the key and ventured inside apartment 303 with Bruce lagging in the rear. He directed his exhausted client, "Sleep on the sofa and don't make a mess; take a shower, too."

To Max's amazement, the place looked meticulous. He further advised, "Remember, Suzy will deliver all your meals going forward. Skulk in this pad; do not journey out." Using his middle finger, he gingerly poked Bruce's chest as a friendly warning, then went into a paper bag and gave the fugitive a red robe he acquired through Suzy. "I'll bring a small bottle of gin plus some clothes for you tonight," Max assured. "They'll be big, however, at least clean."

"Thank you, Max, for everything," Bruce humbly replied.

"I'm close to clearing you by presenting something that causes reasonable doubt. I discovered documents at the Palmer House proving insurance fraud was cooking and even Mrs. Palmer's planned murder," Max propounded. "They were taken from me along with the film I had for a copy, but I'm going to get them back," he confidently avowed. "Then we'll need to contact that lawyer chum of Walter, your brother-in-law."

"I'm responsible for Mr. Gray and Frank's deaths," Ellory lamented. "This guy came searching for me."

Minimizing Bruce's concerns for the two afore-mentioned innocent victims, Max pitched, "Listen... let's just bring these killers to justice."

"Okay." Bruce seemed too galvanized in sorrow to dispute.

Max gauchely spit out a bloody cotton ball into a waste basket. "What happened?" Bruce asked.

"Too long of a story."

Satisfied thinking Bruce appeared safely ensconced

for now, Max egressed apartment 303 and then ener-getically knocked on Pearl's door, apartment 301. It popped ajar as it was already unlocked. Her apartment presented as a deplorable mess with clothes and dishes everywhere, causing Max to stop at the second thresh-old, stonewalling further entry.

He called to her, "Pearl!"

Her flaxen hair over an angelic face came out of a room off the hall and informed, "I have the night off. The Eldorado is closed Mondays and Tuesdays. Tonight, you and I are meeting my friend Georgie at Next Generation."

"Next Generation?" he queried.

"Yeah, it's a hipster joint in Jonesport Harbor," she ardently imparted—showcasing splendidly dark, upturned eyes.

"Never heard of it."

"You're too old to hear of it." She plopped on a peach divan anterior to him and went on, "My queer friend Georgie, we are meeting, is the bartender and closer at the Eldorado. He wants to get away from Mr. Martinelli too. Georgie knows too much," she inferred, exhibiting caution. "It's not safe for him or I to just quit."

Max backtracked beyond the threshold. "Queer?"

"Yes, that kind of queer," she said, but enthusiasti-cally added, "He's the golden ticket to getting into the Eldorado's safe, so be nice to him."

His tone grew impartial. "Gotcha!"

61

AFTERNOON BUZZ

TUESDAY AFTERNOON AT 4:15 P.M., JOHNNY KNUCK-les phoned the Weatherbee Detective agency. Dashing Darlene already departed for the day, so Max took the call; their conversation was swift.

"Johnny, you're late."

"Listen, Mr. Bee," Johnny gravely imparted, "we got big problems."

"Go on."

"Four gangsters in a car grabbed Mrs. Palmer at gunpoint. I'm pretty sure Dutch O'Brien wuz ridin' shotgun."

"Where?"

"Right at duh Palmer house."

"And where are you now?"

"Well, dat's problem numbuh two. Two cops towed my hot-box Buick wit my wallet inside duh glove box," the hood aggrievedly reported. "I'm screwed."

"Why the hell would you leave your wallet in a stolen vehicle?" Max chided as if Johnny had been a kid who stole candy.

"I sort of pretend," Johnny responded blithely, "it's really my ride."

Max shook his head but had no audience to see it. "So, where are you hiding?"

"At my aunt's house in duh village," Johnny disclosed.

"Johnny, I need you later this evening as backup. It's at a nightclub. But first, I have to find Mrs. Palmer, and I don't need you for that part."

"Keep me outta dat part, I'm not messin' wit Dutch O'Brien's guys. Hey, I got no dough."

"I'll spot you ten until Friday when I get some more money from my client's sister."

"I don't feel like bein on duh streets tonight," Johnny self cautioned.

"Too bad. There's a hot dame meeting me there, and she just adores thugs sporting gold chains," Max pitched ruefully.

"Well, I could be persuaded."

"I'll pick you up in the village at ten, near the statue. Oh, one more thing, how is Rico making out in Adamsville?

"Didn't hear from em today cuz I can't go near Pool Palace, but he checked in last night. He said nobody up there has evuh seen dis big hulk yuh are searchin' for."

"I'm not surprised," Max briskly remarked and thought, *"The Adamsville thing had to be a decoy."* The private detective ended the discussion. "Johnny, see you at ten."

Both men hung up their phones.

62

OFFICER FREDDIE BROOKS

AT 5:15 P.M., MAX—STILL DONNED IN HIS GRAY
pinstriped suit and fedora—strolled into the busy
police station lobby. He had after-work plans with an
athlete friend from high school. The Black American,
New Paris police officer in blue instantly flagged Max
down. Officer Alfred Brooks, who everyone called
Freddie, was a flawless patrolman in every aspect.

The cop looked at his watch and then affably reprimanded, "Hey, Weatherbee, you're fifteen minutes late.
Damn, what happened to your jaw?" Freddie Brooks
stood as tall as Max—thinner and leaner—possessing
a full head of black hair on top, plus a side-fade and no
mustache. He, like Max, also served in the Army.

"Don't go there, Freddy. Are we still on for that
beer?" Max pitched.

"Yeah, if you're giving me a ride home," Officer
Brooks keenly negotiated.

"Sure, Freddie."

"I'm talking all the way uptown." Brooks pointed a long finger at Max. "Don't drop me off on the curb like my partner Evans does when you don't see any more white folks on the street."

"Hey, I bet he was just low on gasoline." Both men laughed and exited the station together into the precipitation.

Once the two men were settled in the Ford coupe, Max turned on the wipers and artfully announced, "We have a little mission first."

Freddie grinned. "I wouldn't expect anything less of you, Weatherbee. Beers after that are on you."

Max nodded in agreement. "I got word from a street source reporting a lady being abducted in Roosevelt Heights... Mrs. Wayne Palmer."

"Her husband was recently murdered," added Freddie Brooks.

"We have to go by the Eldorado Club. Joe Martinelli and Dutch O'Brien are involved," Max frankly informed as he eased the coupe off the curb.

"It's closed today, it's Tuesday."

The private detective directed the steering wheel and threw in a little banter. "Ha, you would know."

Officer Brooks slapped the dashboard instead of expelling a laugh.

Max sagely resumed, "But it's a good reason why they could be harboring her there."

Freddie listened to the clangorous wipers, pondered for a second, then articulated, "Well, before we do, take me by Mrs. Palmer's house; maybe there's some clues left behind. If we go to the Eldorado, I'm going to need to call in backup. No way I'm dealing with those cats solo."

By the time they arrived at the Palmer block, today's afternoon rain had converted to drizzle. Darkness had set in on New Paris. The interior lights of the brick structure appeared bright and welcoming.

Officer Brooks vigilantly examined the walkway, then climbed the graceful steps, ringing the bell once. A screen door popped open, and chubby Mrs. Palmer, still in this morning's black dress, came out on the short porch. "How can I help you, officer?" Her buoyant tone aired peculiarly for such a pugnacious woman.

A surprised Freddie Brooks glanced down and asked curtly, "Are you Mrs. Palmer?"

"Why yes." Her big blue eyes sparkled.

Sitting in his Ford parked across the street in front of a sausage shop, Max watched incredulously. *"So much for Johnny's kidnapping,"* he internally reflected.

The muscular policeman removed his cap. "I'm Officer Brooks, investigating a reported abduction. Silly question, ma'am, but did some men force you into a sedan earlier today?"

In lieu of being abashed, the burly widow softly held her chest and guffawed, "Why, no officer. Those men were friends from my church. I volunteer there on Tuesdays." She cordially went on, "Please come in for some coffee."

Officer Brooks dutifully thought he'd better take a more invasive gander, so he accepted her invite. After five minutes, Max furtively exited the coupe, walked with stealth around the connected houses on the Palmer block, and peered in the back window. It happened to be the same window in which he had violated the house earlier today.

Mrs. Wayne Palmer and Officer Brooks were having coffee and socially conversing. Max Weatherbee returned to his coupe and then rolled down the driver's window in a state of bewilderment.

Fifteen minutes later, he heard the Palmer screen door gape again. Freddie Brooks came out giggling, accompanied by Mrs. Palmer directly behind him. The widow waved goodbye to the uniformed officer as he descended the steps.

Freddie Brooks crossed the street, stuck his head into the coupe's open driver's side window, and whimsically concluded, "Damn, Max, that white woman is as nice as apple pie. Looks like your street source needs to get his lenses adjusted. Now let's go get those beers."

The perplexed private detective scratched his head, turned the ignition, and mused, *"Don't try to make sense of it; just do the job. Get those papers from the safe, get your client, Bruce Ellory, off the hook, and be done."*

63

NEXT GENERATION

10:30 P.M., TRAVELING IN THE FORD COUPE, MAX and Johnny accessed a dirt road to Jonesport Harbor on the outer edge of New Paris. Today's rain was gone, but mist remained in the air. They passed numerous shanties, most exhibiting excessive exterior paint wear. Max parked the auto on wet gravel; the two men from different worlds exited and walked toward the loudness. This loudness being the long wooden structure housing a hipster jazz club called Next Generation, where Pearl arranged the meeting.

Hatless, slick-haired Johnny sported an ivory-colored dress shirt plus black trousers, surely his Sunday best on a Tuesday night. Max was still in this morning's gray pinstripe suit and fedora. His head buzzed—compliments of the beers shared alongside Officer Fredie Brooks a few hours prior. The music blared a hundred feet away, and a marijuana smell pervaded the atmosphere. Many of the young men congregating out front were tieless. Max's stern eyes exhibited indignation—he did not fancy any of it.

The sleuth gave a roughneck at the door fifty cents to cover him and Johnny. They entered. An all-black jazz band played fiercely. The unduly jamming aired at a speed unlike anything Max had ever heard before. To Max, the joint felt packed, resembling a can of olives. Pearl and Georgie were already nestled at a small, cozy corner table. The two men sat and joined them. Max spoke loudly over the capophony into Pearl's left ear, "Why did we need to meet way out here?"

"Because Mr. Martinelli wouldn't be caught dead in here," she yelled back.

"I certainly see why," Max agreed. He then imparted loudly into Pearl's ear, "I brought my friend Johnny." Pearl studied the hood up and down amorously.

Suddenly, the melody became soft, and only two instruments hummed. Normal conversation was possible for the moment. Johnny enthusiastically uttered, "Great place."

Pearl reciprocated Max's introduction of Johnny. "This is my friend, Georgie, I told you about." She widened her gaze as she said it, urging him to get to work as if now was a good time while the band recouped their energy.

Max made eye contact with the gentleman in the pink dress shirt. "Nice to meet you, George."

"It's Georgie," offensively contested the late twenties, off-duty bartender possessing a head featuring layers of oily black waves. His tone sounded high-pitched, feminine.

Georgie and Johnny offered no acknowledgment of one another.

To Max, the man named Georgie seemed to be around one hundred fifty pounds. His puppet face seemed naturally tanned. Max focused on the delicate man's gray, almond-shaped eyes, then affirmed, "Looks like you and Pearl have a similar problem."

Before Georgie could respond, Pearl flippantly interrupted, "You two talk… I wanna dance as soon as the music speeds up." The hipster dame grasped Johnny by the top of his sweater and ordered, "Let's go, Tiger!" This stupefied the hooligan as he obediently elevated to a standing position. The two disappeared into Next Generation's crowd.

There initially existed verbal silence at the table as the two remaining men stared at one another. Talking through the stinging pain in his mouth, Max broke the ice, pitching some humor. "Don't ask me to dance."

Georgie, pretending not to notice the private detective's swollen right jaw, leaned rearwards on the wooden chair and curtly responded, "You're not my type. Well, you could be."

The gumshoe averted the invitation and seized the opportune moment. "Okay, let's jump to business while we can still talk." Max reaffirmed Pearl's aforementioned dilemma, "Based on what I understand, Pearl and you have a common enemy, Mr. Martinelli." Max prodded the rectangular pine table using his middle finger. "His crew stole papers and film from me this morning; they must be in the safe at the Eldorado."

Georgie's sockets grew popeyed, then orated, "Sir... you're partially correct. I had to go stock the bar at the Eldorado today. I do so on Tuesdays when they're closed. Mr. Martinelli and his gangsters still showed up, hanging around. I overheard them saying, 'The papers and photos were burned.' That was pretty clear."

Max's face turned deadpan. Georgie continued, "I also heard one of them say that they are keeping your film in the safe."

"Go on." The last part made Max feel a little better.

Georgie caught his breath prior to resuming. "Some non-New Paris photographer is going to try developing your film, Thanksgiving morning. They don't trust any locals. Mr. Martinelli wants to see what else you know by way of that film."

"If I can pull my film out of the safe," Max assured, "I think I can free you of him."

"It's bad working for him. He's crazy." Georgie's almond-shaped eyes started becoming wet as his high pitch escalated. "He had his big thug Junior hang me on a coat hook last Saturday night because he thought I took five dollars belonging to the bar's drawer."

Max's rock face expressed compassion. "How do I get near Martinelli's safe?"

"Come by the Eldorado at 3 a.m. tomorrow night, more correctly, Thanksgiving morning. I'll be closing the place alone and will let you pass through the back door as I'm leaving and give you my key." Georgie buried a generous swig from his glass and then resumed. "You'll have to bust a window during your departure, after locking the rear door, to make it appear like a break-in, or I'm facing big trouble. Mr. Martinelli's security guard doesn't arrive until 4 a.m., so you must utilize the hour."

"When I'm finished, I promise it will look as if an intrusion occurred, and I'll be long gone carrying my film before any prowl car starts fishing around," Max guaranteed. "A peterman is something I'm not. So how bout the combination to the safe?"

Georgie narrated above the provisional soft music; his eyes were dry now. "I know where to find it. There's a storage room connected to Mr. Martinelli's office. On a shelf, you'll see some paint cans. Each can has a set of bogus numbers taped to its bottom. Only the last two numbers are important." Max bobbed his head attentively after each sentence the flamboyant man in the pink shirt delivered. "And ignore the even-numbered cans. So, begin with the first can, then go to can number three, and so on."

"Jeez, how do you know such information?" An awestruck Max queried.

"Because Mr. Martinelli wants his safe cleared out if he's ever arrested. He doesn't want anyone writing down the combination, and Dutch can't remember it, so that's the arrangement. I overheard them talking several times about it at the end of the bar when the club was idle."

Max nodded once more, then praised, "I can't thank you enough, Georgie."

Georgie cast a grave look as the drums started up again hard; the other instruments followed. The band's number felt electrifying. Max gazed forward to the dance floor. Johnny and Pearl looked incandescent, reveling for all to see. Their heads bopped to the intense tune as both bodies rubbed up against one another. Johnny grabbed her short, tight black dress at the hips and shifted her into his crotch.

Max bought Georgie a scotch, and they drank in isolation instead of yelling into each other's ears. When the band took another break, clamorous patron voices replaced rapid jazz music. The two dancers returned to the table. Max had wrapped up his business with Georgie, and his disconsolate face motioned to Johnny that he wanted to leave.

"Mr. Bee, I'm stayin' here wit Pearl," Johnny divulged amid the background noise.

"Okay, fine, but I need you for a mission tomorrow night," Max declared using volume.

"Sure, if I'm not locked up already," foretold the street hustler.

Displaying affirmation, the PI replied, "If my plan works, I'll make a deal with Detective McGann to clear you on the stolen Buick. Believe me, he'd do anything to be the guy who bags Martinelli." He pointed his middle finger into Johnny's sternum. "How you getting back to town from here?"

Pearl stepped in, ogling at Johnny. "Georgie will

give us a ride," she uttered through a giggle, "to my place."

The private detective's intolerant facial expression easily labeled him a prude in Pearl's world. Max skeptically shook his head, rose, and then said, "Johnny, call me at the office tomorrow. I want an update on Rico's accomplishments in Adamsville." Next, Max made his egress to the door, accomplishing what he came here for.

Hours later, at Pearl's unkempt apartment, under the covers, they didn't make love—they had robust sex. After the climax, Johnny sat up in bed with a bedsheet over his private area and smoked. "I really dig you," confided the bravo punk.

She scraped her black cherry nails into his muscular bare chest and cautioned, "Well, you'd better blast out of here before my sort-of boyfriend, Junior, comes by."

"Whoa! Six-foot-eight Junior, who works at duh Eldorado?"

"Yes, him." She presaged.

Johnny got his clothes on quicker than a 1939 Maserati 8CTF, then bolted for the door.

64

DULL WEDNESDAY BEFORE THANKSGIVING

9 A.M., MAX SURREPTITIOUSLY PARKED HIS FORD coupe in the elegant Wickford section of New Paris, one block north from the house with the vines. This was the convalescent-home invalid Mrs. Judith Palmer's majestic dwelling where Judith's daughter Vivian Allard and her bunny-eyed, chemist husband resided.

The PI's surveillance in Wickford on this clear, seasonably warm November day lasted three hours, which ended up mostly spent applying an ice bag to his jaw. Next, he consumed two hours of the same near Mrs. Wayne Palmer's house in Roosevelt Heights. Max went zero for two, meaning nothing had been accomplished; no one came in or out of either residence. He was about as busy as a maître d' in a joint selling twenty-dollar burgers.

"I'm just killing time until 3 a.m. tomorrow morn-

ing, which should make or break the case for my client Bruce Ellory," he internally reflected. The private detective knew there would be no sleep tonight, but if successful, he would administer payback for the asperity inflicted yesterday morning, compliments of Dutch O'Brien and his crew of scoundrels.

After two flopped surveillance details, Max cruised to Chinatown to visit Bruce Ellory. The PI walked mannishly into the ten-story yellow brick apartment building across from Moon's Oriental Laundry. He presented hatless, dressed in a white shirt, no tie, casual charcoal sport coat, black pants, and shoes. As usual, the doorman was nonexistent. Each arm carried a paper bag; he leaned one against the wall and then pushed an elevator button.

Bruce Ellory—donned in a fiery red robe given to him by Suzy—opened the door to apartment 303. The profusely sweating fugitive's face and neck were bedsheet white. What remained of his straggled light brown hair on top of his balding oval head was drenched. "I need that gin," he beseeched Max, pitching an urgent tone.

"Right here, buddy." Max handed over the paper bag containing Ellory's pleasure. "Also got you Chesterfields, towels, shaving stuff, toilet paper, and the clothes I told you about." He gently passed Bruce the other bag. Today's increased swelling in Max's oral cavity made his earnest speech a tad muffled.

"I appreciate it," said Bruce softly.

"Blow the cigarette clouds out an open window,"

Max advised, "because I don't think the guy who rents this place smokes."

"I can't stay here much longer," Bruce desperately divulged, holding the two bags. "I'm not comfortable in somebody else's apartment."

"You have to relax," instructed Max. "The tenant is out of town. I'm getting my film back at 3 a.m. tomorrow morning. I'll clear you with McGann on Friday morning when he comes to my office." Max needed to rest his mouth. He pointed to the right side of his jaw using his index finger, then resumed, "Tomorrow is Thanksgiving, and I think McGann is off. Your brother-in-law Walter Kazarian is also coming to the agency on Friday morning, not at the same time. And we will put his lawyer on board as well. Another Armenian guy... I heard he is good, Sammy Boyajian."

Bruce's recessed brown eyes looked like they could soon explode. "Oh man, you must collect more money from Walter?" Bruce Ellory asked abashedly.

Max shrugged, "It is how I earn a living."

Bruce plaintively frowned. "I'm a loser, existing in the doldrums," he dejectedly conceded.

"Stop. That reminded me, I have some drawing pads and pencils for you in the car." Max propounded, "You can practice your engineering stuff."

"Thank you. Leave them outside the door."

"How is Suzy treating you?" Max inquired.

"Good," Bruce solemnly reported, "She brings me three meals a day, plus takes my garbage."

Max winked a chestnut brown eye gracefully. "She'll take your laundry too."

Cognizant Bruce inquired, "How is your mouth doing?"

"No bleeding today, just pain and swelling." Max changed the poignant subject. "Listen, I'll stop by here tomorrow morning on the way to my mother's house. I can't be late for her Thanksgiving holiday dinner."

The two men said their goodbyes, and then Max briefly returned, leaving the drawing supplies in the hallway, and headed to his nest. When he reached the Keiser Building, Dashing Darlene had left for the day, but a handwritten note remained on her desk.

> *Max, a boring day at our office. One lady called wanting to know how much it would cost to follow her husband around for three days. I almost laughed at her. Anyway, she didn't leave her phone number. Johnny Knuckles called twice and said he would call you back on the hour, every hour, until he reached you. I wish you guys would tell me what you two are up to. You never tell me anything! See you on Friday.*
>
> *Happy Thanksgiving,*
> *Darlene aka Dashing Darlene*

65

TOMMY

9 P.M. WEDNESDAY EVENING, WHITE WINGTIP shoes lead the tall man called Slick, sporting a long white suit, inside the Chadwick Hotel lobby in the Queens Row section of New Paris. As usual, the hatless scar-faced Slick's blonde hair showcased as perfectly parted smack dab in the center. The lobby's atmosphere was crowded, featuring men smoking cigars and well-dressed ladies chatting.

The elderly, bald-headed, thin as a rake manager, Leroy Burton, glanced up from a mahogany counter toward the inbounding gangster. Next, he dexterously shuffled away, entering an office, then locked the door to his sanctum as if he had just seen a gang of out-laws riding into a western town. Slick's lengthy strides were intercepted under a lavish gilded chandelier by yellow-haired Bronc, the expansively framed house detective wearing a wide-brim hat.

"Bout time," Bronc said jovially, looking up at the six-foot-four man.

Slick handed the burly house dick a thick, white letter-sized envelope. "Thanks for giving us a room down the hall from Fatty Arbuckle." The towering man known as Slick spoke with a penetrating, high-pitched drawl. Again, referring to the corpulent, deceased Howard Stanford, he continued, "Are coppers still asking questions regarding the tub of lard's swan dive?"

Bronc squeezed the envelope, gave satisfied eyes, and stuffed it in his pocket. "Not really... nobody cares about the slob," snickered Bronc. "He's always been a nuisance to the bluecoats."

"Where's that other room key I asked for?"

Bronc winked, then handed Slick a key and informed, "Number six hundred twenty is yours for the night."

Slick pocketed his key and further inquired, "Anyone else poking around?"

"A private dick named Max Weatherbee," revealed Bronc.

"Yeah, he's been barking on the wrong side of the fence. He can't do much now since we've iced his client Bruce Ellory at the Duncan Monday night."

"Oh... Mr. Wallace, the vagrant the cops know nothing about, was actually Bruce Ellory, the man you've been hunting?"

"Yup."

Big Bronc guffawed enough for his plump mug to redden like a raspberry. "I had a gut feeling that was him."

"And you have a lot of gut." Slick stuck a gangling arm out. Next, with a thumb and index finger, he pinched Bronc's belly over his tan suit. Both men chuckled.

Slick resumed displaying ascendancy, "There's going to be one more mess before this ends; I'll require your assistance."

Bronc nodded his head deep into chin fat and replied, "Money talks, Slick... especially on a house dick's salary."

The lanky man in the white suit followed Bronc to an inconspicuous hotel service elevator, where he rode solo to the seventh floor. Slick knocked on a wooden door numbered 714, which stood a few units past and across from the room where Howard Stanford had been eliminated.

"Who is it?" a thundering voice beyond the door requested.

"Tommy, it's Slick," imparted the tall man in the crisp white suit.

"It's unlocked!"

Slick walked inside the hotel room, shutting the door behind him. "Hi, Tommy."

The room appeared dark and barren; only a bedside lamp allowed illumination. Slick saw the gorilla of a man called Tommy sitting at a table near a window on the far side of the room. His shadow occupied half the wall behind him, resembling a dark rain cloud. With elbows on the table and two gigantic hands pushed into his uncomely face below a bushel of black hair, Tommy bleated, "Slick... what did ya make me do?"

Slick halted halfway inside the room. "Tommy, you've always wanted to kill people. Years back in college, I remember how you couldn't get enough anger out on the football field; you used to bend the metal locker doors using your bare hands. Then I treated you to beers. It calmed you down."

Tommy started sniffling like a widow at her husband's wake. He oddly remarked through several missing teeth, "Ya were a great quarterback and friend, Slick."

"Because nobody could get near me thanks to you on the line." Slick offered a sinister smile, then recommenced, "Think hard, Tommy. When we went for those post-game beers, you divulged to me that you had thoughts of killing people. It's why I chose you for such an assignment."

"That was over fifteen years ago. I never killed anyone until ya called me a few weeks ago." Ditching his mournfulness, the Gorilla stopped sobbing and then flared his immense nostrils. "Slick, are ya here to settle up on those five murders? I need cash bad. And I'm not killing anyone else... it's outta my system. I'm taking a train away from this town tomorrow and never coming back. Ya promised five hundred per murder. Ya owe me exactly twenty-five hundred by tomorrow, or I'm goin' up to Adamsville to collect it."

"Well, tomorrow is Thanksgiving, the banks won't be open," Slick exhibited an edge of sarcasm in his tone.

The five-time killer Tommy pounded the wooden table using a mighty fist and glowered with black, lifeless eyes. "Since when would ya put money in a bank. I want my payout, Slick!"

The Gorilla put his face back into his oven mitt hands on the table in front of him and started sobbing again. As he did, Slick retreated three feet, rubbed his chin utilizing a left hand, then went into his suit jacket's outside pocket and slid a black glove on a wiry right hand. Inside his left suit jacket's inner pocket, Slick fished out one Luger pistol, attached a silencer, and severed their friendship by saying, "I've got a choice to make. I can give you twenty-five hundred or fill you with holes. I think I'll choose the latter."

The gorilla of a man stood up and charged at the dapper Slick, who aimed at a target he could not miss. Slick's first four rounds stopped the big man in the center of the room, attenuating his assault. Slick backed up to the hotel room's closed door and released four additional rounds, emptying the Luger's magazine.

Dumbstruck, Tommy began bleeding out like a lawn sprinkler. He edged a little more toward Slick, then faltered, falling face down, creating a tumultuous sound as he hit the floor face first, exiting this world.

The next sound in the room was the Luger making a plop as it became purposely dropped next to the colossal cadaver.

Adroit Slick wiped off the doorknob, exited a sanguinary room 714, and took the stairs down one flight. He soon removed a key from his pants pocket, courtesy of Bronc, and then unlocked the door to room 620. He would sleep well in that room tonight.

66

JOHNNY'S NEGLIGENT OMISSION

1 A.M. ON A CHILLY 1947 THANKSGIVING MORN-ing, three blocks beyond Johnny's aunt's house in a low-income section called Coogan's Village, two men sat side by side at an all-night counter. They smoked and ordered hot wieners plus coffee from a phlegmatic, balding man in a filthy, white tee shirt who served as both the cook and waiter. Only one other patron existed at the counter, an elderly man stridently snoring with his face buried into a paper placemat.

A tieless Max had the sleeves of his white dress shirt rolled up as he started the conversation, exhibiting a deprecating tone. "Johnny, what kind of joint is this you took me to? See how dirty my water glass is? I better not catch trench mouth."

"What duh hell is trench mouth?" questioned the

hood Johnny Knuckles, wearing a black leather jacket and white tee shirt underneath.

"I don't know, but my mom always says that when I take her to the cafeteria at Woolworths."

Johnny laughed temporarily till his face turned serious and reported, "Rico has not checked in wit duh guys at Pool Palace. Maybe he got arrested up in Adamsville."

"Would you be Rico's one phone call?" questioned Max.

"Hell no. He don't have my aunt's numbuh. No cats know I'm hidin' out there." Johnny spun his squished hat around till it was backward.

"Sounds smart, Johnny; however, I might be the bearer of bad news." Johnny's eyes became alert as Max inquired, "Does Rico bear a scorpion tattoo on his right arm?"

"Oh shit… yeah. Why?" asked Johnny anxiously.

Max delivered the morbid details grimly. "Because at 11 p.m., they fished a corpse out of the Eastside River that has one."

"Shit!" Pallor suddenly dominated Johnny's dark-shaded, Caucasian face. "I set em up ta die."

"I think I underestimated Adamsville, Johnny," the private detective confessed. "Sorry about your friend."

"It's part of duh game." Johnny shrugged, growing less emotional.

After the two men finished their grub, Max settled the tab, then widened a chestnut brown eye to the balding cook owning a ruddy face. "Should I call a medic," the PI asked, "for you know who?"

The unshaven wiener cook, possessing a calm disposition, gazed at the lone drunkard passed out at the counter and said in a stolid tone, "I'll make him a fresh pot of coffee."

Soon, Johnny and Max were in the Ford coupe, which felt akin to a refrigerator. "Get dat heater box crankin," requested the crushed-hat-wearing hoodlum.

"It takes a while to kick in, Johnny. Anything else from your surveillance you want to tell me?"

Max pulled the choke and started the Ford coupe. Johnny, riding shotgun, began rubbing two cold hands together, creating friction heat for the epidermis of his palms as he disclosed, "Well, when I wuz tailing your fat Palmer lady, a tall, scar-faced, man maybe six feet four, decked in a white suit peered inta the window of Bortone's Coffee Shop while Mrs. Palmer wuz yappin' ta dat foxy dame."

Max pleasantly thought to himself, "*Vivian Allard*." Once the temporary reverie exited his mind, he engaged the clutch, edged the Ford off the curb, and probed regarding the mysterious tall man. "Are we talking about Junior, who works as an enforcer for Mr. Martinelli at the Eldorado Club?"

"No... no, dis guy wuzn't quite Junior's height. I know exactly who Junior is... he messes wit Pearl. Dis guy wuz suave like someone who doesn't get his hands dirty." Johnny paused and pensively looked sideways at a row of concrete tenements the vehicle passed, then solemnly resumed, "Duh funny thing is I knew em from somewhere."

"Oh… that last part scares me. This occurred three days ago. Why didn't you tell me sooner?" Max nearly reprimanded.

"Well, nothin' really happened. He just looked in duh coffee shop window."

"Fuck. Johnny, fuck!" An enraged Max pounded the steering wheel, using the sides of his open hands.

Johnny kept cool. "Relax, Mr. Bee, it wuz only a tall guy in a suit… nothin' suspicious."

"What concerns me is you think you recognized him from somewhere prior. That already makes him suspicious because you associate amongst bad people, Johnny. And Roosevelt Heights is a high-class neighborhood, so this man in white shouldn't be there."

"Okay, maybe I slipped up," Johnny sourly admitted.

"Damn right, Johnny." Max abruptly maneuvered the Ford coupe to the edge of the city street and offered Johnny angry eyes. "I'm paying you to tell me everything." This time, the private detective struck the dashboard in front of Johnny with a closed fist, resembling an irate father.

Max's paroxysm startled the hood.

Max went on, "We're from different worlds, Johnny. You're a thug, always will be, and anyone who looks familiar to you is also a thug."

Max stared straight ahead, shifted the gear, then accelerated the Ford, ignoring the umbrage in Johnny's face as the hooligan warned, "Just make sure I get paid Friday mornin' Mister Different Worlds."

Max slightly relented his impertinence. "Please find out if any of your underworld contacts can recognize this tall man."

"I can't go near Pool Palace, duh coppers are searchin' for me for liftin' dat Buick. But I can make calls from my aunt's house right aftuh we have our turkey."

"I almost forgot. Happy Thanksgiving, Johnny," Max's lack of cadence made it appear dispassionate as he said it.

"Got nothin' ta be thankful for. I'm a thug, remembuh? Gonna skip town once yuh pay me Friday. I ain't goin' back ta no can," the hoodlum imparted.

Max paused, contemplating what he wanted to say, then confidentially assured, "Do what you want, but I think I can convince Detective McGann to give you a pass if I can get that film in his lap by tomorrow."

Still aggrieved, Johnny, unable to envisage such a scenario, pouted his lips like a petulant adolescent and verbalized nothing in return. Unbeknownst to him, the night was about to become unforgettable.

67

THE ELDORADO

AT PRECISELY 3 A.M., MAX AND JOHNNY ARRIVED at their destination. Joe Martinelli's gentleman's club, known as the Eldorado, presented as a low-key structure on the exterior. In front of the blonde brick building, a sign read *ELDORADO GENTLEMEN'S CLUB Members Only*. It was not really a private club; the sign was there to ward off unwanted guests and any riff-raff not associated with the outfit. One solitary place that lit up the area stood across the main avenue—an all-night joint called Anytime Donuts.

Max turned a corner, keeping the Eldorado on his left, went right onto a side street, spun the car around, and then parked it so the private club's inconspicuous rear entrance was in full view and the sidewalk to its front entrance could also be monitored.

"Lay on the horn," Max instructed, "if anyone comes near either door." Next, the PI reached down toward his ankle, removed the Colt from the holster, and handed it to Johnny. He advised the hood, "Just in case." Johnny understood Max's allusion.

The red metal, unmarked rear door was ajar, but just a crack. Puppet-faced Georgie waited behind it as promised. The sleuth gave one soft knock before the bartender fully opened the door for Max to enter. Georgie nodded, then directed, "Don't forget to make it appear like a break-in after you're done."

Georgie handed Max his key, closed the door, and egressed, leaving the uninvited guest alone in the uninhabited nightclub.

Max had never been here; the place was new to him. The outside might have looked low-key, but the inside felt majestic. Although the croupiers were long gone, gilded roulette wheels in its gaming parlor at the lengthy corridor's end served as a vestige of the dynamic atmosphere present just a few hours prior. About a third of the lights burned incandescent. Max realized he had an hour before the security guard arrived at 4 a.m.

Outside, in Max's coupe, Johnny kept surveillance on both entrances. When his vision reverted to the front entrance, a newly parked sanitation truck at the corner was now blocking his view between the entrance of the donut shop across the avenue and the Eldorado's front sidewalk. Unseen by Johnny, two hefty sanitation workers dressed in white exited their truck and slowly crossed the deserted street toward the donut shop. Five men in suits—too far to identify—who were not there a minute ago occupied a compact booth near the joint's front window on the left, still in Johnny's view behind the truck.

In an extensive hallway inside the Eldorado, carrying his kit, Max got down on one knee and easily picked the lock to a door that read PRIVATE. He flipped on the light switch. The office he encountered appeared regal— consisting of a royal red Persian rug, several hunting paintings on its walls, five burgundy leather chairs scattered about, and a marvel of a cherry desk in the room's center. A large metal safe stood in full view behind the grand desk. The spare room to the right was unlocked, and multiple paint cans sat on the shelves with numbers taped underneath, exactly as Georgie had mentioned.

Meanwhile, outside, two New Paris policemen cruised by Max's Ford and shined a light on the automobile for just a moment. Johnny slid down in the passenger seat like a teenager planning to do something naughty on a drive-in movie date. Next, he watched the officers navigate away and then park in front of the Anytime Donuts shop across the avenue, which was mostly obstructed from his view by the sanitation truck.

Back inside, on a pad in the spare room, Max wrote down the last two numbers on each pant can, just as Georgie advised, and ignored the rest.

Outside, from Max's coupe, Johnny still could not see the front sidewalk of the Eldorado but could visualize the left interior portion of the donut shop. Soon after the two cops set foot in the donut shop, he perceived a cluster of rapidly moving shadows reflecting on the donut shop's upper façade beyond the sanitation truck. The five suits congregating at the table were gone. On the left of the obstructed view, through the shop's left window, he could see the two sanitation workers occupying two stools at the counter, so he knew this was not their shadows approaching. The hood's heart raced violently. Even though Max instructed him to honk the horn, Johnny panicked, departed the coupe, and ran to the Eldorado's rear door.

Back inside, applying the information wangled out of Georgie, Max got the safe open using the coded digits located under the paint cans. He saw piles of clear bags containing white powder; a roll of film incongruously sat on top. "*Cocaine,*" Max thought to himself as he stretched an arm to get to the roll of film he came for, his film.

From Mr. Martinelli's office, Max heard the clanging of Johnny's palm on the rear metal door in the back of the club, which overpowered the sounds made by the four men in suits entering the front door.

As Johnny kept pummeling his palm into the red metal door, headlights in the distance began approaching him. Johnny retreated, taking cover behind a row of garbage barrels.

Inside the Eldorado, Max opened and closed the door to Mr. Martinelli's office, then re-entered the long hallway. He was greeted by a tremendous bear hug. "We meet again, Mr. Bill Collector," snickered the six-foot-eight beast called Junior, pitching a reference to when the men first met in the lobby of Pearl's apartment on Monday afternoon.

Max heard someone yell, "Get the Chloroform!"

The unbreakable bear hug made it impossible for

the private detective to move his arms. Employing fortitude, a deft Max utilized the heels of his dress shoes and kicked Junior multiple times in the big man's shins. Junior started screaming in pain, and it almost worked until the thin gangster, called Chuck, who knocked Max's tooth loose on Tuesday, applied a rag over the private detective's mouth and nose. A restrained Max bit Chuck's fingers through the rag, but the drug set in—Max went out like a light.

The fifth suit, broad-shouldered Dutch O'Brien, who was driving the maroon sedan that pulled up to the Eldorado's rear, exited the vehicle and then unlocked its trunk. Next, Dutch held the establishment's back door after it had been opened from the inside by the short, stout, pug-faced man called Wimpy. Soon, Junior, Wimpy, Chuck, and the man known as Silent Sal carried Max's limp body outside with malevolent intentions, each man taking an extremity until he was cast into the vehicle's trunk.

"Junior, wait here until we get back," ordered hoarse-voiced Dutch in a sanctimonious tone.

Obsequious to Dutch's command, Junior closed the red metal alleyway door and then backtracked inside the club. Four men plus their unconscious prisoner Max Weatherbee, rolling around in the trunk, drove off with Silent Sal now at the sedan's wheel and Dutch riding shotgun.

Once the car full of unscrupulous racketeers vamoosed, Johnny quit hiding and placed Max's Colt pistol in a pocket of his leather jacket. He then trotted to the Ford coupe. Before he could open the passenger door, the same prowl car returned—two officers stepped out.

Johnny spoke first. "Glad ta see yuh officers. I need help, my friend Max—"

"Take your hat off, greaseball," dictated officer number one, cutting off Johnny's sentence.

When Johny Knuckles did, a nightstick came crashing down on his head, compliments of officer number two. Johnny's chest hit the pavement, and the streetwise man for hire played possum as the officers tossed his flaccid body onto the Ford's bench seat.

"Let him sleep it off; later, we'll come back and book 'em for that stolen Buick," proudly touted officer number two.

"Yeah, and after that, I'll call Smitty's to have Weatherbee's Ford coupe towed outta here and dropped off in the ghetto. Dutch said for us to head to the pier right now. Let's get movin'," replied number one.

With his head pounding, Johnny lay still and fought the grogginess. After he could no longer hear the prowl car's engine, Johnny aborted his brief quiescence, reached beneath the mat for the key, rose up, and started the Ford. The taillights of the two devious coppers were now deep in the distance as he gave the coupe gas, but the vehicle reacted as though it was stuck in the mud. Johnny jumped out and saw four slashed tires.

"Son of a Bitch!" the forlorn hood yelled into the desolate night.

Notable Characters Introduced in Part 8

Officer Freddie Brooks: New Paris police officer, friend, and drinking buddy of Max Weatherbee, first appearance Chapter 62

Georgie: Pearl's friend, bartender at the Eldorado, first appearance Chapter 63

PART 9

68

MOON CHIN

CHINATOWN, 2 P.M., THANKSGIVING AFTERNOON in unit 303 of the ten-story, yellow brick apartment building across from Moon's Oriental Laundry, Bruce Ellory paced the floor repeatedly. Max's promise to visit him 'in the morning' was increasingly becoming worthless. Bruce's dress pants and shirt sleeves were oddly rolled up because the borrowed clothes belonged to a much taller Max Weatherbee. A soft knock interrupted his wearing out a runner carpet underneath his feet.

Bruce cautiously pulled the door back a crack, saw flaxen hair, and then fully gaped it. Standing next to a bag of discarded Chinese leftover meals from Suzy, Pearl's cherry-lipped smile aired as enigmatic. "*What do you want,*" thought Bruce, but instead said, "Hello again." Her sexy red shoes paired with a short leopard dress—showcasing plenty of cleavage at its apex—presented as meretricious to the stolid Bruce Ellory.

In her high heels, their heights exhibited similarity. "I knew you were here," she disclosed with her entrancing face and jaunty persona.

"It's Thanksgiving. Don't you have family?" There existed an air of annoyance in his voice.

"Not really," she avowed blithely.

"Max was supposed to come by this morning, and he never showed," Bruce imparted, retreating two feet beyond the threshold like she had syphilis.

"Maybe he is at his mom's."

"I… I guess," he stammered.

She leaned her shoulder against the opened door and then playfully asked, "Do you want to go in with me on some opium puffs across the street?"

His annoyed tone started ebbing. "I don't think I know what that is."

"It makes you high a while," she informed, using swaying body movements as persuasion.

Bruce's recessed eyes woefully looked at a half-empty gin bottle on the table rearwards to him. He understood his day was monotonous; the gin failed him in battling this afternoon's severe, raging anxiety. Bruce meekly consented, "How much?"

"I can get us some hits at two dollars and fifty cents apiece. Normally, it is five dollars per person, but sometimes, he will do a two-for-one, especially if I bring in a new customer. Please join me," she exhorted.

"Who is… he?" he queried, displaying apprehension.

"Moon Chin."

"Never heard of him."

Outside on the street, Bruce viewed with uncertainty the large neon sign across the street, which was not visible from the window of unit 303, a rear apartment. It read *Moon's Oriental Laundry*. He positioned himself statuesque on the sidewalk and then nervously gazed left and right at the neighborhood's populated surroundings. Pearl briskly grabbed Bruce's rolled-up dress shirt sleeve and practically dragged him to the adjacent sidewalk, into Moon's laundromat, and over the black and white tile to the counter.

The short salt and pepper-haired Chinese woman dressed in black stood erect and offered attention when the couple paraded through the store. To Pearl, the woman remarked, "Oh... you back again."

Pearl put two hands on the counter's edge and made known via her cherry lips, "My friend and I need a fix."

"Holc on," the older woman in black replied, then vanished within the blackness to her rear like being sucked into a vacuum.

Before long, amid the background darkness, a male face appeared. His black robe made his oblong, lemon-shaped head seem more pronounced. Mr. Ellory, only standing 5'8" himself, towered over the sixty-ish, bald Asian man in slippers. Moon Chin revealed to Ellory, "I am Chin." His monolid eyes were piercing.

The hipster came in betwixt the two men. "Mr. Chin, he's a new customer," she implored, "can we both please come in for five?"

Chin did not quibble. He looked Bruce Ellory up and down. When Mr. Chin became satisfied that he was not anyone pernicious, the Asian store owner raised a panel of wood, which served as a divider between patron and worker. Moon Chin hand signaled for his two visitors to ambulate behind the counter. Mr. Chin subsequently walked into darkness beyond the counter where he originated—his pint-sized body descended stairs into a cellar. Pearl and Bruce followed. Pearl took the lead, stepping as if she had been familiar with where she was going. As they continued, the narrow stairs creaked ominously.

The low-ceiling basement seemed caliginous, dank, and unfinished. Grapefruit-sized rocks jutted out from dirt walls resembling oversized warts. Dozens of wooden crates featuring Chinese writing haphazardly gave it a maze-like appearance. Mr. Chin moved a few wooded boxes using his foot, placed a diminutive hand on a piece of rope, and then pulled.

An archaic door opened, and suddenly, a tall Asian man stood at the secret room's entrance. "They okay," assured Chin to the mammoth man who said nothing.

As Pearl and Bruce entered the smaller room, illuminated by only one single overhead bulb, they saw a young freakish couple in their twenties already lying on its floor with their backs propped on pillows. The couple giggled lazily and smoked through a pipe.

Moon Chin exited. Bruce and Pearl were each handed a pillow by the giant Chinese man, who then nonverbally instructed the duo to the ground to share their own blanket. A bewildered Mr. Ellory stared at the bizarre setup of a lamp, long needle, pipe with bowl, and some other doohickeys he would not call familiar in the middle of the blanket. Pearl relieved doubt, "Don't worry about that stuff; Sen cooks the opium."

"Cook?" Ellory questioned.

The tall Chinese man named Sen sat on the floor, accompanying them, sedulously preparing his accouterments. Next, he heated a tiny ball using a small needle over a small oil lamp. Pungent burning hit Ellory's nasal cavity like nothing he had ever perceived before. When it became time, they shared a bamboo pipe—in the succeeding moments, all of Bruce Ellory's problems inexplicably disappeared.

69

PEARL'S RIDE

3 P.M., THANKSGIVING DAY, IN THE SPLENDID Roosevelt Heights section of New Paris, a maroon sedan pulled up at the deceased Wayne Palmer's house. Broad-shouldered Dutch O'Brien ascended from its passenger seat, climbed the steps, and knocked rapidly on a screen door using meaty knuckles. Chubby Mrs. Wayne Palmer opened the door and then conspicuously furnished Dutch with a fat white envelope which was soon tucked inside the racketeer's inner suit pocket.

---

4 p.m., drug-induced, sedated, Bruce and Pearl dawdled towards the entrance of her yellow brick apartment building in Chinatown. Bruce was opening the glass door just as the two opium smokers heard from behind, "Pearl, get your ass over here!" The same hoarse voice—belonging to Dutch O'Brien—trucu-

lently instructed Bruce, "Keep walking straight ahead, pal. It's a lot better for you if I don't see your face."

Mr. Ellory's hands were trembling as he passed the façade, taking tentative, penguin-like steps into the dwelling's lobby.

The comely hipster buttoned her fur coat and obliviously pranced to the maroon sedan filled with four suit-wearing gangsters. She bent down, glanced into the automobile, and asked, "Where's Junior?"

The stout pug-faced man known as Wimpy exited the passenger's side rear door, then snatched Pearl by her neck. "Get in, Bitch," was all he said, tossing her in the back seat as if she were a garbage bag.

"Help! Help!" Pearl's cry fell on deaf ears. Tires screeched, the sedan accelerated off the curb and vamoosed south through Chinatown.

Now inside the apartment complex, timid Bruce Ellory, following Dutch O'Brien's orders, never looked rearward, missing his chance to see Pearl for the last time.

70

MR. MARTINELLI

THE BOAT'S COMPACT CABIN THAT HELD THE CAP-
tive consisted of a bed, mattress, no linens, and two
piles of steamer trunks. The walls were naked, and no
doubt, it served as a storage room. Max's clothes felt as
tousled as his disconcerted mind. He was positioned
on his backside, lying on an uncovered, stained mattress. Tightness felt in Max's right wrist handcuffed
to the brass rail caused the private detective's brain
cells to vaguely remember the sweet-smelling wet
cloth being reapplied to his face multiple times since
the Eldorado. Envisioning the cloying odor, no longer
present, restimulated his gag reflex, giving him dry
heaves.

When he came to, he asked himself, "*Where am
I? Feels like a boat. How long have I been here?*" He
unsteadily rose and stood beside the bedrail holding
him prisoner, with the cuff sliding to the top of the rail.
Beyond the jade-dyed wave's undulations, the most

salient entity he saw peeping out of the one round cabin window happened to be a coastline, possibly two hundred yards away. The land appeared hazy in the distance, or maybe he was hazy. One thing he knew for sure was that the afternoon had started losing its daylight.

A dazed Max sat on the bed's edge. He heard a doorknob turn and smelled cigar fumes before the mid-fifties, handsome, dandified gangster entered the unlit cabin. Approaching twilight emitted enough residual sunlight for Max to see the starched pinstripe suit worn by a hatless man owning a full head of gray hair featuring a widow's peak. Mr. Martinelli immediately initiated the conversation. "Hey, it's the man who knew too much."

"Fuck you," the restrained sleuth fumed, jutting his jaw.

The average-height, built like a delivery truck, mustached-faced Mr. Martinelli kept his composure. "I wanted to meet the guy who tried sending me to jail. I've got big plans for you; none of them are going to be pleasant," he assured through tobacco-stained teeth.

"Get it over with," Max snapped as he clanged the bedrail, using a cuffed extremity for a temporary tantrum, causing his hand to turn crimson. A few seconds of silence passed, and then Max ascertained, "But first, at least tell me why did you kill Wayne Palmer?"

"I didn't. No way would I kill a guy who owed me eleven thousand dollars. Palmer was a degenerate gambler at my place, the Eldorado."

Surprisingly to Max, Mr. Martinelli's speech seemed articulate and enunciated. Traditional wise-guy lingo was not imbued in his articulation. Max then remembered reading in a newspaper that Martinelli had once gone to law school but flunked the bar exam and then turned to crime.

The upper echelon of the New Paris underworld went on, "We did have some side business dealings outside of the club."

"Yeah, if you call fraudulent insurance schemes business dealings," Max contested.

"It's one aspect of my business."

Max's tone expressed condemnation. "A heathen's business."

Martinelli smirked and talked amid cigar smoke. "Who hired you to dig into my affairs?"

"Investigating Wayne Palmer's death led me to you. My decision."

Martinelli moved on. "Where is that cavone who accompanied you this morning at my club?"

"Cavone?"

"Never mind," Martinelli said, "you're not Italian. We'll locate him." He puffed the cigar. "We know his name is Johnny, and he's an incorrigible menace."

Max's eyes became incandescent, showcasing rage. "He had nothing to do with all of this."

Martinelli changed the subject. "I actually need to thank you for finding Wayne Palmer's notes in his house." The distinguished captor fixed wide eyes on

Max and then inferred, "Palmer's post-mortem note, documents, and photos would've put me in jail."

"That's where gangster scum belongs," Max harshly retorted.

"I'd rather be dead than go to jail," Martinelli divulged, then pointed a manicured finger at Max. "Gold star for you because a few cops on my personal payroll searched Palmer's place before you snooped and didn't discover anything."

"They didn't look too hard," Max remarked.

"Can't wait to see what else you have on that film. It's being processed as we speak for my return to New Paris."

"You'll find nothing else. It was just a backup."

"Smart. Since I found Palmer's 'in case of my death' note, I'm glad the weasel got bludgeoned to death. It worked out in my favor. But regardless, his murder was an unauthorized hit, not sanctioned by my outfit on a man owing me money." He puffed, taking a brief respite before engaging his vocal cords again. "That alone is going to get somebody killed when I return to New Paris," foretold the man in charge.

The arrogance nestled in Mr. Martinelli's voice aired as provocative and accelerated the private detective's anger. He vigorously shook the brass bed rail he was handcuffed to, then spit in Martinelli's direction.

"You possess balls, kid. Perhaps when the ordeal I put you under is over, I'll hire you to find out who really killed Palmer so I can cut em up in little pieces," Martinelli propounded.

"I would rather suck a donkey's hiney," Max flatly repudiated, "than work for you."

"That's what you say now."

The captive once more said, "Fuck you!"

The lewd comment made Martinelli mockingly beckon his fingers, knowing Max's movements were limited. Max countered by throwing an off-balance punch utilizing his free left hand, which missed Martinelli by nearly two feet.

Martinelli nonchalantly dismissed the bodily attack and tranquilly directed, "Calm down, son."

Succeeding the outbursts, Max lost all his energy. He sat back down on the bare mattress. His mood was less hostile when he inquired, "How does Mrs. Palmer play into this? She was seen taking an involuntary ride alongside your goons."

Martinelli precisely orated. "It's a funny situation. Originally, as you discovered, we were going to hit Mrs. Palmer. After the hit, Wayne and I planned on splitting the life insurance payout, and he could clear his gambling debt to me."

Martinelli paused to puff the Cuban maduro, then continued the sequence of events. "Now the crazy twist is before we ice the wife, Wayne gets whacked by an unknown. So, Mrs. Palmer gets a pass but has inherited his eleven grand gambling debt. It took some convincing; however, she agreed to settle, and Dutch stopped by there on his way here to collect it prior to us embarking on our journey. Mrs. Palmer is in the clear; she'll make it to another birthday. I no longer have a reason to kill her. And thanks to what you dug up, I was able to burn any evidence along with the other bogus insurance papers."

"Not bogus… fraudulent. And you kidnapped Mrs. Palmer."

"You call it kidnapping; I call it convincing." The racketeer folded his hands behind a thick back and then stuck out his barrel chest. "You should have been pursuing that dame Palmer was treating around town. Her name is Mona. I had a drink with Wayne and her one evening at a restaurant."

The hostage listened.

"She is a glacier," Martinelli said, "coldest woman I've ever encountered."

Max looked through the cabin's solo window, pondering, *"Bruce's wife, Mona, I gave her too long of a leash."* Next, he questioned, "Where are we going on this boat?"

"Down south to the Caribbean for a nice cocaine run. Going to reinvest Mrs. Palmer's eleven thou and rake fifty off it."

"And your cocaine is going to make a whole group of people run around town acting like a bunch of assholes."

"Who cares," Martinelli responded, "long as they buy the coke. I do admire the way you speak your mind, Weatherbee, just like your Uncle Harry did. He wasn't a pussy, and you're not either." Martinelli backed up to the door without turning his posterior side to the prisoner, glanced at a gilded wristwatch that glistened, then announced, "We'll be leaving soon, just waiting on two VIP passengers."

"What's it got to do with me?"

Martinelli remained reticent about Max's future. "I'm not going to spoil the surprise. In the meantime, I'll have one of the boys bring you a piss bucket. I've posted a guy outside your door all the time. Don't try any silly stuff, or you will get a slug to your head."

Max accepted the threat with a grain of salt. "Just tell me if you have a tall, skinny, polished, blonde-haired guy in a white suit working for you?"

"Nobody in my organization would wear a white suit. We get our hands dirty."

Minutes after Martinelli left, Max again stood peering out the round window and internally reflected, *"Only if Johnny told me about the guy in the white suit looking in the coffee shop window on Monday, maybe I wouldn't be in this mess."* Max comprehended that even if he could escape the cuffs and somehow break the extra-thick glass, the tiny aperture wouldn't allow his rugged body to pass.

A rowboat full of gangsters was now arriving. Darkness began to set in, but through the rays of the ship's bright exterior lights, the PI was able to recognize Martinelli's two secret 'VIP passengers' currently boarding, not by choice, of course. What he saw brought a frown to Max's craggy face.

71

FRIDAY AFTER THANKSGIVING
PART 1

1 A.M., MAX FOUND SHORT-LIVED SLEEP. THE CAP-
tive's stomach gravely sensed the luxury boat drifting.
In the darkness, the cabin door opened, and his ears
heard an uncanny plop strike the floorboards. The
door shut quickly. The sleuth kept silent, wondering
exactly what had plopped on the floor. Then he perceived dull moaning, human moaning. "Who's there?"
whispered the private detective. His whisper went
unanswered. When the moaning ceased, Max dozed
off toward dreamland.

Dawn emitted enough light in the cabin through
the small round window. He knew the ruffled pink
dress shirt, which appeared veneered in ketchup.
"*Georgie,*" said the private detective to himself. The
sylphlike bartender lay on his backside. Max keenly
observed for chest rise. Respirations were null. Mr.

Martinelli's surprise passenger number one, Georgie, the man who let him inside the Eldorado via its rear door, had now been reduced to a corpse.

8 a.m., the door to Max's cabin gaped again. Six-foot-eight, pockmark-faced Junior entered and picked up the corpse using a wrestling hold, dragging Georgie's flaccid body by his heels out of the cabin. Max saw Dutch O'Brien's silhouette just outside the thick door, directing the behemoth with methodical madness, "Dump him overboard; we are in international waters."

Once the cabin door shut, Max, still cuffed to the rail, sprang up like he was lying on hot coals. From the window, he spied stout, pug-faced Wimpy and scrawny Chuck on the deck, loading bricks into a steel drum. They stepped aside. Junior got betwixt the two thugs and stuffed Georgie's dead body deep within the drum—omitting benignant posthumous consideration. The goliath next secured the drum's lid, then heaved it overboard, devoid of assistance. Seconds later, Georgie's metal coffin became engulfed by the ocean.

———

8:30 a.m., in the cute little coastal town of Freeport, sixty miles from New Paris, recently separated Mona Ellory hung up a black hallway telephone. Mr. Winthrop, her white-haired father, played solitaire and asked, "Mona, who was that man on the telephone? It didn't sound like Bruce when I answered."

She raised her sculptured cheekbones and then

shook a heart-shaped face. "You keep asking me the same thing." The elderly man incredulously gazed up from his chair. Mona ebbed her sarcasm and continued, "Oh... it was really nobody, Daddy."

Through the crisp morning's air, the brunette owning umber eyes stared emptily out the picture window at an old swing hanging below a mammoth oak tree.

Old Downtown, 10:05 a.m., in a ninth-floor office inside the archaic Keiser Building, totally unaware of Max's situation, Dashing Darlene's slender frame covered by a pink floral dress sat upright, hoping for any entity of excitement to happen. She just arrived at the office. The client's waiting area ahead of her oak desk appeared desolate. On the wall beyond her right temple, a 1947 Rexall calendar had the boxes prior to November 28th filled in neatly with a big X. The dusky, rectangular interior window possessing blinds between the waiting room and Max's office outlined the fact that the private detective's presence seemed absent. Soon, she noticed a folded paper at the desk's corner. She unfurled it and read.

> *Darlene,*
>
> *In the event of my absence on Friday morning, please do not discuss the Wayne Palmer case or even minuscule details with anyone, especially the police.*

*We are dealing with murderers here, and
your own life would be much in jeopardy.
Just tell the police I went missing, and
you don't know anything. Whatever I get
myself into, I'll get myself out of. If I'm
not in the office by noon, leave. Burn this
note after reading.*

Max

The note made her extremely nervous. Her knees began shaking. Suddenly, the black Western Electric telephone jangled forebodingly. Darlene's brown shoulder-length hair bounced when she nearly jumped out of her seat. She tensely answered, "Hello, Weatherbee Detective Agency."

It was a man who Max once thought resembled a Billiken statue—the one with a voice pitch containing treble like a wino playing a flute inside a garbage can. The Billiken man had been unknown to Darlene.

"Max Weatherbee, please," he tweeted.

"Mr. Weatherbee is not in. Can I please take a message?"

"My name is Hank, ticket agent at the Freeport train station. Please inform Mr. Weatherbee that the woman he inquired about is boarding a train to New Paris right now."

Darlene rightly assumed he meant Mona Ellory, whom she knew now resided at her parent's home in

Freeport. The intern replied, "Thank you, Hank. I'll make Mr. Weatherbee aware of your call."

The line clicked; Hank was gone. Darlene thought, *"I'm useless, I don't know what Mona looks like. Hopefully, Max will be here shortly."*

The black Western Electric telephone jangled once more. "Hello, Weatherbee Detective Agency." She paused to listen, subsequently replying, "Sorry, no, Mrs. Weatherbee, your son Max hasn't arrived yet today." Darlene paid attention assiduously to the incoming statements flowing through its earpiece, then confirmed, "You say he never showed up at your house yesterday for Thanksgiving? And you have not heard from him since Wednesday?" She plaintively sighed, arching pencil-thin eyebrows. "Well, that's peculiar. I'll have him call you right away."

The call was soon terminated, and the phone rang anew. This time, Nurse Cindy's voice traveled over the earpiece, "I need to speak to Max Weatherbee."

"He's not in right now. Can I take a message?"

"That's actually preferable. My name is Cindy. Tell Max, on no occasion, to ever call me again."

"Oh, gee," Darlene sympathized, "why are you so upset? What's this regarding?"

"He stood me up last night. I foolishly waited two hours for him," Nurse Cindy divulged, then slammed the receiver on her end.

Darlene's perfect face grew more alarmed as she rested it on her lanky fingers. Abruptly, two suits with hats strolled into the office.

72

FRIDAY AFTER THANKSGIVING PART 2

MAX HAD PROMISED EARLIER IN THE WEEK TO deliver Bruce Ellory's innocence today—the day after Thanksgiving. Coming for that delivery were the irascible, hulking Detective Dan McGann and his sidekick, the shorter, round, ruddy-faced, wisecracking Detective Skip Cobb. McGann's cubic, unshaven face indignantly peered at the closed white door of the sleuth's office like he was viewing an out-of-order toilet sign.

"Where the Sam Hill is he?" He inquired, using a huffy tone to begin the inescapable discussion.

"Detective, something strange is going on." Darlene hastily arose and revealed, "Max seems to be missing."

"Go on," Skip Cobb interjected gruffly, sticking his protruding belly frontwards. Meanwhile, McGann's boxy torso stood erect.

"The last thing I heard was he planned on going

somewhere late Wednesday night with a guy he calls Johnny Knuckles. I don't know Johnny's actual name; Max really doesn't tell me much. But apparently, he missed Thanksgiving dinner at his mother's house yesterday and was a no-show for a date later that night." As instructed by Max's note, she now realized she shouldn't have dropped Johnny's name. She stopped talking.

"Johnny Knuckles... Johnny Severoni is a true miscreant. We have a warrant out on him for stealing a Buick." The tall, intimidating police detective pinched his chin. "Why would Max get mixed up alongside him?"

Darlene did not reply, but an always omniscient Skip Cobb put two cents in. "No wonder why he's missing," the pudgy detective imparted, "that's bad company."

"Listen, I don't know anymore. It's Greek to me. What can I do to help?" the college intern offered, leaning over the desk between her and them.

"Dig among all his notes in his office; maybe you'll find out something there and call us," Cobb dispassionately directed as if he had something worthier to do, like eat lunch.

"Not sure I'll find anything," Darlene responded, "he burns all his notes after reading." This also meant that Darlene would need to surreptitiously dismantle Max's detective corkboard.

Detective McGann spoke next, prospectively, "Still look and stay by the phone. Maybe he skipped town with Palmer's murderer, Bruce Ellory." Annoyance reverted to his tone as he pointed a thick finger at the young office intern. "If he does show up, have him contact me pronto!"

Succeeding McGann and Cobb's exit, Dashing Darlene tarried in the standing position, brooding about how dire her morning had become. In a whirlwind, Johnny Severoni, aka Johnny Knuckles, and his black leather jacket came barreling around the corner in a melodramatic tirade. Under his dark eyebrows, the sclera appeared fiery. The hood belligerently clenched two scarred fists and banged them several times on Darlene's desk, then demanded, "I want duh money Max owes me! At least fifty dollars; you'd betta find it somewhere!"

"Johnny, why didn't you talk to the cops who just left?" Her articulation was hysterical.

"No cops. I'm not doin' a minute in duh can. Martinelli will orda me killed once I get there." Cynical Johnny's ears turned rose red. "Honey, I ain't no fuckin snitch," the hoodlum upbraided, flaunting an incensed tone.

She took one step rearward, then gasped, exhibiting elongated, frightened eyes.

"Yuh didn't give duh cops Martinelli's name, did yuh?" Johnny interrogated.

"No. Max left me a note advising not to."

"Then why did ya want me ta talk to dem? Forget it. Where's my money?"

"Wait here," she urged. Darlene's shaking hands reached into her purse for keys and then unlocked the door to Max's office. She returned carrying a scanty tin box, the agency's emergency kitty. Even though there was some cash on hand, her fingers nevertheless trembled as she counted multiple bills and announced, "Twenty-seven dollars is all that is here."

Darlene forwarded the twenty-seven in combined bills to him for his remuneration. Johnny grabbed it ungracefully and stuffed the petite wad inside a pocket of his black trousers. "If Mr. Bee evuh gets out of dis situation, tell em I dropped off duh requested material at our usual spot," he asserted.

"Johnny, wait! Where's Max? And Where's the usual spot?" She implored. "Please give me something?"

"Are yuh kiddin'... I told yuh, dat information would get my head busted." The ruffian spun his black boot heel on the marble floor and said no more as he egressed to the hallway. Darlene's inner thoughts told her it was time to close up shop, disregarding Detective McGann's orders to "stay by the phone."

---

1 p.m., amid salty air on the upper deck, mustache-faced Mr. Martinelli sauntered towards the cabin door guarded by a post-adolescent, scabrous-faced goon sitting in a wooden chair with his head down, serving as a mere pawn in the racketeer's retinue. Joe Martinelli kicked the chair, and the cap upon the goon's full head of blonde hair became askew.

"Hey, wake up. Go in there; bring a few guys and uncuff Weatherbee. When you're in the room, keep a gat on this fellow at all times." Mr. Martinelli vigorously poked the skinny man's torso as he briskly rose and continued speaking. "Let him stretch his legs in his cabin. Keep the cuffs off; put another guy at the door with you. I want Mr. Weatherbee to get plenty of rest for the surprise I have planned. Remind him that escape is insuperable."

"Insuperable?" the goon responded.

"It means he can't escape, you fucking idiot," the underworld boss chided.

"Gotcha, Mr. Martinelli," replied the eager-to-render sycophant displaying an obsequious half bow.

The head of the outfit conspicuously proceeded to the neighboring cabin, which housed his second VIP passenger—Georgie, now at the ocean's bottom, being the first. He knocked before encroaching. Pearl's voluptuous frame, still in her leopard dress, presented curled in a ball with her eyes closed. Her red heels were long gone. The cabin was cozy and furnished for a lady.

Mr. Martinelli boldly entered, then sanctioned, "You don't need to remain in your cabin. You are free to walk around my boat. Obviously, you can't abscond."

Pearl goggled one smudged mascaraed eye. "Leave me alone, I'm sick from the waves, and my opium withdrawals are punishing me." Yesterday's angelic face was now pallid.

"It'll pass. Get off that shit." His eyes showed deprecation.

"Bring me a blanket; I'm frozen," she requested, showcasing irritability.

"In a bit."

Pearl opened her other eye and then entreated, "And I have no clothes here."

"We'll stop at Bloomingdale's," the rugged gangster taunted.

Pearl lifted her flaxen hair from the mattress. "I hate you."

Martinelli smirked.

She asked, "Whatcha do with Georgie?"

"We found Ole Pink Shirt's key to my Eldorado Club in Weatherbee's pocket, so we made the homo his own submarine."

"I hate you," she reiterated.

"Take your dirty dress off and get on your back."

"What about Junior?" the hipster questioned in desperation.

"He works for me. When I tell him to dive into a pile of shit, he says, yes sir! Understand?"

"I hate you," she reiterated once more.

Leaving his undershirt and socks on, Martinelli undressed the rest and tossed his pinstripe suit on the vanity as if he was visiting a brothel.

———————————

3 p.m., in the modest Westgate Hotel lobby, the place where Max Weatherbee furtively receives telegrams from associates, Johnny Knuckles entered, accompanied by a petite brunette. They found an unoccupied space at the counter, and he whispered words in the brunette's ear as she jotted down his dictation on paper. Johnny, being partially illiterate—able to read but not write—read his lady friend's note aloud. The wanted hooligan slanted over the counter, processing every word like it was difficult.

Max,

Sorry, I tried to tail Dutch's gang but ran into some dirty cops. If you get to read this, I guess it will be a good thing. The tall man who looked in the coffee shop window is Slick Peterson. He runs the rackets up in Adamsville. I knew that I remembered him from somewhere. He must be involved in Wayne Palmer's murder. Sorry I messed up not getting you such valuable information earlier. We never would have gone to the Eldorado and got into our jam. I took twenty-seven bucks from the girl at your office. You still owe me some money, man, I mean, if you get out of your mess. I had to skip town, too many people are looking for me.

Johnny

Next, the hood sealed and handed the white envelope with the note inside to the roly-poly, half-bald manager. Putting a dollar bill tip on top, Johnny said, "Make sure Max Weatherbee gets dis duh minute he gets back ta town."

"It will go in his box, sir."

Johnny ditched the brunette and then headed to the bus station.

73

THE RETURN OF MOON CHIN

SATURDAY, NOVEMBER 29TH, MARKED TWO WEEKS since Wayne Palmer's murder and Bruce Ellory's engagement in hiding. It was 11 a.m., and beads of sweat poured down the fugitive's forehead as he careened in circles around the living room of apartment 303, still wearing Max's rolled-up trousers. Bruce ceased the erratic circling and began chafing his lower neck with a sharp thumbnail. The skin above his left clavicle was broken, surrounded by abrasions he had been creating all morning.

"Where the hell is Max? Ellory mused, *"He was supposed to be here on Thursday. I'm as good as dead."* The distressed man exited apartment 303, walking by an untouched morning meal Suzy dropped at his doorstep three hours prior.

Upon plodding into Moon's Oriental Laundry, the elderly Chinese counter lady in black possessing salt and pepper hair remarked, "Oh, you come back."

Bruce stood—like a frozen ghost.

"Where you frien?" she vivaciously asked.

"I don't know where Pearl is... but I must see Moon Chin. I need an opium fix." Bruce's mood was sullen.

"Ha ha, I fix you suit." Her tone aired jocular, attempting to humor him.

"Please... I need to see Mr. Chin," he supplicated.

"Hole on." She disappeared among the darkness beyond her with alacrity.

Soon, Moon Chin surfaced.

"Mr. Chin, my nerves are bad; please help me," Bruce Ellory desperately beseeched, exhibiting transparent anxiety.

"You say you a need fix," Moon Chin said, looking hard with stern eyes. "Your pupils should be big as moons if you need a fix. Yours are small like marbles."

"I require it for my nerves."

"It's five dollars. No two for one today," Chin asserted.

"Here." Ellory nervously laid a five-dollar bill on the counter. Moon Chin cupped the bill using a diminutive hand. Bruce noticed all of Chin's fingernails were yellow.

"The opium parlor is full right now," Mr. Chin imparted, then asked, "Are you staying at Pearl's apartment? I can fetch you there in about an hour."

"I'm staying next door in number 303," Bruce Ellory disclosed.

"Okay, I'll contact you in 303."

Mr. Ellory left the laundromat unenthusiastically.

Moon Chin turned a flat neck and spoke to his wife in Mandarin. What he said was, "303 isn't that where Xu Wang lives?" Moon Chin shook his head, perplexed, and then looked at a folded newspaper behind the counter. Next, Mr. Chin picked up a red phone attached to the wall and dialed some digits.

An hour and a half later, six-foot-three Sen, Moon Chin's opium parlor assistant, knocked on the door to Apartment 303. "Mr. Chin will see you now," he made known, airing a masculine voice.

Once again, Bruce Ellory was led down the basement stairs of the Chinatown laundromat, this time by Sen. Moon Chin did not tag along. A different secret door opened in the same manner as the last by pulling a rope. This room looked larger, even dingier than the room Pearl and he occupied on Thursday. Inside the dirt floor, cave-like chamber, Bruce saw half a dozen diaphoretic men on wooden gurneys. The poor souls, being the pits of society, waiting for attenuating relief from intrinsic suffering via a needle prick.

An uncouth young man with shoulder-length hair sat in a chair sporting a tourniquet on his right arm. Bruce had never seen such long hair on a man. The petite Chinese fellow who knelt beside him tapped the addict's veins while holding a syringe in his other hand. The bleak environment served as a prelude to danger, causing Bruce Ellory to verbalize to Sen with great alarm, "There must be a mistake; get Mr. Chin. I want the opium parlor... not dope!"

Just seconds after Ellory uttered opposition, Sen

brutally forced Bruce's frail body into an unoccupied mangy chair. The other smaller Chinese man in the space dropped his former duty and deftly applied a tourniquet to Bruce's upper extremity. Mr. Ellory scratched and clawed before the immense shouldered Sen manually secured Bruce's wrists to the wooden arms of the chair using large hands transversely. Sen offered a sinister, tight lip, non-tooth-bearing smile as he stepped on Ellory's shoes, hampering further movement.

Bruce Ellory cowered then screamed, "No, please.... no!" The utterance ended up being his last words on earth, as the heroin bolus from a syringe, fit for a horse, was injected into Bruce's right antecubital vein by Sen's accomplice to murder. It did not happen quickly. At first, he lost consciousness, then erratic shallow breathing followed. Next, all in the room heard gurgling through Mr. Ellory's oral cavity before he vomited. Bruce Ellory's heart stopped beating. His kismet had been finally sealed.

Minutes later, the chamber door opened. White wingtip shoes led six-foot-four Slick Peterson, wearing his signature ivory suit, into the noxious room. Moon Chin trailed a yard behind him. Slick faced off with Mr. Chin's enforcer, Sen, who stood only an inch shorter. The petite Chinese man who administered Mr. Ellory's death dose looked way up at Slick. Ignoring the junkies in the background, camaraderie was shared as the four men of malice all looked low at Bruce Ellory's dead body slumped in the chair until Slick said, "Thanks for the call, Mr. Chin. I thought my associate Tommy killed this wimp Monday night." The tall man in angelic white then imperiously ordered, "Dump the chump's body in an alley. An alley where it will easily be found."

The next morning, the Armenian rug dealer, Walter Kazarian, Bruce Ellory's sister Susan's husband, brought the newspaper in from the doorstep and flumped it on the kitchen table. On the front page, the headline read:

> *Wayne Palmer's Killer, Bruce Ellory,*
> *Heroin Addict, Found Dead, Overdosed*
> *in City Alley. Police say Palmer Case*
> *Officially Closed.*

Notable Characters Introduced in Part 9

Moon Chin: Owns laundromat in Chinatown with hidden opium parlor underneath, first appearance Chapter 68

Sen: Moon Chin's 6'3" enforcer and opium parlor assistant, first appearance Chapter 68

Joe Martinelli: Head of the New Paris syndicate, owner of the Eldorado Gentlemen's Club, first physical appearance Chapter 70

Diego: Santa Pedro lawman, first appearance coming in Chapter 74

PART 10

74

SANTA PEDRO

THE ONE-WEEK JOURNEY HAD TERMINATED. MAX was weakened from insufficient food. Skinny Chuck kept a gat on him as the deckhands handcuffed Max's wrists inside his denuded cabin. An eight-day-unshaven, light-bearded private detective faltered off the ship, which led to getting pushed in the rear with each stumble by an uncouth deckhand sporting a filthy striped shirt.

The Caribbean land he set foot on appeared warm and tropical. Its roads were dirt. Horses and buggies outnumbered the sparse, outdated American automobiles. Up the hill, one unsophisticated deckhand continued shoving Max in an unduly manner. When Max saw hatless Mr. Martinelli standing without a hair out of place in the bygone era town square donned in a cream-colored suit, he meekly asked, "What's happening to me?"

"Simple. You tried to send me to jail, so now you're

going to jail instead." Martinelli gave penetrating eyes. "Prison is the worst thing for a man's soul. Ever do time, Weatherbee?"

"Fuck you," a gaunt Max mumbled, barely audible. The prisoner's body hunched forward, and its owner would have fallen flat on his face if he was not held up by two deckhands. Meanwhile, Martinelli puffed his cigar.

Beyond the town square, Max's malevolent captors dragged him through a rocky street—like in a Hollywood Western—towards an adobe shanty featuring obsolete bars on its windows. The dwelling's interior floor was bare cement; a darker-skinned man with a bushy mustache sat behind a desk to the left.

"Diego, put him in a cell and get him a bath; he fucking stinks," Martinelli directed, using a domineering tone. "And get our cocaine loaded; we're not staying on this sewage-infested island very long." The short Indigenous man wearing a tan uniform fully arose halfway through the racketeer's second sentence.

The man, called Diego, pleaded, maintaining a Spanish accent, moving chubby hands erratically, "Señor, I can't keep him here more than thirty days. He must see the judge."

"Enough bafflegab. We're not doing the judge," Obstinate Mr. Martinelli chided, demonstrating ascendancy. "Just keep changing his name like a vagrant and stick a new charge on him." Martinelli set down a wad of U.S. bills on Diego's shabby desk. "This is probably what this piss hole job pays you for a year." The gangster's phiz turned salmon as he glowered. "He'd better be right here when I get back in a few months."

"Sí, Señor." Diego's face grew happy.

Next, Joe Martinelli pivoted sharply, facing Max, then pointed at a damp, empty jail cell, and taunted, "Like your new residence, Weatherbee? Sorry, we didn't festoon it with pretty balloons for ya."

Max's eyes were shuttered—he was powerless but cognizant enough to understand the cell that presaged his fate.

"See, if you just tried to kill me," Martinelli arrogantly boasted, "I'd have mercy and killed you nice and quick."

"I'll kill you if I get back to New Paris," Max listlessly muttered, just enough for the head of the outfit and the scoundrelly lawman called Diego to perceive.

Martinelli smirked. "Well, that's much better than going to jail; you're a fast learner, Weatherbee."

Control of Max's torso soon switched from the deckhands to three of Diego's guards, who lugged the cuffed detainee into his cell.

75

MEANWHILE, BACK IN THE STATES

DASHING DARLENE SAT STOOPED. HER BONY elbows rested on the desk—a new desk. She had been assigned to an alternative detective agency by Professor Whitley in Max's absence. A short, square-bodied sleuth sporting a flat coiffure sloped over her, exhibiting derision through bad breath. "You don't look happy here," he quipped.

Darlene was not known to be reticent. "I'm… not," she replied, tartly digging a violet fingernail into her cheek.

The pizza face of the young intern's new boss turned deadpan.

A phone jangled. She answered with sadness embedded in her tone, "Hello… Parker Detective Agency."

————

Nurse Cindy, decked in candy stripes under a long black coat, returned to a place she had visited her last two evenings before work. A place that had special meaning—the city park where the twenty-eight-year-old nurse experienced her favorite afternoon in years a few weeks ago. She missed the man she hardly knew.

Amid frigid December air, Cindy peered over her shoulder. If this had been a dream, Max would appear. Cindy was not dreaming. She could smell the aroma of hot peanuts one pushcart vendor offered ten yards behind her. The pretty redhead leaned forward over the rail with glossy hazel doe eyes as she threw pieces of Wonder bread into a green pond. A dozen ducks came—Cindy left.

In the Wickford section of New Paris, a phone call originated from a second-floor, spacious, opulent bedroom at the house with the vines. Accompanied by her fine Veronica Lake hairdo, Vivian Allard, Wayne Palmer's younger sister, appeared all dolled up and looking for somewhere to go. Mrs. Allard waited, propping a receiver to her ear accompanied by a petulant frown. When the recipient answered on the other line, Vivian instructed through her rugged voice, "Pick me up at seven. Wickford Pharmacy."

She impatiently listened.

Vivian Allard spoke truculently towards the mouthpiece, "My husband won't even know I left; he never leaves that foolish laboratory."

After the call was terminated, Mrs. Allard remained seated on the grand bed and offered a sinister, fiery-eyed stare into a gilded 1920s art deco mirror on the wall. The reflection of herself between the two high mahogany bedposts made her look like a queen in a castle—an evil queen in an evil castle.

———————

Three thousand miles west from New Paris in San Francisco, idiosyncratic Johnny Severoni—aka Johnny Knuckles—garbed in a leather jacket and crushed pork pie hat, set up billiard balls inside a dingy joint called Big Al's. He slyly gazed at his new opponent and announced, "My name is Johnny. I'm a newbie tuh dis town."

The young San Fran local nodded his head.

The New Paris shyster removed the rack; a cigarette hung loosely out of his mouth as he told a fib. "Can't say I'm any good at pool, but I'll take a chance against yuh for a sawbuck."

———————

In a cluttered, tobacco-smelling office of the downtown precinct, big and tall, rectangular-faced Detective McGann sat behind a colossal desk. Altitudinous stacks of files close by its edges were tall enough to hide his massive buzz-cut head and play peek-a-boo. Half-bald, ruddy-faced Detective Skip Cobb sat in between McGann and those high-piled files.

Cobb was not in any mood to play peek-a-boo.

Instead, he said, "Well, Dan, the Wayne Palmer case is laid to rest."

"Yeah, we knew all along Bruce Ellory did it. He must've killed Weatherbee too when Max found out that Ellory really murdered Palmer," theorized Detective McGann through jagged teeth, slanting backward in the chair.

Detective Cobb nodded in agreement with McGann's theory and added, "Weatherbee had to have been clipped off somewhere. We searched his apartment and office, but nothing was missing. He certainly didn't leave town. His suitcase never left the closet."

"We do know that Weatherbee snooped around town asking about Ice Box Collins," McGann added.

"Dangerous game, but Collins was in the can at the time of Palmer's murder." Cobb went on, "And that tail you put on Mona Ellory was a dead end, as we thought."

McGann orated, "Yes, she already had a new boyfriend, a banker. She was meeting him every Friday at the train station. I checked the guy out; no way he killed Palmer. Like Palmer, he is a well-to-do married guy who fools around on the side."

"Money will do that," hypothesized Cobb.

"I heard she broke it off already. She jumps about," McGann speculated. "She'll be on to something new up in Freeport."

"Well, good thing you at least checked her out."

McGann bobbed his head, then changed the subject. "Officer Freddy Brooks is taking Max's disappearance pretty hard."

"I heard," acknowledged Cobb, lighting up a cigarette. "I don't want to tell him that Weatherbee's body
is probably going to turn up under a rock someplace."

McGann widened his eyes humorously, then suggested using persuasion, "How about us takin' that Flor-
ida vacation with the wives and a playing a lot of golf."

"Dan, now you're talkin," Detective Skip Cobb
agreed without dither, slapping his bowling ball belly.

———————

Sixty miles from New Paris, in the quaint town named
Freeport, Mona Ellory remained seated by a picture
window at her parents' single-story house. Mona's
white-haired father, Mr. Winthrop, queried out of the
background. "Mona, are you okay? You have not talked
much since Bruce's funeral."

"I'm fine, Daddy," she responded impassively.

"Someone has been calling here, hanging up the
telephone on their end." The old man's voice was croaky
as he paused and continued. "Mona, do you know anything about that?"

She abstractedly looked at the old swing in the yard
through ice-cold eyes. "No, Daddy, I don't."

———————

Slick Peterson's white wingtip shoes led him to a kitchen
table. He tossed today's newspaper on it and examined
a headline.

Former State University Football Player's

Decomposed Body Found in Carr's Pond,
Tommy Kostopoulos. Police have no leads.

The tall, villainous man grinned.

———————

Thick-mustached Walter Kazarian, the brother-in-law of the departed Bruce Ellory, stood beyond a counter in his spacious Persian rug store donned in a sharp rust-colored suit. A slim, creepy male customer owning jet-black hair pussyfooted into the establishment. Mr. Kazarian's fixed mocha eyes reacted as if he had never seen the man before.

"Good afternoon. I need a rug for my parlor. Nothing fancy," requested the bunny-eyed man.

"We have a non-Persian section for folks on a budget," the high-forehead Middle Eastern Kazarian pitched with disfavor.

"Perfect."

The bizarre-looking man paid for his rug and soon pulled up out front with a modest black-colored van. Walter Kazarian's stock boy loaded the rug into the van's rear. The side of the vehicle was lettered ALLARD CHEMIST. Professor Allard, who was not in his laboratory as his wife assumed, drove off furtively possessing venomous intentions.

———————

Mrs. Wayne Palmer, all 200 pounds of her, walked into the New Paris Savings and Loan Bank. When it was her turn to see the teller, she handed over a long, rectangular check and smugly said, "I want Mr. Case, your manager, to notify me immediately once it clears."

"Yes, Mrs. Palmer." The twenty-ish female teller gawked at the figures on the check with protruding eyes.

Mrs. Wayne Palmer imparted, "It's life insurance, sweetie."

———————

The luxury boat was heading back to New Paris minus one passenger—Max Weatherbee. Hatless, gray-haired Mr. Martinelli zipped the fly of his pinstripe dress pants and exited Pearl's cabin.

Pearl's upturned eyes cried as she curled her body at the edge of the bed.

Six-foot-eight pockmark-faced Junior entered two minutes later. A no-makeup-wearing Pearl anxiously disclosed, "Do you understand what your asshole boss just made me do?" She got up, rinsed her mouth with a glass of water, and spat in the sink.

The mammoth man brusquely stuck a paper bag beneath Pearl's mattress.

She questioned, "What's that?"

"The Smith & Wesson pistol we took off Weatherbee," Junior divulged with his deep voice. "Do you know how to use it?"

There were flames in her eyes; she could now abort her forbearance. "Oh, fuck yeah, I do."

76

BACK UP IN ADAMSVILLE

IN A PLUSH ADAMSVILLE APARTMENT, THE SIX-foot-four spindly man, who Johnny Knuckles mentioned in his last letter to Max, called Slick Peterson, grandiloquently entered the parlor. Wearing his signature white suit and wingtip shoes, Slick was handed a cocktail from a jewelry-cladded hand featuring exceptionally polished fingernails.

Vivian Allard, the daughter of the comatose Judith Palmer and sister of the bludgeoned Wayne Palmer, spoke in a dispassionate tone. "Cindy, the red-headed nurse who works at Saint Elizabeth's Home, called and said my mom will be gone by tomorrow." She reached up and picked at Slick's baby blue bow tie like it was tree bark, then continued, "Her legs are purple, plus she is hardly breathing. Soon, the convalescent home can't take any additional money from my late father's estate for her care." The more she talked, the more her green egg-shaped eyes became heartless. "It's all mine."

Jaunty Slick extended a left arm, supinating his palm enthusiastically. "Babe, now we're on easy street. Time to leave that loathsome spouse of yours."

She ignored the second part of his statement. "It had been my idea to rub out my brother Wayne," her truculent voice asserted, seeking credit. Vivian sported a red rayon, sloped-shoulder dress, spotlighting gold-tipped arrows embroidered at the chest.

"You possess gumption, honey, but remember... I hired the killing machine," he countered, exercising his high-pitched voice.

"Tell me of him," Vivian exhorted, accompanied by a curious glance. "You said the fellow's name was Tommy."

Slick reminisced about the gorilla of a man Bruce Ellory encountered one horrific November Saturday night. "I met Tommy years ago in college on the football team when I became their quarterback. He played as an oversized linebacker who loved to hurt people. I had beers with him after games, and on a few occasions, he told me he had urges to even go as far as killing people."

She pretended to be interested and playfully yanked down on his suit's lapels. "Tell me more, dear."

Slick's long, eager face showed he seemed head over heels for the devious peek-a-boo hairstyle dame. His story resumed. "See," he said, "I wasn't in the rackets up here yet, so it didn't mean much to me at the time. But years later, when you and I planned to kill your brother, Wayne, I looked him up because I heard he'd been strapped for cash, not doing well." Slick shook his tumbler enough for the ice cubes to clank. "Plus, I surely wouldn't use an intown, recognizable mug, so I offered Tommy the job. It would have been one and done, but our pencil neck witness Bruce Ellory and that big whale Howard Stanford couldn't keep their traps shut, which led to extra casualties."

"It was just supposed to be my brother Wayne killed. How many folks were actually murdered?" She didn't ask with sorrow but more for her own amusement.

Applying his unoccupied hand, the tall man started counting on lanky fingers, resuming the oration. "Let's see: ole handsome Wayne, the fat sleuth Howard Stanford who visited your house, two lowlifes at the Hotel Duncan, a Puerto Rican guy Max Weatherbee sent to Adamsville, that Bruce Ellory cat and Tommy." Slick double-counted his gangly thumb and index finger to make a seven. Next, he closed his fist, sticking out the same index finger and thumb like a gun, then added, "I politely sent dumb dumb Ellory a warning note at the beginning, urging him to skip town after I clocked him over the head with a bar stool."

She backed up as if he were a Poison Ivy plant. "Slick," she asked, "why did you kill Tommy?

"Simple. Easier to kill him than pay him. He wasn't connected to any outfits, so nobody really cared. My friend Bronc, the house dick, over at the Chadwick Hotel even took care of dumping Tommy's monstrous body for me in Carr's Pond." Slick peered over his glass with sparkling eyes. He went on, "Anyway, no more witnesses. Let's have a toast."

"Wait. What about the good-lookin' private detective who came to my house?" she inquired, sarcastically adding, "Not that fat one."

"He's gone missing. I learned from Bronc that your 'good-lookin' PI had been barking up the wrong tree. His name is Max Weatherbee. He erroneously stayed busy snooping after some stripper your brother was fooling around with. This led him to the attention of Joe Martinelli."

She gave no-nonsense eyes and replied, "I know Weatherbee is his name; I told you I didn't want him touched. He wouldn't be a threat once you eliminated the witness, Mr. Ellory."

"I had nothing to do with Weatherbee's disappearance. He walked into his own trap." Slick ran a long finger along the part separating his perfectly divided blonde hair while collecting thoughts. "I heard through the grapevine that your brother Wayne had some shady business dealings alongside Martinelli, and this put Weatherbee on the wrong trail. I must say you got the private dick off your own back by convincing Ellory that you really wanted revenge on your brother's killer, pitching your 'I'll fill 'em with slugs' intentions. Well done, sweetheart."

"Why, thank you. So, you're not in cahoots with Mr. Martinelli?"

"I stay clear of Martinelli's crew. My racket is up

here in Adamsville. And why did you say Mr. Weatherbee was a no-touch? You dig him or something?"

She leaned against the back of the sofa. "A girl could easily."

Slick let that one pass, and they brought their martini glasses together for a toast. He raised a glass first. "To Tommy."

She followed. "To Tommy."

The man in the white suit downed the concoction by way of two big gulps and questioned, "What kind of mixed drink is this?"

She answered incongruously, "My husband is picking me up soon."

"Huh?"

"I don't stutter." Her tone now aired bellicose.

"Wait a minute, sweetheart. You told me you were leaving him for me."

"Oh... should I inform you? You've just been murdered for homicide number eight," she disclosed. "I'll use your line, 'easier to kill him them than pay him.' This time, him being you."

"Stop foolin' around." He didn't fancy her enigmatic talk. "Honestly honey, what kind of drink is this?" he asked again, wrapping a free hand around his protruding Adam's apple. "My throat feels funny."

Vivian Allard replied, "The kind that makes a turd like yourself go poof." Next, she smiled wickedly via glazed lips and further articulated, "When I was in my hubby's chemist lab, I asked the dingbat what would happen if someone took a sip out of the bottle with the big skull and crossbones on it. He divulged to me, 'In ninety seconds, the ingesting person will be dead.' So, if he's correct, you've got about thirty seconds remaining to live. Now, there really will be no more witnesses."

Slick's eyes turned ablaze. He coughed. Whitish foam trickled from his mouth. The cocktail glass shattered on the floor, and soon, the towering fiend fell to his knees, gasping.

She stood erect and spoke to the contorted human mass on the floor below her. "I do have to applaud you for doing my dirty work. Speaking of dirty work, my husband, Professor Allard, is on the way here now, transporting a nice, tall rug to wrap you up nice and snug. He actually picked it out all on his own without my direction. Don't worry; we'll dig your body deep in the woods. We can't leave you here in case the poison is traced back to his lab."

The contorted human mass attempted speech, but fresh foam oozed out of his oral cavity. The foam's velocity started ebbing as he neared his journey to perdition.

"I'll need a cowgirl hat... we're selling everything and moving to Texas," she envisaged blithely.

The former dapper man owning the white wing-tip shoes, who once stalked Bruce Ellory, expelled two final gasps of foam twelve inches from the femme fatale's black stilettoed pumps.

When his respirations ceased, Vivian Allard lit a cigarette. Wicked laughter filled the room.

77

THE END

APPROACHING FRIGID NEW PARIS DECEMBER waters, the luxury boat swayed gracefully amongst the current. Pearl, with her flaxen hair tucked into a sailor's cap further garbed in a deckhand suit, obviously oversized for her, tiptoed inside Mr. Martinelli's cabin office.

The head of the New Paris outfit sat journaling behind a sleek bamboo-legged rattan desk. He looked up, baffled for a split second, processing the unfamiliar deckhand's diminutive size. Once he recognized her angelic face, the gray-haired man featuring a widow's peak commented, "Oh, it's you."

She stood ten feet away, in the front of the desk, exhibiting morose eyes and said nothing.

Not appreciating the interruption, the criminal society's top echelon questioned, "What the hell do you want? He paused, offering lecherous dark eyes. "I don't require you just yet."

Mr. Martinelli did not engage in additional conversation and resumed journaling something that would be meaningless in thirty seconds. Still standing in the same spot, the hipster fished out Max's Smith & Wesson from a small purse. The initial shot sailed four inches wide of his temple, sinking into the plaster wall. The detonation jolted Martinelli to an erect position in the chair. He finished half a sentence. "What the fuck—"

The subsequent bullet hit him above the nose, smack in the middle of the glabella. The man so many feared had spoken his last words. His dead head swan dived onto the desk's leather-outlined blotter.

For a moment, she felt power like she'd never felt before.

The cabin door gaped with a billowed force. Dutch, Chuck, Pug Face, Silent Sal, Junior, and two deckhands came running about, surrounding Pearl, who turned motionless, dropping the gun in a desultory manner. Everyone in the room gazed at Joe Martinelli's crop of gray hair sitting on the bloody desk top resembling a coonskin cap. They all looked at Pearl next. Amongst the bedlam, Junior got in front of Martinelli's killer and intervened, yelling, "Nobody touches Pearl!"

A scrawny, shaggy-haired deckhand furtively slithered along the wall, ignoring Junior's request, and grabbed Pearl rearwards. Through the chaos, six-foot-one broad-shouldered Dutch superciliously growled over everybody in the room, asking, "Who's in charge now?

All at the same time, Dutch's cronies Chuck, Silent Sal, and pug-faced Wimpy blurted out, "You are, Dutch."

For a moment, every person in the room froze like a tableau. They shared one common thing, no one possessed clarity about what the next move was going to be.

The newest head of the New Paris outfit, Dutch O'Brien, tactfully uttered his first orders using a hoarse voice, "Okay, leave the girl alone; I need Junior. We'll say Weatherbee did it, then jumped overboard." He stared down at the discarded revolver on the floor and added, "I see it's his gat anyway."

Pearl chimed in, "The cops aren't going to believe that; his uncle had been one of them."

Dutch gave her a hard look. "I don't talk to cops. I'm talkin' about what we'll tell all the thugs in the underworld." The new boss soon faced the men in the room and directed, "Let's dock in New Paris and go sell our cocaine."

Meanwhile, back on the tropical island of Santa Pedro, time stood still. Through a thick Spanish accent, "I have some hot soup for you, Señor Max; you are looking better," said the bushy mustache jailer named Diego, peering keenly in between the bars.

Standing inside the cell, showing apprehension towards the crooked lawman's solicitous ministration, Max inquired, "Why are you doing all this for me?"

The private detective turned prisoner, with the ruffled clothes, promptly retreated two steps, which allowed Diego, dragging a chair, to enter. The captive added, "Let me guess, you need to keep me alive until Martinelli returns."

Diego used a jocular tone. "Maybe Señor ... maybe not."

Max sipped his soup as the two men from dissimilar worlds sat and played chess placidly.

Half an hour later, Max announced, "Checkmate!"

Diego rose, walked out of the cell, and winked at two armed guards in tan uniforms standing close by. The cage door was left open.

"Aren't you forgetting something?" hinted Max, still seated on his cot.

"I told you if you win me in chess, you free to go."

Flummoxed, Max asked, "Is this a deranged joke?"

Diego motioned for Max to exit the cell.

The sleuth obeyed, then queried, passing the lockup's entrance, "What about Martinelli and all that cocaine he purchased here?"

"Ha ha, Señor Max," Diego said, "there was only cocaine in the bags on top of the pallets."

"And the bags on the bottom of the pallets?" Max questioned.

"Ha ha... flour Señor. We took his eleven grand, though."

Once Diego evinced his contempt for Mr. Martinelli, Max's eyes became relaxed, realizing the open iron door behind him did not mean he would be on the way to the gallows.

Diego continued bringing to light Max's afore-mentioned statement made last week, "Señor Max, you said you wished to kill Señor Martinelli when you arrive home. So do us a favor here in Santa Pedro and make good on your promise."

Max nodded, not realizing Pearl had already beaten him to it, and egressed the adobe structure solo amid the eighty-degree sunshine. Cloistered no more, he plodded up the dirt road—horse manure pervaded the air. Once he got to the rustic town square of the island seventeen hundred miles away from anyone who could be trusted, Max Weatherbee mused—*"Gotta find the tall man in the white suit. Now, just how the hell am I going to get back to New Paris?"*

The answer to Max's question was that it really did not matter because Slick was already six feet under the dirt.

Back in the States, Vivian Allard and her chemist husband had settled their affairs and crossed the state line. Three duffel bags of moolah rested on the back seat of a brand-new Oldsmobile driven by Professor Allard.

Vivian Allard's boisterous voice spoke first. "This road looks desolate. Are you certain you know the way to Texas?"

"Yes, dear," replied the professor.

"Keep your eyes on the road, will ya."

"Vivian, you didn't help me dig Slick's grave."

"Grave digging is not ladies' work."

Surrounded by woods, Professor Allard pulled the Oldsmobile to the side of the road.

"What are you doing?" she snarled.

"I have to pee."

"Find a tree and make it quick," Vivian sharply barked.

"Yes, dear."

Professor Allard did not get out of the car. Instead, he reached under the seat and firmly grasped the bone-handle of the kitchen knife resting below him.

Stay tuned for other Max Weatherbee stories, including the *No Escape from Death* prequel, *Two Birds, One Stone* in Allan Kevorkian's next release—*10 Twisted Pulp Fiction Tales.*

ACKNOWLEDGMENTS

I would like to thank the following:

- My beta readers (sons Allan Kazar and Bedros, Alyson and Steve Santaniello, Jeff Tracy, Jennifer Kevorkian, Lorna Jaymes, and Patty Mariani) for taking the time to read this story and offer feedback.

- Steven and Dawn Porter from Stillwater River Publications for making my dream possible.

- Graham Gifford from the New Hampshire Telephone Museum, who gracefully took the time to answer my questions regarding telephone communication for the period.

- Tabitha Lord Jorgensen, Rhode Island author and friend, who took the time to do a Zoom call with me.

- My late father, Allan Kevorkian Sr., who introduced me at a young age to film noir movies and pulp fiction reading.

- My wife, Jennifer Kevorkian, who encouraged me to pick up this story again after I left it behind uncompleted during the years of my mother's illness.

- All the film noir and vintage pulp fiction fans out there. Without you, I would not have had the motivation to pen this story. I wrote it for you!

ABOUT THE AUTHOR

Allan, a native Rhode Islander, has always been a big fan of film noir and vintage pulp fiction stories. His ethnic background is Armenian and Italian, which he enjoys incorporating into many of his characters. Allan has worked as an RN for most of his adult life but recently decided to try his hand at writing noir stories.

His first two books, *No Escape From Death* and *10 Twisted Pulp Fiction Tales*, are heavily influenced by classic film noir movies and pulp writers such as Richard Stark, Cornell Woolrich, Raymond Chandler, Harold Masur, Dashiell Hammett, Mickey Spillane, and the many stories featured in *Black Mask*. Allan puts his own touch in all his work, including some fresh humor along the way.

In his free time, Allan enjoys exploring off-the-beaten-path places in small-town USA, hitting the gym, and going on moderate hikes. During family vacations with his wife and two sons, he organizes a pseudo murder mystery, assigning hotel staff as suspects and giving them each a character name. At the end of the trip, the family votes to decide, "Who did it?"